GLANCES OF LOVE

LUCID

Made with ♥ on the Notion Press Platform
www.notionpress.com

To everyone I love.

Contents

Preface

Art often mirrors the human soul, capturing the echoes of joy, despair, and everything in between. For Mareek Masood, the melodies he brought to life resonated with millions, but hidden beneath the applause and acclaim lay a man at war with himself. This is not just a story of music, love, and fame—this is a story of obsession, betrayal, and the cost of promises made in the shadow of vulnerability.

What drives a man to kill? What binds him so tightly to the memory of love that he begins to destroy all who threaten its sanctity? This book delves into the mind of a man who lost his way, following a path shaped by childhood loneliness, stolen genius, and the haunting specter of unfulfilled vows.

Yet, amid this chaos lies an intricate web of relationships: a psychiatrist who seeks the truth but hides his own motives, an imaginary friend who becomes the cornerstone of his reality, and the silent body of a lover that becomes his sole companion.

This is a journey into darkness—a psychological exploration of love turned toxic, guilt turned fatal, and genius turned deadly. Every note of Mareek's music carries a piece of his story, but as the truths unravel, the harmony of his life becomes dissonant.

This book invites you to step into Mareek's world, to question the fine line between genius and madness, and to witness how the brightest stars can cast the darkest shadows. As you turn these pages, remember: every story has its silences, and some silences are louder than the loudest applause

Acknowledgements

Every story is a journey, and this one would not have been possible without the unwavering support, guidance, and inspiration from those around me.

First and foremost, I express my deepest gratitude to my family and friends for their encouragement and belief in my vision. Your patience and understanding during the countless hours I spent immersed in this world mean more to me than words can ever convey.

To the readers who pick up this book—thank you for giving this story a place in your life. Your curiosity and willingness to explore the depths of the human psyche are what make writing worthwhile.

A heartfelt thanks to the creative souls who unknowingly inspired elements of this narrative. Whether through music, art, or life experiences, your influence added texture and depth to this story.

To my mentors, teachers, and fellow writers who have guided me along this journey—thank you for helping me hone my craft and teaching me to find my voice. Your advice and feedback have been invaluable.

Lastly, to the characters in this book—fictional as you may be, you've lived vividly in my mind and heart, teaching me lessons about love, loss, and the fragile nature of humanity.

This book is as much yours as it is mine. Thank you all for being part of this journey.

Foreword

Every story carries with it a mirror—reflecting not only its characters but also the complexities of human nature. *Glances of Love* is one such tale, weaving the fragmented threads of love, obsession, morality, and loss into a haunting melody that lingers long after the final page.

As you journey through the life of Mareek Masood, a man celebrated for his art but tormented by his promises, you will encounter a world where the boundaries of right and wrong blur, and where the weight of one's choices shapes not just their own destiny, but the lives of all they touch.

This book does not seek to comfort. It seeks to challenge. To ask difficult questions. To hold a mirror to the parts of ourselves we would rather leave unexplored. What drives a man to madness? How does love transform into something darker? And at what cost do we cling to promises that define us?

Mareek's story is, at its core, about the human condition. It is about the beauty and burden of creation, the depths of grief, and the inescapable pull of our past. While the narrative unfolds against the backdrop of fame and artistry, its true essence lies in its raw, unflinching portrayal of a soul unraveling.

For those who pick up this book, I offer only this: approach it with an open heart and an open mind. You may not agree with Mareek's actions. You may find yourself recoiling at his choices. But, as with all great stories, there is something here that will resonate deeply, a silent truth that lies just beneath the surface.

This book is not merely a story—it is an experience. One that asks us to reflect, to feel, and, perhaps, to see the world—and ourselves—differently.

Enjoy the journey.

Lucid AKA Farhan Sheikh

1

All the noises are silent now, the concert of the best DJ and singer among all the college students has finished. **Rakesh Agarwal**, a senior at the College of Technology Delhi (PMD College), stands at the center of it all—both revered and misunderstood. Loved by many, yet often considered rude, Rakesh's pride stems from a brilliance that is impossible to ignore. His music—an exquisite blend of talent and emotion—has captured the hearts of all who hear it. It's easy to see why: when you craft something as remarkable as his songs, pride is a natural companion.
But behind the success lies a journey shaped by hardship. Born into a lower-middle-class family, Rakesh's father, a hardworking cab driver, struggled to make ends meet. Despite these challenges, Rakesh's exceptional intellect and determination earned him a place at one of the best engineering colleges in the country, paving the way for the man he is today. His music, a testament to his genius, remains the soundtrack of his rise—a rise driven by both talent and the memory of a difficult past.
His life changed after an incident in his sophomore year. In his freshman year, he fell love with a girl named **Ayesha**. They both love each other. Ayesha was a muslim, when they. Whenesfully went into sophomore year, some extremists in the area found about them, they started giving threat to rakesh and ayesha, telling them to leave each other, otherwise they'll kill both of them. Ayesha was frightened because of her fear. She started to ignore Rakesh and his whole existence. At this time, Rakesh was fully shattered. He started to take addictive products to get some relief from the stress he had.

When Ayesha heard about him, she went to see him.

"Rakesh?" Ayesha called softly as she entered his room.

"Who's there?" Rakesh's voice was thick and slurred, clearly intoxicated.

"Ayesha," she replied calmly, trying to steady herself in the face of what she was walking into.

"Ayesha, wait, I..." Rakesh's words trailed off, his body unsteady, and he suddenly collapsed.

"Are you okay?" Ayesha rushed to him, grabbing him to help him stand.

"No!" he shouted angrily, pushing her hands away.

"Why?" Ayesha asked in a whisper, the pain in her voice evident.

Rakesh's bloodshot eyes fixed on her, a look of raw frustration. "You really want to know why?" he asked, his voice laced with bitterness.

"Yes... I do," Ayesha stammered, her heart racing.

"Because of you!" Rakesh snapped, his voice rising. "You've made my life hell! What's wrong with you? You were so quick to leave me, scared of some extremists who are all talk—empty threats that will never be carried out. They'll never..."—he trailed off, his anger bubbling over.

He collapsed onto the sofa, his hands covering his face in defeat. "Thank you, ma'am," he said with sharp sarcasm, "You may leave now."

Ayesha stood frozen, her heart breaking at his words. His hostility was more than she could bear. She felt a weight in her chest as she watched him lose consciousness and slump into a restless sleep. Tears welled up in her eyes, but she wiped them away quickly, trying to hold it together.

With a final look at him, her chest tight with sorrow, Ayesha turned and walked out of the room, leaving him to the chaos of his thoughts.

On her way home, Ayesha's heart pounded in her chest as a group of boys from the extremist group blocked her path.

"Where were you?" one of them asked, his tone sharp and demanding.

"I was at a friend's place," she replied, her voice trembling with fear.
"You have friends in a boys' hostel?" they spat, their anger evident in every word.

Ayesha, her panic rising, pushed past them and broke into a run. But the goons were fast, and no matter how hard she tried, they quickly caught up to her.

"You have committed a sin," one of them sneered. "You must be punished."

"Burn her alive!" another shouted, his voice filled with venom.

Those were the last words Ayesha heard before they dragged her to the ground. The sun blazed in the sky as they set her on fire, the flames consuming her as she screamed in agony. Her cries for help echoed into the air, but no one came. Not a single soul stood up for her.

The people around her were nothing but monsters in human form—men and women who had lost their humanity. They watched with twisted pleasure, cheering and laughing as a young girl was burned alive, simply because she had dared to love someone outside her religion. They believed they were doing their God's work, that by taking her life, they were securing divine favor.

To them, it wasn't a crime. It was an act of holiness. And as Ayesha's life faded, the crowd reveled in the darkness of their actions, blissfully ignorant of the pure hatred they had unleashed.

Rakesh was in shock after the incident. During his hard time, there was nobody to help him, except his addictive products. They were his only supporters at that time. Since then, he has started to talk less to people. He lost his ability to smile after this incident. Even despite these big incidents, those goons are still roaming freely in the world of corruption. He made music his support for everything and became one of the best at music. The more disturbed the person, the more great his work.

After his performance ended, Rakesh went to a terrace where he usually drank alone. It was his usual spot, a quiet place where he could unwind. But tonight, something was different. When he arrived, he noticed someone sitting there.

"You again?" Rakesh asked, his tone sharp.

"I'm a first-year student here," the boy replied.

"Good. But why are you here?" Rakesh questioned, annoyance flickering across his face.

"I wanted to meet you," the boy said earnestly.

"I'm not interested in talking to you. Now leave," Rakesh said bluntly.

"Sir, please. I really want to talk to you. If you want, I'll do anything for you," the boy pleaded.

"I don't need you to do anything for me," Rakesh yelled, frustration seeping into his voice.

"Sir, please. It'll only take a few minutes," the boy insisted.

Rakesh sighed, the persistence of this boy wearing him down. This was the sixth time he'd shown up. Finally, Rakesh relented, though his tone was curt. "Fine. But listen—you have a quarter of a quarter of an hour. That's it."

"That should be enough," the boy said, and a small, triumphant smile broke across his face.

"Your time starts now," Rakesh said, folding his arms.

"I want to learn music from you," the boy declared.

"I'm not a teacher," Rakesh replied flatly.

"I know. But even if you teach me half of what you know, it would mean so much to me," the boy said, his voice filled with determination.

"I won't teach you anything," Rakesh retorted.

"Why not?" the boy asked, his eyes wide with genuine curiosity.

"Because I don't want to," Rakesh said firmly.

"Sir, please," the boy pleaded again. "I'll do anything for you if you just teach me some music and mixing."

Rakesh stared at him for a moment, clearly irritated but also sensing the boy's desperation. After a few more minutes of pleading, Rakesh finally gave in. "Fine. I'll teach you music. Be here tomorrow at 5 A.M. sharp. For now, just leave me alone and let me get back to my stuff."

The boy nodded eagerly, gratitude shining in his eyes. "Thank you, sir. I'll be here."

He left the terrace, leaving Rakesh alone once more.

At 5 a.m., a sharp knock echoed on Rakesh's door. He opened it, his expression blank and unreadable. "So, you've come on time. Good for you," he said in a flat tone.

The visitor didn't respond, nor did he hesitate. He stepped inside, his gaze sweeping over the room—a cramped space filled with musical instruments. Guitars leaned against the walls, a keyboard sat on a cluttered table, and sheet music was scattered across every available surface.

"You didn't tell me your name," Rakesh said after a moment.

"**Mareek Masood**," the man replied, his voice calm and measured.

Rakesh nodded curtly. "Fine. Let's get started."

For several days, the practice and training sessions went smoothly. Rakesh maintained a distant stance—neither friendly nor overly strict toward Mareek. His instructions were precise, his expectations clear, but his tone was devoid of warmth. Mareek, however, didn't mind. He was thrilled to learn music and absorbed every note, chord, and rhythm with unrelenting enthusiasm.

But something about Rakesh's demeanor bothered him. It wasn't strictness—it was detachment. Mareek sensed that Rakesh wasn't just hurrying through the lessons because of efficiency; he seemed eager to be rid of him.

Mareek, despite the coldness, made numerous attempts to build a connection. He tried to share moments of laughter, ask questions about Rakesh's life, and occasionally brought small tokens of gratitude—a cup of tea, a few snacks. Each attempt was met with polite indifference. Rakesh neither rejected his efforts nor reciprocated them.

Rakesh's aloofness wasn't born of disdain, though; it was fear. He believed attachments led to inevitable pain. To him, relationships were messy, complicated, and ultimately hurtful. Mareek's eagerness to connect only reinforced his resolve to maintain emotional distance.

Still, Rakesh couldn't completely hide the depth of his mind. While he avoided personal topics, he often shared his thoughts on life, music, and his personal philosophies. He spoke of discipline, self-reliance, and the importance of guarding one's emotions. These musings had a profound impact on Mareek, who began to see Rakesh as more than just a teacher.

In this short span of time, Rakesh's ideology began to shape Mareek's outlook. Whether Rakesh realized it or not, he had become a significant influence on the young man's life—a teacher not just of music, but of thought and resilience.

"Your music has improved so much, Mareek," Max said with a nod of approval.

"Thanks to him," Mareek replied with a small smile, a flicker of gratitude lighting up his face.

Max's expression darkened. "Aren't you admiring him a bit too much these days?" he asked, his tone turning serious.

Mareek frowned. "What's wrong with that?"

"Plenty," Max said, leaning forward, his voice firm. "You're idolizing him like he's some kind of god. That's not a good thing, Mareek. The only person you're allowed to admire is yourself. You shouldn't put anyone on a pedestal when you are the greatest person to exist in this whole world."

Mareek's face flushed with anger. "I'm nothing compared to him," he snapped.

"That's just your illusion!" Max yelled, his voice echoing in the small room. "You've convinced yourself that he's above you, but he's not. You're diminishing yourself for no reason."

Mareek's voice faltered. "What am I supposed to do, then?"

Max sighed, his frustration still evident. "Stop idolizing him. Respect him if you must, but don't worship him. You're the greatest—don't ever forget that."

With that, Max stood up abruptly, his chair scraping against the floor. He marched to the door, slamming it shut behind him with enough force to rattle the walls.

Left alone in the silence, Mareek sat motionless, replaying Max's words in his mind. Though spoken with anger, they carried a harsh truth that struck a chord. He realized he had been blinded by admiration, losing sight of his own worth in the process.

From that moment on, Mareek resolved to change. He would still respect Rakesh, but he wouldn't worship him.

"Mareek, tonight I'll have my last concert as a student here at this college," Rakesh said, his tone flat and indifferent. "I want you to accompany me as an assistant DJ."

"I'll be there, but do you trust me with this job?" Mareek asked, unsure.

"No, I don't, but I don't have any other options," Rakesh replied, his voice devoid of any emotion.

"Alright, I'll be there," Mareek agreed, feeling the weight of the situation.

The concert began at 7 P.M. Mareek took the stage first, effortlessly getting the crowd into the vibe. His energy was high, but when Rakesh joined him, the attention quickly shifted. Without a word, Rakesh began his set, and within moments, he reclaimed the spotlight, his presence commanding the crowd. Both DJs were caught up in a silent, almost mechanical rivalry as they mixed their beats, the competition palpable but never expressed.

The concert wrapped up at 11 P.M. Mareek, exhausted but satisfied, sat beside Rakesh on the terrace. "It was good, sir," he said, trying to gauge Rakesh's reaction.

Rakesh stared ahead, his expression unreadable. "Mareek, I always drink alone after concerts," he said flatly. "But tonight, you're here. For once, someone feels like a friend."

Mareek hesitated, unsure if Rakesh meant what he said. "Thank you... sir," he replied cautiously.

Rakesh didn't acknowledge the gratitude. "I've had a bit too much to drink. I'm saying things I don't usually say. Let me show you something."

"Okay, sir," Mareek responded, following Rakesh to his room.

Inside, Rakesh showed him his work—his songs, his compositions, his lyrics—without any fanfare. "These are amazing, sir," Mareek said, genuinely impressed but also sensing the lack of warmth in

Rakesh's demeanor.

"Thanks," Rakesh said, his voice still emotionless. "You can leave now."

Mareek, unsettled by the abrupt change in Rakesh's tone, simply nodded. "Okay, sir," he said and walked out.

"You attended my concert?" Mareek asked, looking at Max with a curious expression.

"Yes, I did," Max replied, his tone casual, as if attending the concert was no big deal.

"How was it?" Mareek pressed, genuinely interested in Max's thoughts.

"Amazing, of course," Max said, offering a confident smile. He didn't need to elaborate further—his approval was evident in his simple answer.

"Do you know the story of Rakesh?" Mareek asked, his tone shifting, becoming a bit more serious.

"Yes, I do," Max answered, his gaze drifting toward the horizon as if remembering something from the past.

"How do you know that?" Mareek asked, surprised by how quickly Max seemed to know.

"The whole college knows about it!" Max said with a shrug. "it's been the talk of the campus for a while now. Everyone knows about Rakesh's past and the tragedy with Ayesha."

Mareek nodded, processing the information. "What do you think about it?" he asked, still trying to understand how Max viewed the situation.

Max took a deep breath, his expression thoughtful. "It's all about ideologies," he began, as if preparing for a long explanation. "It's all about how you think, your way of seeing things, your principles. We can't really say what's wrong and what's right because it all depends on your perspective. The way we interpret the world, the way we define morality—it's all subjective. Morality isn't universal. The boundaries of morality shift depending on the person. What's considered moral by one person could be seen as immoral by another. It's all relative. It's all about perspective."

He paused for a moment, letting his words settle. "For example, if you look at this whole situation from the perspective of an extremist, their actions might seem justified. From their frame of reference, they're protecting what they believe in, doing what they think is right. But if you look at it from Rakesh's point of view, what happened is a sin. And the thing is, you can't really say either perspective is right or wrong. It's just how they view the world."

Mareek was silent for a moment, reflecting on Max's words. Max had a way of making complicated ideas seem simple, but it also made Mareek uncomfortable. "But isn't there a limit to that?" Mareek asked. "I mean, at some point, don't you have to draw a line? You can't just say that everything is okay based on how someone sees it. Some things are just wrong, right?"

Max smiled slightly, almost as if he were amused. "Sure, you could say that. But who decides where that line is? Who gets to determine what's right and what's wrong? Throughout history, there have always been people who have thought they were doing the right thing, only to have their actions condemned later on. The whole concept of morality is fluid. It changes over time, depending on who's in power, who's telling the story, and how society evolves."

He leaned forward, his voice growing more intense. "These things have been happening for centuries. People who challenge or oppose a dominant belief have always been persecuted—sometimes even killed—by those who claim to be defending their faith or their cause. It's not new. It's been going on for as long as history has been recorded."

Max then relaxed back into his chair, his tone shifting to a more reflective one. "There's a big difference between a religious person and an extremist. Not every religious person is an extremist, and not every extremist is truly religious. Most extremists don't really understand the essence of their religion—they're not scholars or deep thinkers. They've been manipulated by those in power, who use religion as a tool to control the masses. They think they're protecting their faith by killing those who oppose it, but in reality, they're just following a narrative that's been handed to them. It's not about religion; it's about power and control."

He paused again, letting the weight of his words sink in. "Morality, in the end, is a matter of perspective. What's wrong for one person might be right for another, and sometimes, it's hard to say who's truly right. We all live in our own little bubbles, shaped by our experiences, beliefs, and the influences around us. That's why I can't really take sides in this. I can't relate to Rakesh's perspective or the extremists'. I'm just someone trying to understand the world without getting caught up in the labels."

Mareek, who had been listening intently, frowned in frustration. He wasn't used to hearing such complex philosophical arguments. "You yap a lot," he muttered, his patience wearing thin.

Max grinned, his demeanor unchanged. "That's who I am."

Max was a childhood companion of Mareek, a friendship that flourished under unique circumstances. Their first encounter took place in a public park, where Mareek often found himself in a state of solitude, marginalized by his peers due to the prejudices associated with his religion. He faced significant discrimination, with many parents forbidding their children from playing with him. This pervasive ostracism left Mareek feeling isolated during his formative years, grappling with loneliness and rejection. Everything changed when Max entered his life.

From the moment Max chose to engage with Mareek, a remarkable bond began to form. Unlike others, he saw past the superficial barriers and connected with Mareek on a deeper level. Their interactions became a regular occurrence, transforming them from mere acquaintances into inseparable best friends. Together, they navigated the transition into college life, eagerly enrolling in the same institution and sharing a dormitory. Mareek chose to pursue a degree in Computer Science Engineering, while Max opted for Mechanical Engineering. Despite their differing academic pursuits, their shared living space allowed them to maintain their close friendship.

As college life unfolded, it became apparent that Max was inherently introverted. He preferred the comfort of solitude over the allure of social engagements. Parties and clubs held little appeal for him; Max found solace in the confines of their shared room. After classes concluded, he often chose to remain indoors, immersing himself in academic pursuits or engaging in contemplative reflection. This inclination toward seclusion was a defining characteristic of his college experience, offering Mareek a sense of companionship while providing Max with the peace he valued. Mareek was average in his studies, and so was Max. Max, however, was an orphan, and he never visited Mareek's home. He carried the weight of a silent shame, fearing that Mareek's parents wouldn't approve of an orphan entering their house. Mareek, perhaps sensing Max's reluctance, never questioned it.

The College of Technology Delhi, known for its fast-paced, competitive environment, was buzzing with excitement on the eve of placement day. As the final day of college approached, students were engrossed in last-minute preparations—rehearsing their mock interviews, perfecting their resumes, and scrambling to get that one final recommendation. In the midst of all this, Rakesh, the most beloved yet enigmatic student of the campus, sat alone on the terrace of the hostel, his back leaning against the cold stone wall, staring blankly at the city lights below. The bottle in his hand was his only companion, a cruel reminder of how far he had fallen from the person everyone once admired.

He had it all—or so everyone thought. Rakesh, the DJ, the genius composer, the man who could make a crowd move to his every beat, the one whose songs had become anthems for the youth. On the outside, he was everything people aspired to be. But tonight, as he sat alone in the darkness, there was nothing left of that man. No excitement about the placement. No passion for the music that had once been his lifeline. All that remained was a hollow shell of the person he used to be, drowning in the emptiness of his own existence.

His mind drifted back to the days before everything had changed—the days when he had been in love. Ayesha. The girl who had filled his heart with hope, the girl whose laughter had once been the sweetest melody he knew. They had shared dreams, plans for the future, and a love that transcended all boundaries. He had tried to fill the void with his music, but the more he composed, the deeper the loneliness grew.

Rakesh took another swig from the bottle, the sharp burn of alcohol doing nothing to numb the pain. He stared at the empty streets below, his mind racing through the past, through the decisions that had led him here. Every step, every choice he had made seemed meaningless now. The praise, the applause, the endless streams of compliments—it had all felt so important at the time, but now it was nothing more than a cruel joke. What was the point of all this? What was the point of living when everything you had ever wanted had been ripped away?

"Rakesh?" The voice startled him. It was familiar, but it didn't register immediately. He turned around slowly, his vision blurred from the alcohol, and saw Mareek standing in the doorway.

Mareek hesitated before stepping out onto the terrace. He knew Rakesh well enough to understand when something was wrong, but he also knew how proud Rakesh was, how difficult it could be for him to show weakness. Mareek had watched Rakesh over the year.

"I came to wish you good luck for tomorrow," Mareek said softly, trying to break the tension in the air. He stepped closer, cautiously, unsure of how to approach him.

"Luck?" Rakesh scoffed, a bitter edge to his voice. He took another long swig from the bottle, his eyes never leaving the distant skyline. "What's the point of luck, Mareek? What's the point of anything?"

Mareek frowned, walking closer, but keeping his distance. "Rakesh, you've worked so hard for this. The placement—it's everything we've been preparing for. You're going to do great."

Rakesh let out a dry laugh, but it wasn't a laugh at all—it was a sound of someone who had lost all sense of hope. "Great? You think that matters? All these years, all this work, all this effort—what's it for? A job? A future? None of it means anything. It's all just a distraction. I've spent my whole life chasing something that doesn't exist."

Mareek took a step back, taken aback by the coldness in Rakesh's words. He had never seen him like this—so distant, so broken. "What are you talking about? You've got everything, Rakesh. You've got your music, your future, your friends. People look up to you."

Rakesh's eyes snapped toward him, a fire flickering behind the emptiness. "People?" he spat. "People look up to me, but do they know me? Do they know what's inside? Do they know how much it hurts just to get out of bed every day? All this success, all these accomplishments—it doesn't matter. Because the one person who mattered to me the most is gone."

Mareek's heart sank. He knew Rakesh's pain—Ayesha. It had been the one thing that had been eating away at Rakesh for so long, and yet, he had never truly spoken about it. It was always there, lurking in the background, in the way Rakesh withdrew from everything. But now, the dam had broken. Rakesh was finally talking, finally opening up, and it was clear just how much pain he was in.

"I... I don't know what to say, Rakesh," Mareek said, his voice faltering. But you can't just give up. You've got so much ahead of you."

Rakesh's expression softened for a moment, but the bitterness returned quickly. "What's ahead of me, Mareek? A job I don't want? A life I don't want? I'm done pretending that everything's okay. I'm done pretending that I'm fine when I'm not. I can't keep living like this."

Mareek felt a knot tighten in his chest, a sense of dread creeping over him. He knew what Rakesh was hinting at, but he didn't want to acknowledge it. "Rakesh... Please. Don't talk like this."

Rakesh stood up, his movements slow, almost deliberate. He reached for the bottle, taking another drink before looking at Mareek. "You want to help me, Mareek? You want to do something for me? Then bring me my guitar."

Mareek stared at him, confused. "Your guitar? What do you need that for?"

Rakesh gave him a wry smile, but it didn't reach his eyes. "Just bring it. Please."

Mareek hesitated, but then nodded, his heart pounding. He turned and quickly ran to Rakesh's room to fetch the guitar. It didn't make sense to him, but he did it anyway, hoping that somehow, playing music would bring some clarity, some peace to his teacher.

But by the time he returned, the terrace was empty. He stood there, frozen, his mind racing as he scanned the empty space. The guitar slipped from his hands, hitting the ground with a hollow thud. His heart leaped into his throat, and panic set in as he rushed toward the edge of the terrace.

Rakesh was gone.

Mareek's eyes widened in horror as he saw the faint trace of movement below. He couldn't breathe. His legs felt like they were made of stone. He reached out, trying to shout, but the words wouldn't come. The realization hit him like a physical blow—he was too late.

He dropped to his knees, his hands shaking uncontrollably as he reached into his pocket and pulled out the room key. Rakesh's room key. The key to the place where all his pain had festered, the place where his music had once been his only escape. But now, that room would forever be empty. The silence would never be filled again.

Mareek stared at the key in his hand, the tears welling in his eyes. He collapsed to the ground, the night air cold against his skin as the sounds of the college life continued below him, oblivious to the tragedy that had just unfolded on the terrace above.

Mareek sat on the terrace, staring down at the lifeless body of Rakesh sprawled on the ground below. The night air was cold, but he didn't feel it. A single thought consumed his mind: Rakesh's music.

As the reality of the situation settled in, Mareek's lips curled into a subtle smirk. Rakesh was gone. The genius who had once overshadowed everyone else, the man whose name echoed in every corner of the college, was no more. Mareek's heart didn't race from shock or grief—it beat steadily, calculatingly. He thought of all the times Rakesh had shown him his music, those unsung masterpieces that only existed within the confines of his room. And now, all of that was unclaimed, left behind like an inheritance waiting for someone to pick it up.

Mareek leaned back against the railing, his eyes shifting from Rakesh's body to the stars above. Why should it all go to waste? he thought. Rakesh was gone, and the world would never hear his brilliance unless someone stepped in. Someone who could bring it to life. Someone like Mareek. He chuckled softly to himself. No one has to know.

With a sudden sense of purpose, Mareek stood up and walked briskly back into the hostel. The key to Rakesh's room was in his pocket, given to him just moments before Rakesh leapt to his death. It was almost poetic, Mareek thought. Rakesh had unwittingly handed over his legacy.

Mareek pushed the key into the lock, the door creaking open to reveal the room that had been Rakesh's sanctuary. He stepped inside and flicked on the light, surveying the space with an appraising eye. The desk was cluttered with notebooks, sheet music, and scattered USB drives. The guitar leaned against the wall, its strings gleaming faintly under the fluorescent light. This was it. The treasure trove.

He moved to the desk and picked up one of the notebooks, flipping through the pages. Each song was a masterpiece, the kind of work that could catapult an artist to superstardom. Mareek read through the lyrics, nodding to himself. These songs could be mine now, he thought. Rakesh is gone. No one will know. No one will care.

He pulled a bag from the corner of the room and began packing everything: the USB drives, the notebooks, even the loose scraps of paper with unfinished ideas scribbled on them. He worked quickly, methodically, his mind already racing ahead to the possibilities. He saw himself on stage, basking in the applause of thousands. He saw his name at the top of charts, interviews where he would talk about his "process" and "inspiration."

Mareek didn't flinch as he took everything. There was no hesitation, no pang of guilt, not even a moment's pause to reflect on what he was doing. To him, this was simply an opportunity. Rakesh had been a genius, yes, but he was also weak, a man crushed by his own emotions and demons. Mareek didn't have those weaknesses. He had ambition, and now he had the tools to turn that ambition into reality.

As he zipped up the bag and slung it over his shoulder, Mareek glanced around the room one last time. It was strange, he thought, how quiet it felt now. This room had been filled with Rakesh's presence, his energy, his genius. But now it was just a space, an empty shell. Mareek felt sentimentality as he turned off the light and locked the door behind him.

Walking back to his own room, Mareek didn't once look back. The image of Rakesh's body on the ground was already fading from his mind, replaced by visions of his own future. He didn't see himself as a thief, or even as someone taking advantage of a tragedy. To Mareek, this was survival. This was ambition. Rakesh had left behind something extraordinary, and Mareek was simply smart enough to seize it.

When he reached his room, Mareek placed the bag on his bed and unzipped it, pulling out the notebooks and USB drives. He flipped through one of the notebooks again, humming the melody to himself. It felt good—powerful, even. The compositions were magical, and Mareek knew they would be enough to sustain him for years.

He leaned back in his chair, holding one of the notebooks in his hands. "This is my time now," he whispered to himself, a sly grin spreading across his face. He didn't feel guilty. He didn't feel remorseful. If anything, he felt triumphant. Rakesh's genius would live on, but under Mareek's name.

As the night wore on, Mareek began to plan. He would release the songs one by one, timing each release perfectly to maximize impact. He would tweak the lyrics slightly, just enough to make them his own. He would craft a story—a narrative about his "struggles" and "journey" in the music world. No one would ever question it. No one would ever know.

Rakesh had once been a mentor, a friend, a guide. But in Mareek's mind, he was now something else entirely—a stepping stone. Mareek's path to fame and success was clear, and he wasn't about to let anything, or anyone, stand in his way.

The campus buzzed with muted chaos. Rakesh's death was still the talk of the town, whispered about in quiet corridors and passed around in hurried, grief-stricken conversations. While some mourned, others were too preoccupied with their placements to delve into the tragedy. Mareek, on the other hand, stayed eerily silent. He avoided the groups of students gathered to dissect the suicide or talk about Rakesh's brilliance. He stayed away from the candlelit vigils held in Rakesh's memory. Instead, he worked. Quietly. Methodically.

Mareek couldn't get Rakesh's music out of his head. The compositions, the lyrics—every piece of it felt like a treasure trove too valuable to be buried along with Rakesh's memory. Yet, something gnawed at him. It wasn't guilt—Mareek had long abandoned guilt in the pursuit of his ambitions—but doubt.

He sat in his room, staring at the USB drive that held Rakesh's unsung masterpieces. Hours passed as he debated his next move. He wanted the fame, the recognition, but he wasn't entirely sure he could claim the music as his own.

That's when Max walked in. "You look like you've seen a ghost," Max said, dropping his bag on the floor.

Mareek waved the USB drive in his hand. "I've been thinking about this. Rakesh's music... It's brilliant. It's a waste to leave it unheard. But..." He trailed off, unsure how to frame his hesitations.

Max leaned against the doorframe, crossing his arms. "But you're afraid people will find out it's not yours?"

Mareek nodded. "Exactly. I mean, it's his work. People loved him for his music. How could I just... take it?"

Max smirked, shaking his head. "You're overthinking this, Mareek. Look, Rakesh is gone. Dead. Do you think he'd want his music to die with him? If anything, you're doing him a favor by sharing it with the world. Besides, who's going to know? You're the only one with access to it."

"But claiming it as mine? That's..."

"That's smart," Max interrupted. "You're not just claiming his music,

Mareek. You're giving it life. You're giving it a platform. And let's be real, no one's going to ask questions. You were his assistant, his apprentice. People already know you're talented. They'll believe it's yours."

Mareek looked at Max, trying to gauge his sincerity. Max's confidence was infectious, and Mareek couldn't deny the allure of the idea.

"You think I can pull it off?" Mareek asked, his voice hesitant but hopeful.

Max leaned in, a sly grin on his face. "I know you can. You've got the voice, the skills, and now you have the songs. This is your shot, Mareek. Don't let it slip away."

The next day, Mareek took the first step. He locked himself in his room and started practicing Rakesh's compositions. With each song, his confidence grew. By the end of the week, he felt ready.

His first release was a haunting ballad that Rakesh had composed but never sung. Mareek posted it online, claiming it as his own. The response was immediate and overwhelming. The song went viral within hours, with comments flooding in about Mareek's raw talent and the brilliance of the composition.

Max was there to celebrate, raising a toast to their newfound success. "See? I told you," he said, grinning. "This is just the beginning."

Mareek nodded, the USB drive clutched tightly in his hand. For the first time, he felt unstoppable.

Over the following months, Mareek released more of Rakesh's songs, each one met with critical acclaim. His name became synonymous with genius, his voice celebrated as the next big thing in music. Max played his role perfectly, handling the technical aspects and ensuring every release was flawless.

As Mareek's fame grew, the story of Rakesh began to fade into the background. No one questioned the origins of Mareek's music. To the world, he was the brilliant artist behind the magic.

Mareek didn't feel guilty—not even for a second. To him, this wasn't theft; it was destiny. He had taken what was left behind and made it his own. In his mind, Rakesh's death wasn't a tragedy; it was an opportunity.

And Mareek seized it with both hands.

By the end of his second year, Mareek had released over sixteen songs, each one carving out his name in the college and even beyond. The songs felt fresh, authentic, and deeply emotional, and their popularity skyrocketed with each release. It was as though Mareek was a prodigy no one had seen coming.

The crown jewel of his rising fame was the song "Love Chilly"—a hauntingly beautiful piece that delved into the dual nature of love. The song portrayed love as both a warming flame and a freezing frost, capturing the paradox of how it could heal and destroy simultaneously. Mareek had only slightly adjusted Rakesh's original lyrics to fit his own voice and personality. Yet, it was Rakesh's genius composition that had made the song transcend the boundaries of mere music—it was raw poetry woven into melody.

The first verse painted love as a cozy embrace:
*"Soft as the morning sun, a touch that mends the broken;
Words unspoken, hearts entwined, warmth in each token."*

Then, the chorus shifted into its chilling side:
*"But love is chilly, freezing in the night;
A storm that strips you bare, no warmth in sight.
It lifts you high, then lets you fall,
Love gives its all, then takes it all."*

"Love Chilly" quickly became a sensation. Uploaded on streaming platforms and shared widely on social media, it racked up views faster than Mareek could have imagined. Students hummed it in hallways, strangers sent him messages about how it moved them, and even local radio stations picked it up for rotation. Max, ever the opportunist, was ecstatic. "This song? It's a masterpiece! I told you, Mareek, you're unstoppable. We need to capitalize on this momentum. Next month, we'll record two more singles. Keep the fire alive."

Mareek grinned, leaning back in his chair. "I knew this one would hit. There's something in its honesty, its duality. People feel it because they've lived it."

But deep down, Mareek knew it wasn't his honesty that people were resonating with—it was Rakesh's. Every word, every note of "Love Chilly" carried Rakesh's emotional depth, the pain of his lost love and the bitterness that had defined his final years. Mareek didn't care, though. Guilt was a foreign concept to him now. He only saw the adoration pouring in, the likes, the shares, the endless stream of comments praising his "genius."

"Do you think anyone will ever connect the dots?" Mareek asked Max one evening as they celebrated another milestone for the song. Max shrugged, swirling his drink. "Not unless you slip up. You've got the voice, the stage presence, and now the reputation. Who's going to question you? People believe what they're shown, and right now, they're seeing you. That's all that matters."

For Mareek, that was enough. "Love Chilly" became more than just a song—it was his identity, his calling card, and his golden ticket. Every time he performed it, the crowd erupted, swaying to its bittersweet melody. It solidified him as not just a musician, but a storyteller, someone who could capture the complexity of human emotions.

And yet, as Mareek stood on stage, soaking in the applause, he never once thought about Rakesh's pale, lifeless body on the ground below the terrace. Not once did he let the memory of Rakesh's broken soul interrupt his meteoric rise.

In Mareek's eyes, Rakesh's songs were no longer Rakesh's. They were his. And he planned to ride them to the very top.

By the start of his third year, Mareek had achieved what most could only dream of. His songs were everywhere, his name was becoming synonymous with musical genius, and fame had enveloped him in its intoxicating embrace. But the source of his success—the hauntingly beautiful compositions of Rakesh—remained locked away in his mind, a secret he refused to acknowledge even to himself.

Returning to college had become a formality, a tiresome routine he had no patience for. While his peers poured over placement materials and juggled their academic schedules, Mareek was fielding calls from producers and planning his next releases. His heart wasn't in the campus anymore; it was out in the world, where his songs had already taken root.

One quiet evening, Mareek sat in his dorm room, staring at his half-packed bag. The USB drive containing Rakesh's unsung masterpieces sat on the desk, catching the faint glow of his desk lamp. It was his ticket to a future he believed was rightfully his, a future he no longer needed college to pursue.

Max didn't come by that night. He had a way of knowing when to show up and when to stay away, and tonight, he stayed away. Whether it was indifference or an unspoken understanding, Mareek didn't know and didn't care. Max had always been pragmatic, never one for farewells or sentimentality.

The next morning, Mareek walked to the administration office alone. The campus buzzed with the usual morning energy, students rushing to classes or fretting over upcoming placement interviews. To Mareek, it all seemed trivial. He handed in his withdrawal papers without hesitation, his decision made.

Back in his room, he zipped up his bag and took one last look around. The room felt empty, not just of belongings but of meaning. It had been a space of transition, a waiting room for a destiny he was now ready to claim.

He left without a word to anyone. As he boarded the train that evening, the campus shrank in the distance, a chapter he was eager to close.

Max, true to his nature, didn't appear to see him off. He stayed on campus, immersed in his own world. Whether he approved of Mareek's actions or not didn't matter; he simply didn't care. Recognition and fame were never his goals, and Mareek's departure was just another ripple in the larger tide of life.

For Mareek, though, the journey ahead was everything. The USB drive in his pocket, filled with Rakesh's unsung creations, was a weight he didn't acknowledge but carried nonetheless. To the world, he was a rising star. To himself, he was unstoppable. Rakesh's memory and the truth of the songs no longer mattered. Mareek's story was his alone, and he was determined to write it in the bright, blinding light of fame

2

Years passed, and Mareek's life had transformed into the embodiment of success and extravagance. He was no longer just a promising name in the music industry; he was *the* name. Sold-out concerts, chart-topping albums, and an ever-growing fanbase had made him a global sensation. Mareek was a millionaire now, living in a sprawling mansion in the heart of the city, surrounded by luxury and adoration. His music had become the anthem of countless lives, though the origins of his success—the songs born from Rakesh's genius—remained hidden behind the curtain of his fame.

Despite the whirlwind of his life, Mareek maintained one peculiar constant—Max. The two hadn't parted ways completely, but their friendship had shifted. Max hadn't changed much; he still lived a modest life, avoiding the spotlight. While Mareek had ascended to dizzying heights, Max had stayed firmly rooted, indifferent to fame and fortune.

Once a week, without fail, Max would visit Mareek, but only at his house. He never attended Mareek's lavish parties, nor did he accompany him to concerts or public appearances. Max wasn't part of the entourage or the image Mareek presented to the world. He was just... Max.

On one such evening, Mareek was sprawled on a leather couch in his grand living room, a glass of whiskey in hand. The room was adorned with trophies, platinum records, and photographs of him performing in front of massive crowds. Max sat across from him, as he always did, sipping a plain soda he had grabbed from Mareek's fridge.

"Still the same old Max," Mareek said with a smirk, swirling his drink. "You visit me every week, yet you never ask for anything. No money, no favors. It's like you're here to keep me grounded."

Max shrugged, leaning back in his chair. "I don't need anything from you, Mareek. I'm here because I want to be. That's all."

Mareek chuckled, though there was a faint bitterness to it. "You're probably the only person in my life who doesn't want something from me."

"Maybe that's why you still tolerate me," Max replied with a faint smile.

There was a long silence, punctuated only by the faint hum of the city outside. Mareek's gaze drifted to a grand piano in the corner of the room. It was purely decorative; Mareek rarely played instruments anymore. His team of producers and sound engineers handled everything now.

"You ever think about the old days?" Mareek asked suddenly, breaking the silence.

Max raised an eyebrow. "What about them?"

"College. The late-night jam sessions. Rakesh..." Mareek trailed off, his voice losing its edge.

Max didn't respond immediately. He studied Mareek carefully, as though trying to gauge the sincerity behind the question.

"I think about it sometimes," Max admitted. "But not the way you do."

Mareek looked at him sharply. "What's that supposed to mean?"

"It means I don't carry it with me like you do," Max said calmly. "You might not admit it, but Rakesh's shadow still looms over you. Every song, every stage you step on—it's all built on what he left behind."

Mareek's jaw tightened, his fingers gripping the glass a little too hard. "I don't owe anyone anything. I took what was given to me and made it into something bigger than he ever could've imagined."

Max tilted his head slightly. "Maybe. Or maybe you've spent all these years trying to outrun the truth."

The tension in the room was palpable, but Max didn't press further.

He had never been one to argue or moralize. He said what he felt needed to be said and left it at that.

Mareek drained his glass and set it down with a loud clink. "You should go. It's getting late."

Max stood without argument. "Same time next week?"

"Yeah," Mareek muttered, not meeting his gaze.

As Max walked out, Mareek sat in the silence of his opulent living room. He stared at the piano, at the gold-plated awards lining the shelves, at the life he had built. For a moment, just a fleeting moment, he felt the weight of it all pressing down on him. But then he shook it off, as he always did.

Max, meanwhile, walked out into the night, unaffected by the wealth and glamour he had just left behind. For him, Mareek's world was alien, almost unreal. He visited not out of admiration or envy, but out of a strange, unspoken loyalty to the person Mareek used to be—the boy who once sat on a terrace, strumming a guitar, dreaming of a future neither of them could have imagined.

Years of success had buried the past beneath layers of fame, but tonight, as Mareek sat alone in his mansion, sipping whiskey and reflecting on the years gone by, a fleeting memory began to resurface—one that he had long since pushed deep into the recesses of his mind. It was a memory from his childhood, a time when he was still the shy, awkward boy, before the world knew his name.

Mareek had never been popular in school. He wasn't athletic, he didn't fit the mold of the "cool" crowd, and he spent most of his time reading books or listening to music. But there was always one bully—Raj—a boy who tormented Mareek relentlessly. Raj found pleasure in mocking him, calling him names, pushing him around, and making him feel small. The taunts and jabs continued for years, until one day, the bullying crossed a line.

It was in the schoolyard after hours, just as Mareek was finishing his music practice. Raj, surrounded by his group of friends, approached him, this time with a crueler intent. He knocked Mareek's books out of his hands, then shoved him hard into the dirt. "You think you're better than us, huh?" Raj sneered. "You're nothing but a freak. Who would ever care about someone like you?"

Mareek stood up, dusting himself off, his heart racing in anger and humiliation. He wanted to fight back, to say something—anything—that would make Raj stop. But all he could do was stand there, seething, too afraid to do anything. That's when Max had appeared out of nowhere, as he often did during those school days.

Max had always been a little older, a little wiser, and in many ways, a mentor to Mareek. He wasn't one to speak much, but when he did, his words had a weight that couldn't be ignored. Max saw the situation unfold from across the yard and had approached Mareek. Without hesitation, he pulled Mareek aside, away from the scene.

"Don't let him walk over you like that," Max had said. "If you want respect, you have to take it."

Mareek looked at Max, his chest tight, unsure of what to do. "But I can't. He's too strong. What if I make it worse?"

Max's eyes had narrowed, his voice low and steady. "Sometimes you need to make it worse. Show him that you won't be the punching bag anymore. If you don't, you'll never be anything."

Max had offered Mareek a solution, one that seemed drastic, but for some reason, in that moment, Mareek trusted him completely. He didn't want to live in fear anymore. He didn't want to be the person who cowered in the face of cruelty. Max's advice was simple: *Make him regret it.* The words hung in Mareek's mind like a dark promise.

So, Mareek did what Max suggested. That evening, after school, as Raj was walking home, Mareek followed him quietly. There was a place near the edge of town, an abandoned alleyway that no one really used. Raj was alone, probably thinking about his next target, when Mareek caught up to him.

"What do you want, freak?" Raj spat, turning to face Mareek.

Without a word, Mareek did the unthinkable. In a blind rush of rage, he pushed Raj to the ground. The bully scrambled to get up, but Mareek was already on him. The punch came without warning—a forceful, desperate swing. Raj, taken off guard, crumpled to the ground, his face bleeding. Mareek stood over him, heart pounding, the adrenaline coursing through his veins. Raj didn't dare move, his shock evident in the way his body trembled.

"You ever touch me again," Mareek said, his voice thick with emotion, "and I'll make sure you regret it."

Raj didn't answer. He lay there, stunned and defeated, and after a long moment, scrambled to his feet, running off into the night.

The deed was done. Mareek had shown Raj that he wouldn't be walked over anymore. He had taken the advice Max had given him and had stood up for himself. But as the adrenaline faded, as the tension in his body ebbed away, Mareek realized something—something that made him feel uneasy deep in his gut.

He had crossed a line. He had done what he thought was necessary, but it had left him feeling hollow. There was no satisfaction in what he had done. In fact, there was a gnawing feeling, an unsettling knowledge that perhaps he had become something darker. But the damage was done. The decision had been made.

That night, when Max came by, he didn't ask any questions. He didn't comment on what had happened. He just looked at Mareek and nodded, as if he knew what had taken place.

"Good," Max had said, his tone unreadable. "You did what you had to do. Sometimes, life demands you act. It's a part of growing up."

Mareek had swallowed hard, but didn't say anything back. He wasn't sure if he felt pride, guilt, or something else entirely. All he knew was that his world had shifted. He wasn't the same person anymore. He had taken a step into a much darker version of himself, and now there was no going back.

Years later, as he sat in his mansion, surrounded by the life he had built from music and fame, Mareek couldn't shake that memory. It hadn't been the first time he had made a choice that would define him, nor would it be the last. But in that moment, when Raj had crumpled before him, something inside him had snapped, something that he would never be able to fully understand or undo. Max had been there, in the shadows, advising him to take control of his life. But as Mareek looked at the glittering success he had now, he realized that Max's advice—however well-intentioned—had changed him in ways he didn't want to acknowledge. He had taken what was given to him, just like he had taken Rakesh's songs, and he had built a world that was both his creation and his curse.

Max's words echoed in his mind once more, and Mareek couldn't help but wonder if, somewhere deep down, Max knew exactly who he had become.

Several years had passed since that fateful day when Mareek had crossed a line with Raj. His world had become filled with fame, music, and the power that came with success. But no matter how much he achieved, there were some things, some moments, that lingered like shadows, haunting his thoughts. One of those shadows was Raj. Though the bully from his childhood had disappeared from his life, there was still a lingering curiosity about what had become of him.

It wasn't that Mareek wanted to seek closure or redemption—no, it was more than that. There was something about Raj, something unresolved, that had stayed with him over the years. It was as if the unfinished business of that moment still gnawed at him. But he hadn't given it much thought until that night when Max arrived at his mansion.

Max, as always, was a quiet presence. He wasn't interested in the trappings of fame, the concerts, or the wealth that surrounded Mareek. He wasn't there for the limelight, and that's what had always intrigued Mareek about him. While others treated him like a distant friend, Max had always been someone who observed quietly, rarely offering advice unless it was absolutely necessary.

They sat together in the spacious living room, the noise of the outside world far away behind thick walls of glass. The conversation had drifted, as it often did, to the past. The success, the music, and the people they used to know. Eventually, like a creeping thought that couldn't be ignored, Mareek brought up Raj.

"Do you ever wonder what happened to Raj?" Mareek asked, his voice calm but with a subtle edge that betrayed his curiosity.

Max, who had been staring out the window, turned slightly toward him, his expression unreadable. "Raj?" he repeated, as if the name had been a distant echo from a long-forgotten past. "Why would I wonder about him? We left all that behind, didn't we?"

Mareek's jaw tightened, and he leaned forward slightly, his eyes fixed on Max. "I think about him sometimes. You know, the way he just disappeared after that day. I wonder what he's become. I want to see him again."

Max shook his head slowly, his eyes darkening slightly. "That was a long time ago, Mareek. What good would it do to drag that part of your life back into the present?"

"I don't know," Mareek replied, his voice lower now. "I think I need closure. I think I need to understand what happened to him after everything... after what I did to him. It's been eating at me for years. I want to see him. I want you to bring him to me."

Max was silent for a long time, the air thick with tension. He leaned back in his chair, his fingers absently tracing the edge of his glass. It was rare for Max to seem unsettled, but now, his calm demeanor was laced with something different—something Mareek couldn't quite place.

Finally, Max spoke, his voice steady but firm. "I'm not doing that, Mareek. I'm not bringing Raj to you. You have no reason to see him again. He's not part of your world anymore. It's better left forgotten."

Mareek's eyes narrowed. "Why not? You brought him to me back then, when I needed to take control of things. I need to know where he is now. I need to see him face-to-face."

Max's eyes flickered for a moment, then returned to Mareek with a gaze that was as cold as the glass in his hand. "You think you need to see him to get closure? What will it solve? What do you want from him, Mareek? You've already done what you needed to do, and he's gone. You don't need anything from him."

Mareek stood up, his frustration building. "You don't get it, do you? I need to face him. I need to confront the past once and for all. I can't keep running from it. I can't keep pretending like it didn't happen."

Max remained still, watching him, his expression a mask of calm. "You're running from something, alright. But it's not Raj, and it's not your past. It's you. You're running from the fact that you don't know what to do with the person you've become. You're afraid of facing who you are."

Mareek froze, his breath catching in his throat. The words cut deeper than he cared to admit. For a moment, he wasn't the famous, wealthy artist he had become. He was just a young boy again, standing in that alley, feeling the weight of his choices bearing down on him.

"I don't need you to remind me of who I am," Mareek snapped, his voice sharp, though there was a tremor of vulnerability beneath the harshness.

Max didn't flinch. "Then stop pretending. Stop pretending that seeing Raj will fix anything. It won't. It never does."

The silence between them stretched on, each man lost in his own thoughts. Mareek couldn't understand why Max was being so stubborn. He had always been the one to guide him, to offer clarity in moments of confusion. But now, Max wasn't budging, and Mareek couldn't quite figure out why.

"I thought you were my friend," Mareek said quietly, his voice softer now, the edge gone but replaced by something heavier. "I thought you'd understand."

Max looked at him, his expression unreadable, and for a moment, Mareek wondered if he had made a mistake by asking.

"I am your friend," Max replied finally. "But a real friend doesn't help you make the same mistakes over and over. You've got to let the past go, Mareek. Raj is a ghost now. Bringing him back won't change anything."

Mareek clenched his fists, a deep sense of frustration washing over him. "You don't understand. I have to do this. I can't live with this uncertainty."

Max sighed, setting his glass down on the table with a soft clink. "Then you're on your own with this one. I won't be a part of it. You've got to deal with it yourself, Mareek. You've always had that ability. Don't stop now."

With that, Max stood up, his movements slow and deliberate.

Without another word, he turned and walked toward the door, leaving Mareek alone with his thoughts.

Mareek sat back down, his mind a whirlwind. Max's refusal, his words, everything—had struck a nerve. But deep down, somewhere within him, he knew Max was right. He had always been right. The question now was, could he face his past and truly move on? Or would he continue to run from it, as he always had?

As the door closed softly behind Max, Mareek sat in silence, the weight of his choices heavier than ever.

Mareek sat in the dimly lit room, his thoughts swirling like a storm within him. The world outside, filled with the noise of success and achievement, seemed far away now. The weight of the conversation with Max still pressed on him, heavier than the plush leather chair he sat in. He had never before felt so unsettled by the quiet, calm demeanor of his friend. Max, the one who never sought fame or wealth, the one who always seemed to have a deeper understanding of the world, had always been the anchor in Mareek's chaotic life. But this time, something was different. This time, Max had refused him.

Mareek leaned back in his chair, closing his eyes for a moment. The words Max had said earlier echoed in his mind, a constant refrain that he couldn't escape. *You think you need to see him to get closure? What will it solve?* And then, the final blow: *A real friend doesn't help you make the same mistakes over and over.*

He had been right, of course. Max was always right, even when it stung. But Mareek couldn't shake the feeling that he had to do something—he couldn't just leave things with Raj unresolved. He needed to know what had happened to him, what had become of the boy who had shaped so much of his own story. But now, Max wouldn't help.

What was it that always made Max so different? He didn't have a phone, never carried anything that could connect him to the digital world. No social media, no emails, no messages. In fact, Max was as disconnected from the world as someone could be. Yet, there was something about him—a quiet, undeniable presence that seemed to transcend the limitations of the material world. It was as if Max existed on a different plane, one where the need for gadgets and technology didn't matter.

Mareek's mind drifted to times when he had needed Max the most. There were moments in his life, during those years of growing up, where everything seemed uncertain, chaotic. In those moments, when Mareek felt he couldn't go on or when he faced crossroads he didn't know how to navigate, Max had always appeared. Always. Even though Mareek had never called for him, even when there was no way to contact him. It was as if Max knew exactly when to show up, when Mareek needed him most.

It was a strange feeling—a kind of spiritual connection. Mareek couldn't explain it, but he believed it to be true. He had always thought of Max as his guiding star, the constant presence in his life that never faltered. And now, when he needed him the most, Max had turned his back. Not because he didn't care, but because he knew Mareek had to make this decision alone.

But Mareek couldn't bear the thought of going down this path without him. There was a part of him that believed, deep down, that Max was the only one who truly understood him. After all, how could anyone else, with all their material distractions, ever truly understand the pull of the past? No one could. Only Max had the clarity to see things for what they were—and only Max could help him sort through the complicated mess of his emotions.

Mareek closed his eyes again, trying to center himself. He had done it before. He had faced countless obstacles alone, overcome so many hurdles without Max by his side. But this—this felt different. His connection with Max wasn't just a fleeting friendship—it was something deeper, something more spiritual, even if Mareek had never fully understood it.

"Max," Mareek whispered aloud, as though speaking his name could somehow summon him. "Where are you? I need you."

And just as he said it, there was a shift in the air. It wasn't like the world around him physically changed, but he could feel it—something intangible, something unexplainable. It was as if the space around him had become charged with a quiet energy. He sat up straight, a sudden realization flooding over him.

Max didn't need a phone. He didn't need any kind of modern technology. All he needed was that quiet understanding, that connection between them that had always transcended the material world. And it was in those moments of pure, unspoken need that Max would always come.

Mareek stood up from his chair, his heart beating faster now. He felt it—something deep in his chest, the familiar pull that came whenever Max was about to show up. It was a strange sensation, like an invisible thread connecting their souls, always drawing Max back when Mareek needed him.

Without thinking, Mareek moved toward the door of his house, stepping outside into the cool night air. He knew what he had to do. It wasn't about asking for help anymore; it was about trust. He had to trust that Max would show up when he needed him most.

He wasn't sure how, or why, but he just knew. Max would come.

The night was still, and for a moment, Mareek wondered if he was fooling himself. But the certainty in his chest told him otherwise. This was more than just a fleeting hope. He had always felt this spiritual connection with Max, and it had never steered him wrong before.

As he stood there, staring out into the night, a faint figure appeared in the distance. The familiar silhouette of Max, walking slowly toward him. There were no grand gestures, no announcements. It was just Max, as always, coming when Mareek needed him most.

Max didn't say a word as he reached Mareek. They simply stood there, facing each other in the quiet, sharing a moment that spoke louder than any words ever could.

Mareek didn't need to explain himself. Max had already known what he needed.

Without a word, Max placed a hand on his shoulder, offering the silent reassurance that only he could give. The connection between them was deeper than anything Mareek could explain, but it was enough.

"Come on," Max said, his voice soft but steady. "Let's go."

Mareek nodded, a weight lifting from his chest as they walked side by side into the unknown. The past, Raj, everything—none of it mattered right now. Because Max was with him, and that was all that mattered.

The next morning, the quiet of the early hours settled over Mareek's house like a heavy blanket. The world was still, with only the distant sounds of birds breaking the silence. The lingering thoughts of the previous night weighed on him, but something within him had shifted. The connection he shared with Max, that quiet understanding, was still vivid in his mind. But today was different. Today, Mareek had made up his mind—he would go on this journey alone. He would find Raj without Max's guidance, without anyone holding his hand through it.

As the sunlight filtered through the window, Mareek stood up, his movements steady but determined. The decision to go to his village and find Raj had been growing inside him for days, but now it felt like something he had to do. Raj was the missing piece of his past, a chapter that needed closure. Mareek didn't know what he would find when he went back, but he had to try.

He packed a small bag with essentials—water, a few clothes, and a few personal items. But as he reached for his phone, his mind wandered to the strange connection he shared with Max. He realized, with a sort of clarity, that even though Max was not physically with him, he didn't need him in the way he had thought. If Max were meant to show up, he would. And he would be there at the right moment, as always.

Mareek's car rumbled down the familiar, winding road as he approached the village. The sun had begun its descent, casting a warm orange glow over the landscape. His thoughts were scattered, consumed by a restless energy he couldn't shake. He had come all this way to find Raj, but he wasn't entirely sure what he expected to find once he did. Raj was a name from his past—someone he hadn't thought about in years. But something, some inner pull, had driven Mareek to make this trip, a sense that perhaps there was something left unresolved, something that needed to be confronted.

The village was small and quiet as always. Mareek's heart beat a little faster as he reached Raj's house. He parked the car in front of the modest home, taking in the familiar sight of the worn-out gate and the small, overgrown garden. His fingers hovered over the door handle, unsure if he was truly ready for what lay ahead.

He stepped out of the car, each step toward the door feeling heavier than the last. The house stood still and quiet in the early evening light. As Mareek knocked on the door, the sounds of a creaky floorboard echoed inside, and a figure appeared at the entrance.

It was Raj's father, his face weathered and tired, but his eyes sharp and alert despite the years. His graying hair and bent posture spoke of age, but his gaze still carried a sense of resolve, a deep-rooted sense of having lived through hard times.

"Can I help you?" Raj's father asked, his voice calm but guarded.

Mareek hesitated for a moment, unsure of how to begin. The words didn't come easily, but there was a quiet determination in him that finally broke the silence. "I knew your son, Raj. I was looking for him. Do you know where he is now?"

Raj's father blinked, his expression unreadable. There was a long pause as the older man studied Mareek, then something shifted in his eyes—recognition, perhaps, or simply a moment of understanding.

"He's not here," Raj's father said, his voice low. "He left a long time ago."

Mareek's stomach dropped. "Where did he go?" he asked, unable to keep the desperation from his voice.

Raj's father sighed, rubbing his hand over his weathered face. "He left this village... started a new life. He's running an NGO now in the nearest city."

Mareek stood still, trying to absorb the information. Raj, the same boy who had once been so different from the person he was now. It was hard to imagine him running an NGO, let alone being involved in something that helped others. The memories of their time together were too sharp, too angry for him to picture Raj as someone trying to make a positive impact on the world.

"An NGO?" Mareek asked, his voice tinged with disbelief. "What kind of NGO?"

Raj's father nodded slowly. "Yes, it's for kids—troubled kids who need a second chance. He's working with them, helping them find a better path. I don't know all the details, but he's been doing this for a while now. It's the only thing that seems to give him peace."

Mareek's mind raced. The man Raj had become was nothing like the one he remembered. The Raj he knew was brash, reckless, and full of anger. And yet here he was, someone who had chosen to help others, perhaps in an attempt to redeem himself.

"I... I need to find him," Mareek said, more to himself than to Raj's father. "Can you tell me where this NGO is?"

Raj's father looked at Mareek for a long moment, his expression unreadable. After a while, he spoke. "It's in the city, not far from here. You'll find it easily—there's a street near the main road, and you'll see the kids gathered around there. It's a small, unassuming place. But that's where Raj is."

Mareek's chest tightened. He felt a strange sense of purpose wash over him. He had come here to find Raj, and now, it seemed, he was closer than ever. But there was still something lingering in his mind—something unresolved. He wasn't sure if he was ready to face the man Raj had become, but the pull to find out, to understand, was too strong to ignore.

"Thank you," Mareek said, his voice quiet, almost reverent. "I'll go to the city. I need to talk to him."

Raj's father gave a brief nod, his expression softening slightly. "I hope you find him, son. Raj is... a good boy. He just made some wrong choices when he was younger. But he's trying now. He's trying to be better."

Mareek paused before leaving. The weight of those words hung heavily in the air. Was Raj really trying to be better? Or was this just a façade to hide the guilt and regret he must have carried with him all these years?

Without saying another word, Mareek turned and walked out of the house, his mind racing. The drive to the city was quiet, save for the hum of the car's engine and the occasional thought that flitted through his mind. He was headed toward a man he hadn't seen in years, a man who had once been the source of so much anger and fear for him. Now, all those feelings felt distant, foreign even. Was he really ready to face Raj? To confront the boy who had once tormented him, who had left without any trace?

As Mareek drove, the weight of his own choices pressed down on him. He had made mistakes, too, after all. There was no denying it. He had hurt people along the way, and now, he wondered if this search for Raj was more than just about closure—it was about seeking redemption, about understanding that people could change, and maybe, just maybe, he could change too.

The city loomed ahead, its skyline towering in the distance. Mareek didn't know exactly what he was walking into, but he knew that this was something he had to do. There were no guarantees, no promises that the person Raj had become would even be the same as the boy Mareek had once known. But Mareek had come this far, and now he couldn't turn back.

With a deep breath, Mareek pressed down on the accelerator, heading toward the city—and toward Raj.

As Mareek drove through the winding roads toward the city, the quiet hum of the engine was a constant companion, but his mind was elsewhere, caught in the past. The events of the last few days played like a montage in his head: his conversation with Raj's father, the uncertainty he felt about the man Raj had become, and the ever-present memory of Max's words.

Max had never mentioned Raj. Not once. Yet somehow, Max's teachings and his way of seeing the world kept echoing in Mareek's mind, especially now as he drove toward the city. It was almost as if Max's philosophy, which had shaped so many of Mareek's decisions in the past, was still guiding him in ways he couldn't fully understand.

Max had always been a person of few words. His advice was often cryptic, indirect—more a whisper in the back of Mareek's mind than something clear-cut. But somehow, over time, Max's perspective on life had shaped Mareek's worldview. Max had a unique understanding of people, of change, of time. He saw things from a broader perspective, one that could see a person not just for who they were, but for who they could become.

"Everything changes, Mareek," Max had once said, when Mareek was questioning his path. "Time, circumstances, experiences... they shape people, for better or worse. No one stays the same. You have to understand that."

At the time, Mareek had shrugged it off as just more philosophical ramblings from Max. But now, as he drove, those words began to settle in. Change was inevitable. People were always evolving, sometimes in ways that were impossible to predict. Raj, the man who had once been a bully in Mareek's life, might be someone entirely different now. He might not even be the person Mareek remembered.

What struck Mareek most was that Max had never said anything specific about Raj—yet here he was, driving into the city to find him. Why? Was he seeking redemption? Closure? Or was he simply trying to prove that people could change, that someone as terrible as Raj could have found a different path?

As the city's skyline loomed ahead, Mareek's mind returned to the present, to his purpose here. He wasn't just looking for Raj because of their past. No, it was more than that. He wanted to see if Max's words held any truth. If Raj had indeed changed, if he had grown into a better person, it would mean that change wasn't just a theoretical concept—it could be real. And if Raj could change, could Mareek? Could he evolve into someone better, someone less consumed by his own ambitions?

The city streets grew busier as Mareek drove through the heart of it. The sound of honking horns and the hustle of the crowds filled the air, but Mareek was focused. He thought about how, all those years ago, he had seen Raj as nothing more than a bully. The Raj he remembered was a boy who had tormented him, who had sought power in the most demeaning ways. But if he had truly changed—if he had truly left that life behind—what would that mean? Could he even forgive Raj for the things he had done?

Mareek shook his head, trying to clear the fog in his mind. The questions swirling around him felt like a whirlwind, but deep down, he knew he had to confront Raj. He needed to see if the person Raj had become was someone he could respect, someone who had grown beyond the man who had once terrorized him.

When he finally arrived at the building where Raj's NGO was located, Mareek took a deep breath before getting out of the car. He paused for a moment, looking up at the structure. The glass windows reflected the sunlight, but they seemed distant, like a barrier between the past and the present.

He walked inside, approaching the receptionist and asking for Raj. After a few moments, the receptionist nodded and made a call. Minutes later, Mareek was led down a long hallway, where the walls were adorned with photographs of smiling faces—people from all walks of life, each with their own story. It was strange. Was this the same Raj who had once bullied him? Could he really have transformed into this person who helped others?

Mareek's thoughts were interrupted when the door to an office opened. Raj stepped out, and for a moment, Mareek didn't recognize him. The man before him was older, more mature, his demeanor calm. The cocky, arrogant Raj he had known seemed like a distant memory, as though it had never existed.

"Raj," Mareek said, his voice low.

Raj looked up, his face softening when he saw Mareek standing there. For a moment, the two men just stared at each other. There was no recognition, no anger, just silence. Then Raj spoke.

"Mareek," he said, his voice hesitant. "I didn't expect to see you."

There was a long pause, as if both of them were trying to gauge the other's intentions. Raj motioned toward the office door.

"Come in. We can talk."

Mareek hesitated for a moment before stepping inside. As he entered, he couldn't help but notice how different Raj looked. His clothes were simple, his posture more relaxed, and there was an air of responsibility about him that hadn't existed before. It was as if the weight of the world was now on his shoulders, but in a way that spoke of growth, of understanding.

They sat down, and the conversation began slowly, tentatively. Mareek didn't know what to say. He didn't know if he should bring up the past, or if he should simply ask about Raj's work now. But then Raj spoke, breaking the silence.

"I know what you're probably thinking," Raj said, looking down at his hands. "I'm not the same person I was back then. I've changed. And I know that doesn't erase what I did. But I've tried to make up for it. I've been working with people who need help, who are struggling with the things I used to struggle with. It's not much, but it's something."

Mareek listened, not interrupting. Raj's words seemed genuine, and for the first time, Mareek felt like he was hearing the truth. Maybe Raj had changed. Maybe he wasn't the same person who had tormented him all those years ago.

As the conversation continued, Mareek realized that Raj wasn't just talking about his past, but also about the lessons he had learned, the mistakes he had made, and the way he had tried to move forward. It wasn't an apology—it was an acknowledgment, an understanding that change was possible, and that it was something he had actively worked toward.

Mareek didn't know what to say in response. He couldn't tell if Raj was truly changed, or if he was just putting on a front. But in that moment, he didn't care. Raj had made his peace, and perhaps that was all that mattered.

As the conversation between Mareek and Raj continued, the tension that had been hanging in the air slowly began to dissipate. There was no anger, no animosity—just the uneasy but genuine exchange between two men who had once been on completely different paths. Raj spoke with a calmness that Mareek hadn't expected, explaining how he had left behind the person he used to be, how he had tried to make amends through his work at the NGO. It was clear Raj had found a sense of purpose in helping others, a way to balance the mistakes of his past.

Mareek sat in silence for a moment, processing everything Raj had said. The years of bitterness, the desire for revenge, the self-centeredness—it all seemed so distant now. But despite hearing Raj's story, something still gnawed at Mareek. There was a void inside him, something he hadn't been able to fill no matter how much fame or success he'd achieved. He was rich, popular, and well-known, but peace of mind seemed to always slip just out of his reach. The pain, the emptiness—he hadn't been able to shake it.

As he looked at Raj, something clicked in Mareek's mind. Perhaps the answer wasn't found in his music or in the fame he chased. Maybe it was somewhere else—somewhere he hadn't even considered before.

Raj's words had struck a chord with him. The NGO, the work he was doing—maybe there was something in it that could help him find peace, something beyond himself, something that wasn't about success or recognition.

"Raj," Mareek said slowly, his voice softer than it had been before. "You've mentioned how you've found a way to make things right, through your work here, helping others. I... I don't know if I'm ready to say I've made things right, but I need something. I need to find some sort of peace. Something that gives me a purpose beyond just... myself."

Raj looked at Mareek with a quiet understanding, his eyes no longer filled with the arrogance or self-preservation Mareek remembered from years ago. There was something genuine in them now, something Mareek hadn't expected but couldn't ignore.

"I know what you mean," Raj replied quietly. "This work—it's not easy, but it's rewarding in ways that I never imagined. I'm not just giving back to others, I'm giving back to myself. It's been a way for me to heal."

Mareek felt his heart rate quicken as he listened. He had been chasing fame, looking for validation in all the wrong places, and had never once considered something deeper, something that could help him heal his internal wounds. The pain that had been building inside him, the restlessness he had never been able to satisfy—it seemed like Raj had discovered a solution to all of that.

"I don't know what you're doing exactly here," Mareek said, "but I want to help. Maybe... maybe if I contribute to something bigger than myself, something that matters, it'll give me a sense of purpose. A sense of peace. Can I be a part of this? I don't know how, but I want to try."

Raj leaned back in his chair, his expression thoughtful. It was clear that Mareek's words had struck him in a way he hadn't anticipated. He was silent for a moment, almost as if weighing Mareek's offer, but there was a flicker of recognition in his eyes.

"If you're serious about this," Raj said, "you're welcome to join. We can use all the help we can get. But I have to warn you—it's not as glamorous as it may seem. It's about helping people who are struggling, people who are fighting battles that are much harder than what we've been through."

Mareek nodded, feeling the weight of Raj's words settle into his chest. He wasn't looking for glamour. In fact, he wanted the opposite. The fame, the lights, the accolades—they hadn't brought him the satisfaction he craved. Maybe this was what he needed—a chance to make a real impact, to help people who had suffered more than he could ever imagine.

"I don't care about glamour," Mareek said firmly. "I just need something that matters."

Raj smiled faintly, the first real smile Mareek had seen from him in years. It was not the smug grin of a man who had once felt powerful, but a quiet acknowledgment of the person who stood before him now. "Alright then," Raj said. "Let's get you started. We can always use someone who's willing to put in the work."

As Mareek stood up to leave, he felt a strange sense of calm wash over him. The road ahead wouldn't be easy, and he knew it would take time to adjust to the kind of work Raj was doing. But for the first time in a long while, Mareek felt like he was heading in the right direction.

Raj's words echoed in his mind as he left the office. Helping people, giving back to the community, and finding peace through service. Maybe this was the beginning of something new, something that could offer him the mental peace he had been searching for all his life. For the first time, Mareek wasn't focused on the next song or the next performance. He wasn't thinking about the crowds, the money, or the fame. Instead, he was thinking about what really mattered—what could make a difference not just in his life, but in the lives of others.

He had no idea how he would fit into Raj's world, but that didn't matter. All that mattered now was the quiet hope that maybe, just maybe, helping others would help him find peace within himself.

Mareek sat in his luxurious, albeit lonely, apartment, staring out of the window at the busy city below. It had been two days since his trip to Raj's village, and he couldn't shake the feeling that something had changed inside him. The entire time he was there, the thought of giving back to others, of being part of something bigger than himself, lingered in his mind like a quiet whisper. But he knew that before making any decision, he needed to talk to Max.

Max had always been there for him in one form or another, even if it wasn't always the most conventional support. Mareek respected his opinions, even if he didn't always follow them. Max had a different way of looking at the world, one that often made Mareek pause and reconsider his choices. And now, after everything that had happened with Rakesh, the success, and the emptiness that followed it, Mareek knew he needed to have a conversation with Max before taking any further steps toward this new path.

He had never been the type to wait around, but in this case, he couldn't shake the need to talk things through. For the past two days, he had gone about his usual routine—taking meetings, responding to messages, and even recording a few tracks for new songs—but his thoughts kept drifting back to Raj's NGO and the possibility of a different life, one that wasn't about the next hit song or the next concert. But instead, something more meaningful.

Max hadn't shown up yet, though. That was normal. Max was never predictable in the way he came and went, but when he arrived, it was always with his quiet wisdom that seemed to make everything clear.

It was late in the evening on the third day when Mareek's doorbell finally rang. He hadn't expected Max so soon, but then again, Max never worked on anyone else's timeline. Mareek stood up and opened the door, his heart a little lighter at the sight of his old friend.

Max stood in the doorway, his usual quiet self, with his unkempt hair and clothes that looked as if they hadn't been washed in days. Mareek wasn't surprised. Max had always been the type to live life in his own way, no matter how it looked on the outside.

"Come in," Mareek said, stepping aside to let Max into his apartment.

Max nodded and walked in, looking around as if he hadn't seen this place in ages. "Nice to see you haven't changed," he said, his voice casual as always.

Mareek didn't waste any time. He walked over to the couch and sat down, motioning for Max to join him. "I've been thinking," Mareek began, his tone serious. "About the NGO, about what Raj's doing, and... about what I've been doing."

Max didn't respond immediately, just took a seat and watched Mareek with a quiet, assessing look in his eyes.

"I went to his village," Mareek continued, leaning forward, "and I saw his father. Raj runs this NGO now, helping kids, people who've been through tough lives, people who need a second chance. He told me that this work has been the only thing that's given him any peace after everything he's done in the past."

Max still didn't speak, but his eyes flickered with interest.

Mareek sighed, running a hand through his hair. "I think... I think I need to do something like that. I need something real, something that matters. I've spent so much of my life chasing fame, success, and recognition, but none of it feels like it's enough. I'm not happy, Max. I don't think I've ever been happy."

Max remained quiet for a moment, then spoke in his usual calm voice, "So, you want to help people? That's what you're telling me?"

"Yeah," Mareek replied, nodding. "I've been chasing all the wrong things, Max. I don't want to keep living in this cycle of trying to one-up myself or others. I want something that... I don't know. Gives me peace. Gives me purpose. I'm thinking of joining Raj's NGO. I don't know what I can do to help, but I want to try."

Max's gaze softened slightly, but there was still a hint of skepticism in his eyes. "You're serious about this?"

"I think so," Mareek answered, feeling a sense of clarity wash over him. "I know it sounds crazy. I've always been about the spotlight, the music, the fame. But none of that's real, Max. None of it fills the emptiness I feel inside."

Max leaned back on the couch, his arms folded as he processed what Mareek had said. After a long silence, he spoke again, his voice low and thoughtful. "You're right about one thing: the emptiness. That's something everyone faces eventually. The question is, why wait until it's too late? You've got the chance to change now, Mareek. If you think this NGO work is what you need to find some peace, then go for it."

Mareek stared at Max, feeling a mix of gratitude and doubt. He wasn't sure if he was ready to fully give up everything he'd worked for, but at the same time, he knew he had to try. He'd spent so long focused on external success, thinking that would make him happy, but deep down, he knew it wouldn't.

"Thanks, Max," Mareek said quietly. "I'm not sure what the future holds, but... I think I'm ready to find out. I need something to give me a reason to get out of bed in the morning, something that's not just about me."

Max gave a small, approving nod. "You know, I don't think this is about being a hero or changing the world in some grand way. It's about finding your peace. That's the only thing that really matters."

Mareek nodded slowly, his thoughts racing. "I think you're right. I've been running from myself for too long. Maybe now it's time to stop and face who I really am."

Max didn't say anything else, but there was a certain understanding in his eyes, an acknowledgment that Mareek had made a decision that would change his life. Mareek felt a sense of relief, as if he had finally stopped chasing an illusion and started to search for something real. It wasn't going to be easy. It wouldn't be glamorous. But for the first time, it felt like the right choice.

"I'll start tomorrow," Mareek said, his voice filled with quiet determination. "I don't know where this road leads, but I'm ready to walk down it."

Max stood up, ready to leave. He didn't need to say anything else. Mareek knew Max's thoughts were his own. Sometimes, words weren't needed to communicate the things that mattered most.

"Good luck, Mareek," Max said, his voice low and sincere.

"Thanks, Max," Mareek replied. And for the first time in a long while, he meant it.

The next morning was a new start for Mareek. The sun had barely risen, but he was already on the road, his mind buzzing with anticipation. He drove to the NGO's office, a mix of excitement and nervousness churning in his stomach. It felt like he was about to step into a completely different world—a world where his fame and past didn't matter, where the only thing that counted was the impact he could make.

As Mareek pulled up to the NGO's office, he noticed Raj was already waiting for him outside. The same calm, grounded presence Mareek had noticed the other day was still there. Raj's demeanor hadn't changed; he was still the quiet, reflective person he had always been, but now there was something more. A sense of purpose, a sense of fulfillment that Mareek couldn't ignore. Raj smiled when he saw Mareek approach.

"Good to see you here," Raj greeted, his voice warm yet steady. "Ready to get started?"

Mareek nodded, a slight but genuine smile forming on his lips. "Absolutely. Let's do this."

Raj led Mareek inside the building, showing him the office space, which was much more organized than Mareek had expected. The walls were adorned with photographs of the people the NGO had helped—smiling faces, families reunited, individuals empowered. It was clear that this was more than just a charity; it was a movement, one that brought real change to people's lives.

"Alright," Raj began as they sat down at a desk together, "We have a few things to go over. I know you're here to help, and I think you'll fit right in with our team."

Raj walked Mareek through some of the ongoing projects. There were initiatives for underprivileged children, women's empowerment programs, and mental health awareness campaigns. Mareek was intrigued by everything, his mind working overtime to absorb all the information. It was a lot to take in at once, but he was eager to dive in.

"You'll be helping with the outreach programs," Raj explained. "We need to connect with local businesses, schools, and communities to raise awareness about our work. You'll be managing some of the social media and public relations, too. But more than anything, we need someone who can connect with people and share our message. That's where you come in."

Mareek was surprised at how well Raj had thought through his role. It wasn't what he expected at all—he thought he might be doing menial tasks, something far removed from his usual lifestyle. But Raj had seen something in him, something that he could bring to the table, and it made Mareek feel both humbled and determined.

As they went through the details of Mareek's responsibilities, the door opened and a new voice interrupted their conversation.

"Hi! You must be Mareek," a cheerful voice said. A woman with short black hair and a welcoming smile stepped inside. She was wearing glasses and a casual blouse, exuding an air of friendly professionalism.

"This is Sufiya," Raj introduced her. "She's one of our biology teachers, and she's been with us for a few years now. She's also a key contributor to our education programs."

Sufiya extended her hand to Mareek. "Nice to meet you. I've heard a lot about you." There was a warmth in her voice that made Mareek feel instantly comfortable.

"You're a biology teacher?" Mareek asked, a little taken aback. "I thought this was all about social work and community development."

Sufiya laughed lightly. "It's a bit of both, actually. Education is at the heart of everything we do. We run various educational workshops in the community, especially focusing on children and young adults. We believe that the power of knowledge is one of the most effective tools for change. I teach biology, but I'm also involved in many other aspects of the NGO—training, organizing events, and outreach."

Mareek nodded, impressed. He had never really thought about how education and community development intersected before. He realized that Sufiya's role was pivotal in shaping the future of the people they were helping.

"Together, we work to create a platform where people can empower themselves through learning," Raj added, giving Sufiya a nod of approval. "Each one of us brings something different to the table. And we're glad to have you here to contribute."

Mareek felt a sense of unity in the room, a feeling that he had never experienced in the world of fame and concerts. Here, people were working together for something greater than themselves, and Mareek couldn't help but admire that. He realized that for all the success he had achieved in music, he had never experienced the kind of fulfillment that these people had. They were changing lives, and Mareek was about to become a part of that.

"Thanks," Mareek said, his voice steady but sincere. "I'm looking forward to it."

Raj smiled, clearly pleased with Mareek's enthusiasm. "We're glad to have you. Let's get started then."

For the rest of the day, Mareek was thrown into the work. He spent time with Raj, Sufiya, and the other contributors, learning the ins and outs of the NGO's operations. He was introduced to more people, each one more passionate than the last. They all had their own stories, their own reasons for being there, but they shared a common goal: to make the world a better place, one small step at a time.

Mareek had always been surrounded by people who admired him for his music, people who saw him as a star. But here, he was just another person trying to do something good. He wasn't treated like a celebrity; instead, he was respected for his willingness to help, for his desire to be part of something bigger than himself.

As the day came to a close, Mareek felt a sense of peace settle over him, a quiet contentment that had been missing from his life for so long. He had entered this world uncertain and full of questions, but now he was beginning to find his place. He could see how his skills could be used for something meaningful, something that would not only bring him fulfillment but also help others along the way.

When he left the office that evening, the setting sun painted the sky with hues of orange and pink. Mareek drove back to his apartment, reflecting on the day. It was a new chapter, a chapter that had begun with uncertainty but was already beginning to feel like the most important journey of his life. He knew that whatever lay ahead, he was exactly where he needed to be.

As Mareek drove back home that evening, his mind was a storm of conflicting thoughts. The streets outside seemed to blur, the familiar landscape losing its meaning as his mind turned inward. He wasn't used to feeling this way—this unsettled, distracted. He had always been certain about everything, especially about love. It was something he didn't believe in. Mareek had never had a crush, never felt that kind of pull toward someone that everyone seemed to talk about. To him, love was a fleeting emotion, a weakness. It was something people got tangled up in, and he had no interest in it.

But today, there was something different. Something about Sufiya had managed to slip under his skin, without him even realizing it. He couldn't quite explain it, but there was an unfamiliar flutter in his chest, and it made him uncomfortable. He tried to dismiss it, but the more he thought about her, the more he couldn't shake the feeling. This was uncharted territory for him—he wasn't supposed to feel like this. He had always kept his distance from such emotions, priding himself on his independence and detachment.

It wasn't just the way she spoke or the way she looked at him. It was something deeper—something about the way she lived her life. She had purpose. She knew who she was and what she was doing. She was confident in a way Mareek had never seen before, a quiet strength that didn't need validation. People like her were rare, and he couldn't help but admire that. But did that mean he was attracted to her? Mareek wasn't sure. He had never felt anything close to what people described as "love."

Still, his thoughts kept drifting back to her, and the more he tried to push it away, the stronger the feeling grew. It wasn't love, he told himself. Maybe it was admiration, maybe respect. But even as he tried to convince himself, a part of him knew that wasn't quite it either. There was something about Sufiya that had planted a seed in his mind, and it was growing, whether he wanted it to or not.

When he reached his house, he couldn't stop thinking about her. This feeling, whatever it was, didn't sit right with him. He had always been in control of his emotions, but now it felt like he was losing grip. It wasn't love, not for a second. But it was something, and that thought made him uneasy. He didn't know how to deal with it, so he pushed it aside, focusing on the next step in his journey, the NGO, and his mission to find peace away from the chaos of his past life.

But as Mareek sat down on his couch, the weight of the day's events settled on him, and he couldn't help but think of Sufiya once again. Why did he feel this strange sense of longing when he was around her? He didn't believe in love, but in this moment, it felt like something he couldn't ignore.

Mareek always used to avoid the feeling of loving someone, as same as rakesh, he was afraid of attachments. He doesn't want to get connected with anybody.

For to his surprise, as Mareek sank deeper into his thoughts, there was a sudden knock at the door. He wasn't expecting anyone, not at this hour. His heart skipped a beat as he got up to answer. To his surprise, it was Max, standing there with his usual calm demeanor.

"Max, what are you doing here?" Mareek asked, his voice carrying an edge of curiosity. Max had been elusive lately, only showing up sporadically. Mareek had almost forgotten what it felt like to have him around for more than just a few minutes.

"I had a feeling you might need to talk," Max said with a smile, though it was barely there. His eyes, however, were sharp, as if he had been sensing something all along. Max had always been perceptive, often understanding Mareek's unspoken thoughts better than anyone else.

Mareek hesitated for a moment, not sure if he wanted to open up. But he knew Max, and he knew that once he started talking, there would be no turning back. So, with a sigh, Mareek led him inside.

As they sat down, the silence stretched between them for a while. Mareek's thoughts were still scattered, but he couldn't ignore the nagging feeling about Sufiya. There was something about her that he couldn't shake, and he found himself wanting to share it with someone who might understand, even though he wasn't sure if he understood it himself.

"Max," Mareek started, his voice uncertain, "there's this woman I met at the NGO. Her name is Sufiya." He paused, unsure how to continue. "She's different. You know, not like anyone I've ever met. She's confident, smart, independent... I don't know. She's been on my mind a lot lately."

Max's expression remained unchanged as he listened intently, his eyes never leaving Mareek's. He didn't interrupt, letting Mareek speak freely, knowing that sometimes Mareek needed time to sort through his own thoughts.

"I don't know why I'm telling you this," Mareek continued, a sense of unease settling in his chest. "It's not like me to talk about feelings... I don't believe in love, you know that. I've never had a crush, never been interested in any of that. But with her... it's different. I don't even know what it is, but it feels... important."

Max didn't respond immediately. He leaned back in his chair, his gaze thoughtful. Mareek could feel the weight of his silence, but he didn't rush him. Max had always been good at giving him space, letting him figure things out on his own.

Finally, after what seemed like an eternity, Max spoke.

"You're confused," he said, his voice calm but filled with understanding. "But that's not a bad thing. It just means you're starting to feel something you've never felt before. And that can be uncomfortable."

Mareek was silent for a long time, mulling over Max's words. He didn't want to admit it, but deep down, he knew that Max was right. This was unfamiliar territory, and he didn't know how to navigate it.

"I don't know what to do, Max," Mareek admitted, his voice barely above a whisper. "I can't stop thinking about her, but I don't know what that means. I don't know what I'm supposed to do with these feelings."

Max nodded slowly, his expression unreadable. "Sometimes you don't have to know right away," he said. "You just have to be honest with yourself. If you're thinking about her this much, maybe it's worth exploring. But don't let it control you. Don't lose yourself in it."

Mareek nodded, feeling a sense of relief wash over him. For once, someone was telling him to embrace the uncertainty, to not have all the answers right away. Max's advice was always simple but powerful.

"I don't know if I'm ready for this," Mareek said, his voice tinged with doubt.

"You don't have to be ready," Max replied. "You just have to be open to it. If it's meant to be, it'll happen. But you have to be honest with yourself first."

Mareek sat back, his thoughts swirling around him. It felt like a turning point, but he wasn't sure which direction he should go. For so long, he had kept his distance from emotions like this, but now, everything was different. Maybe it was time to stop running from it. Max stayed for a while longer, but eventually, as always, he left quietly without saying much. Mareek sat there, still processing everything Max had said. He wasn't sure what would come next, but he felt a sense of clarity that he hadn't felt in a long time.

The next day, as Mareek drove back to the NGO, his thoughts were clearer. He still didn't know what he felt for Sufiya, but he was beginning to accept that he didn't need to have all the answers right away. For the first time, he felt like he was ready to face whatever came his way—whether it was love, friendship, or something else entirely. And maybe, just maybe, that was enough for now.

The second day at the NGO was far from what Mareek had anticipated. As he drove up to the gates, he noticed a familiar sight—there, standing outside, was the crowd of media and fans, eagerly waiting for him. The cameras flashed in the distance, and the reporters' voices pierced the air with rapid questions. They were all curious, wondering if Mareek, the famous DJ and singer, was about to leave his music career behind to devote himself to the work at the NGO. The questions seemed endless, and the crowd's energy was palpable.

Mareek had been in the spotlight long enough to know how to handle these situations. He knew the routine—how to smile, nod, and give a few well-rehearsed answers to keep everyone satisfied. As he stepped out of his car, he could already feel the weight of the media's gaze on him. They wanted answers, and they wanted them now. But for Mareek, this was just another day in the life he had created. The interviews, the meet-and-greets with fans, it had all become too normal.

"Are you planning to leave music, Mareek?" one reporter shouted.

"Will your commitment to the NGO interfere with your career as a musician?" another asked.

He responded with a practiced calmness. "I'm still figuring things out. Music is part of who I am, but helping people is just as important. I'll continue to do both for as long as I can."

The questions continued to rain down on him, each one more pressing than the last. Mareek's patience was wearing thin, but before he could answer the next barrage, he felt a gentle pull on his arm.

Sufiya.

Without a word, she appeared beside him, her presence like a shield against the crowd. Her hand gripped his firmly, guiding him through the chaos of reporters and cameras. The moment her hand touched his, Mareek felt a sudden sense of calm. Sufiya didn't hesitate; she gently pushed through the throng of media, her calm demeanor starkly contrasting with the frenzy around them.

"Mareek, let's get inside," Sufiya said, her voice steady and authoritative.

She didn't look back at the reporters as she led him to the NGO office. Mareek, still in a bit of a daze from the commotion, let her guide him. He had to admit, there was something undeniably reassuring about her presence. She wasn't intimidated by the media, and she didn't hesitate for a second in taking control of the situation.

Once inside the building, Mareek let out a deep breath, his heart still pounding from the interaction with the media. He glanced at Sufiya, who was now standing next to him, her hand still resting lightly on his arm.

"Thank you," Mareek said, his voice quieter now. "I don't know what I would have done without you back there."

Sufiya simply nodded, her expression warm but calm. "It's nothing," she replied. "You don't have to deal with all of that alone. We're here to focus on the work that matters."

But as the door to the NGO's office closed behind them, the media outside wasn't about to let them go so easily. Within hours, the headlines started to pop up online, some of which focused not just on Mareek's decision to spend more time at the NGO but also on the fact that he and Sufiya had shared a moment of closeness. Speculation ran wild about their relationship. Some outlets suggested they were romantically involved, while others simply noted their growing bond as colleagues.

"I don't know what they're talking about," he muttered to Raj when they were alone. "She was just helping me get through the crowd."

Raj raised an eyebrow but didn't press further. "People love a good story, especially when it comes to famous people like you. Just be careful, Mareek. Things might get complicated if you let it go too far."

But despite Raj's cautionary words, Mareek couldn't shake the feeling that the attention was starting to feel too heavy, too overwhelming. The media was already making assumptions about his relationship with Sufiya, and he wasn't sure how to handle it. But Sufiya, ever calm and composed, didn't seem bothered by any of it.

A few days later, Mareek was standing outside the NGO office, waiting for Sufiya, when one of the reporters approached him again. "Mareek, is it true that you and Sufiya are more than just colleagues? Are you romantically involved?"

The question took him off guard, but he couldn't deny that it had been on his mind too. He had no idea what was happening between them, but whatever it was, he wasn't ready to label it. He didn't know how to explain it to the media, to anyone.

He opened his mouth to speak, but before he could answer, Sufiya appeared, her gaze sharp and focused. She stepped in front of Mareek, her presence commanding the attention of the reporter.

"We're here to do important work, not entertain baseless rumors," she said, her tone firm yet calm. "If you're done here, we'll be inside."

And just like that, Sufiya took control of the situation once more, leading Mareek away from the reporters and back into the safety of the office. She didn't seem phased by the questions or the media frenzy, but Mareek couldn't help but feel a sense of gratitude toward her. She wasn't just protecting him from the media—she was protecting him from himself, from the overwhelming pressure that fame brought with it.

But the rumors didn't stop. As the days went on, the media continued to speculate about Mareek and Sufiya. They tried to capture every moment they spent together, looking for any sign that their relationship was more than just professional. And although Mareek had no interest in feeding into those rumors, he couldn't deny that a part of him was curious about Sufiya, about the strange, unspoken connection they seemed to share.

But for now, Mareek chose to focus on the work at hand. The NGO was his priority, and he knew he had to stay focused on that. The music, the fame, the media—all of it could wait. There was a greater purpose here, one that was more important than anything else.

And so, he continued his work with Sufiya, with Raj, and with the rest of the team, hoping that eventually, the noise outside would fade, and he could find the peace he was desperately searching for.

One evening, as Mareek was returning home after a long day at the NGO, he took the usual route through the busy streets of the city. The sun had just begun to set, casting a soft golden hue over everything. As he was driving, he noticed a familiar figure by the side of the road, her scooter parked awkwardly, and Sufiya crouching beside it, trying to figure out what was wrong.

Mareek slowed down and pulled over. Stepping out of his car, he approached her with a concerned look.

"Sufiya," he called out, "Are you alright?"

Sufiya looked up, her face a mixture of frustration and mild embarrassment. "Hey, Mareek," she said, standing up from her crouched position. "Yeah, it's just the scooter. I think something's wrong with the engine. It's not starting."

Mareek looked at the scooter, then back at Sufiya. It was obvious that she was trying to handle the situation on her own, but it seemed like a bigger issue than she was letting on. "Need any help?" he offered, already reaching for the tools in his car.

Sufiya shook her head. "No, it's okay. I can handle it. But thanks."

Mareek hesitated. He could see that she was struggling, but at the same time, he knew that she didn't like asking for help, and he didn't want to push her further. However, as he stood there, he couldn't help but think of an easier solution—just a simple ride to the office or home.

"Hey, listen," Mareek said after a moment of contemplation. "Why don't you give me a lift? I can drive you to the office or wherever you need to go. I'm sure this will take a while, and I don't mind. It'll save you the hassle."

Sufiya looked up at him, her expression unreadable for a moment. She clearly didn't want to make things more complicated. "I'd love to, but with the media around lately... I don't think it's a good idea. They'll jump to conclusions again."

Mareek could understand her hesitation. Lately, with all the attention from the media and the rumors about their relationship, it had been hard for Sufiya to do anything without being noticed. But he wasn't going to take no for an answer.

"Sufiya," Mareek said with a small grin, "The media's going to talk whether we do something or not. Let's just go. I promise no one will notice us."

She sighed but gave in, knowing that there wasn't much to be done anyway. "Okay, fine. But you owe me one."

Mareek chuckled. "Deal." He got into the passenger seat, and they drove off, heading toward the office.

As they cruised down the street, the city lights flickering by, Mareek leaned back in his seat and turned to Sufiya, who was focused on the road ahead. The silence between them felt comfortable, but after a few moments, Mareek decided to break it.

"Sufiya," he began, his voice casual, "How do you manage everything? I mean, the NGO, the work you do there, your personal life... and how do you even make a living?"

She glanced at him quickly, a bit surprised by the question. "I'm not sure what you mean," she replied, her eyes quickly returning to the road.

Mareek adjusted his position in the seat, his curiosity getting the best of him. "Well, you're here all the time, working with Raj and the others. But it's not like you're getting paid much for it, right? You're so dedicated to helping people, I can't help but wonder how you make ends meet."

Sufiya looked thoughtful for a moment. It was clear she hadn't expected such a direct question, but after a beat, she spoke up.

"I teach biology at a local school," she said, her tone a little more guarded now. "That's how I earn my living. The NGO's not my primary source of income, but it's something I'm deeply passionate about."

Mareek nodded, impressed by her dedication. "That's admirable.

Most people would have a hard time balancing all of that. Teaching, working here, and still trying to have a life."

Sufiya smiled faintly, but there was a hint of exhaustion in her eyes. "It's not always easy, but I manage. I've always felt a calling to do this work. It's important to me."

Mareek was silent for a while, mulling over her words. There was a sense of respect in his mind for Sufiya's determination, but at the same time, he couldn't help but feel that there was something she wasn't telling him. Something deeper about why she chose to live her life this way. But he didn't push. It wasn't the right time.

Instead, he changed the subject, asking about the work at the NGO and how she thought things were progressing. They fell into a more comfortable conversation as they continued their drive, the earlier tension lifting. Despite the media's constant attention and the pressure on both of them, in that moment, Mareek couldn't help but feel at ease.

Sufiya had always been a mystery to him—someone who seemed to carry a quiet strength, someone who balanced her responsibilities with a level of grace that was rare in people of her age. Mareek had always admired that about her, but tonight, there was something else. Something unspoken between them that lingered in the air, even as they spoke of mundane things. It was subtle, but it was there.

He didn't quite understand what it meant yet, but it was a feeling he couldn't shake.

As the car hummed quietly down the road, the soft glow of the streetlights passing by, a rare stillness settled between them. Mareek glanced at Sufiya from the corner of his eye, noticing the way her shoulders had slightly tensed, her focus remaining solely on the road ahead. He had always sensed that there was more to her than what she let on, a story hidden beneath the calm exterior she maintained so well.

Finally, Sufiya spoke, breaking the silence in a soft voice that held a vulnerability Mareek hadn't expected.

"You asked me how I make a living," she said, her tone now more reflective. "But the truth is, I don't really have a personal life. Not anymore, anyway."

Mareek looked at her, curiosity piqued. He could hear the faint sadness in her voice, the words hanging heavy in the air. She wasn't the type to share much, and this felt like a rare glimpse into her world.

"My parents died in a car accident when I was younger," she continued, her gaze fixed firmly on the road. "It was just... gone, one day. They were my world. After that, my older sister, Alfa, became everything to me. She raised me, made sure I didn't fall apart, even when everything seemed to shatter."

Mareek could feel the weight of her words. He understood loss, even though the details of her story were different from his own. "I'm sorry to hear that," he said quietly, the words almost seeming too small for the grief she must have carried for all these years.

Sufiya gave a small, wistful smile, her fingers tightening slightly on the steering wheel. "You don't need to apologize. It happened a long time ago, but the memories... they still stick. Alfa works as a receptionist at a hotel now, and she's been the one holding everything together. She's my strength." There was a quiet pride in her voice as she spoke of Alfa, a silent gratitude that shone through despite the sorrow in her words.

Mareek was silent for a moment, processing the depth of what Sufiya had shared. He'd never imagined this part of her story, this hidden chapter of her life. It made sense now why she seemed so guarded, why she focused so heavily on her work with the NGO. She had been shaped by the pain of losing her parents, the need to survive on her own, with only her sister as her anchor.

Then, Mareek turned his gaze toward the window, lost in his own thoughts. Something stirred within him—a sense of connection, a shared understanding between them. He'd never really opened up to anyone about his own family, and yet, here he was, listening to Sufiya's story, realizing just how much they had in common, even if their circumstances were different.

He took a deep breath, his voice quieter now, tinged with the honesty he rarely showed. "I know how you feel," he began. "My mother died while giving birth to me, and my father... well, he ran away when I was still really young. I don't even know the reason. One day, he was just gone, leaving us behind." Mareek paused for a moment, his hand tightening around the seatbelt. "My sister, Sara, she raised me. She had to. And our father... he wasn't a good man. When he lived with us, he used to beat me and Sara, mostly when he was drunk. I don't even know how we made it through those years. But Sara... she kept us going. She was the one who fought for us, made sure we survived."

Sufiya's expression softened, her gaze shifting toward him briefly, a deep understanding reflected in her eyes. It was a rare moment for Mareek, one in which he allowed his guard to fall completely. To speak of his father, the man who had abandoned him, and the abuse that had marked his childhood, was something he had never done before. But in that moment, with Sufiya beside him, it felt different. It felt safe.

"I'm sorry about your father," Sufiya said, her voice gentle, but there was no pity in her words, just understanding.

Mareek nodded, the memories of his father still haunting him even after all these years. "I don't even remember him clearly anymore. He was just a shadow in our lives, a nightmare we had to survive. But it was Sara who really raised me. She had to take care of everything. I never really had a chance to be a kid. I just grew up fast."

"I get it," Sufiya murmured. "You had to fight for yourself, just like I did. We didn't really have the luxury of being innocent, of having a carefree childhood."

Mareek let out a quiet breath, feeling the weight of their shared experiences settle between them. It was an unspoken bond, forged from pain, survival, and the deep scars they both carried. He'd never expected to open up like this, especially not with someone like Sufiya, but somehow it felt... right.

They drove in silence for a while, both reflecting on their words, the stories they had shared. For Mareek, it was an unsettling yet cathartic experience. He had always kept his past locked away, buried beneath layers of fame and success. But in this moment, with Sufiya, it felt like he could finally be honest about who he was, who he had become.

As the car approached the NGO's office, Mareek glanced over at her, a sense of appreciation flooding him. "You know," he said, his voice softer now, "I think we both made it through because we had someone to fight for. You had Alfa, and I had Sara. We weren't alone, even when it felt like we were."

Sufiya gave him a small, bittersweet smile. "Yeah, we weren't alone," she agreed, her voice quieter now, but still filled with that same quiet strength. "I guess we've both had our battles. But at least we're still standing."

As they pulled into the parking lot, the weight of their conversation lingered in the air, but there was a sense of peace that followed. Mareek had never expected to share so much with her, but now, as they faced the challenges ahead, he felt like he understood her better. And maybe, just maybe, she understood him, too.

Mareek sat down on his couch, his thoughts drifting back to the conversation he had with Sufiya. Her words about her own tragic past hit him in a way he hadn't expected. He thought about the struggle she'd endured, losing both parents, and how she had no personal life to call her own, always pushing forward for the greater good.

It was in that moment that he realized how much he had taken his sister Sara for granted. He remembered the countless times she had put her own dreams on hold, sacrificing everything to make sure he was okay. He picked up his phone and dialed Sara's number, feeling an overwhelming wave of gratitude.

When she answered, her voice was calm but warm as usual. "Hey, Mareek. What's up?"

He could hear the faint sound of dishes clinking in the background, likely from her work at the restaurant. "I just wanted to thank you, Sara," Mareek said, his voice softer than usual. "For everything. For raising me. For being there when Mom wasn't... and Dad didn't care.

I don't think I say it enough, but I'm really grateful."

There was a pause on the other end of the line, and for a moment, Mareek wondered if she was surprised by his sudden vulnerability. But then she spoke, her voice filled with the same gentle strength that had always comforted him. "You don't have to thank me, Mareek. You're my little brother, and I promised Mom I'd take care of you. It's not a burden, it's what family does."

Mareek felt a lump form in his throat, the words of gratitude coming more easily now. "Still... I don't know how you did it. You were always so strong, even when things were hard. I don't think I could've done it without you."

Sara's laughter was a soft, comforting sound. "You never had to do it alone, Mareek. You were always the little brother I wanted to protect. And now, you're doing so well for yourself. I'm proud of you."

Mareek sat back in his chair, letting her words wash over him. He had always believed that he had been the one to take care of others, especially in the hard times. But now, hearing Sara's voice, he realized how much she had sacrificed for him. How much she had given up for his sake.

"Thanks, Sara," Mareek said quietly. "I love you."

There was a moment of silence before she responded, her voice soft and reassuring. "I love you too, Mareek. Always have, always will."

With that, they ended the call. Mareek sat there for a while, reflecting on everything that had led him here. The pain, the loss, the struggles—and the people who had always been there, even when he couldn't see it.

Mareek leaned back in his chair, his thoughts drifting to an old conversation he had with Sara. It was years ago, right after he had started gaining fame as a DJ and singer. He had called her, eager to offer her a way out of her difficult life in the small restaurant where she worked tirelessly every day.

He remembered the exact words he had said, the hope in his voice: "Sara, you don't have to stay there anymore. You can come live with me. I'll take care of everything. No more long hours, no more stress.

You deserve so much more than that. Just come, we'll figure it out together."

But her response had been different from what he expected. She had hesitated before speaking, her tone calm, yet firm. "Mareek, I appreciate it. I really do. But I can't just leave everything behind. That's my life. I've built it up, and as much as I'd love to be with you, I can't just walk away from it."

She had always been the practical one, the grounded one. Mareek knew it was difficult for her—working long hours in a job that didn't pay nearly enough for all the effort she put in. But Sara had always had a sense of pride in her independence, a quiet strength that came from surviving their childhood together. She had never been one to take the easy route, even when it would've made sense for her to accept his offer.

Mareek had tried to convince her. "I can give you anything you want, Sara. I can get you a better job, better opportunities. You won't have to struggle anymore. We've been through so much, but now I can help you. You deserve it."

But Sara had stayed firm. "Mareek, you don't need to do that for me. You've worked hard for everything you have, and I'm proud of you. But I'm okay. This is where I belong for now. Maybe one day, things will change, but I'm happy doing what I'm doing."

In that moment, Mareek had felt a mix of frustration and admiration. He didn't understand why she wouldn't accept his help, but he also couldn't help but respect her determination to continue on her own terms. She was, as always, strong and resilient, refusing to let go of her own path.

That conversation had stuck with him. He often thought about it when he saw Sara working tirelessly, when he saw how little time she had for herself. He wished he could do more for her, but he also knew that Sara's pride and independence were part of who she was. She had fought through their hard years together, and now she was carrying on in her own way.

Even now, Mareek thought about that offer—wondering if it had been the right thing to do, or if, like Sara, he too was trying to define his own path in the world. He felt conflicted, but the thought of her still working long hours in that restaurant made him want to change things for her. However, deep down, he knew Sara had her own way of doing things. And that was what made her who she was. Mareek's mind wandered back even further, to darker times, when the struggles of their childhood were far more painful. His memories of those years were clouded with shame and regret, yet there was no escaping them.

He remembered how hard it had been for Sara, especially when they were living in a cramped, dimly lit apartment. Their father had long since disappeared, Mareek and Sara were left to fend for themselves. Mareek was still a child, too young to understand the weight of their circumstances, but Sara, barely a teenager, had already shouldered responsibilities far beyond her years.

The rent was due, and the bills kept piling up. Mareek's mind raced back to those moments when he would lie awake at night, the sound of their empty stomachs growling louder than any noise in the world. It was Sara who would keep him calm, telling him everything would be okay, though Mareek could see the exhaustion in her eyes.

One cold evening, when they had no money left, no food, and no way out, Sara had done something Mareek could never forget. She had taken him aside, her face grim, her voice barely a whisper. "Mareek, I have to do something," she had said, her eyes never meeting his. "I'll be back soon."

He didn't understand at the time, too young to grasp the depth of her sacrifice. He had gone to bed that night, stomach empty, and when he woke up the next morning, Sara was gone. She had returned late, the tension in her body telling him everything. He never asked her what she had done, but it was clear. It was clear from the way she acted, from the silent tears she tried to hide, and the deep sorrow that lingered in her eyes every time she looked at him.

It wasn't long before Mareek learned the painful truth—Sara had resorted to selling her body to feed them. At first, he didn't fully understand the weight of it. He was just a boy, clinging to his sister for survival, not realizing how much she was sacrificing for him. But as the years passed, the weight of her actions became undeniable. Mareek would never forget the times he would find Sara sitting in silence, her face pale, her hands shaking, as she tried to forget what she had done.

Despite it all, Sara never let him know the full extent of her pain. She kept the facade strong, always the protective sister, always the one who would assure him that they would be okay. But Mareek knew. He knew that the world had broken her in ways he couldn't comprehend, and yet she had kept going. For him. For them.

Now, as he thought about those dark days, Mareek felt a sense of guilt and shame he couldn't shake. He had never fully understood what Sara had gone through, the lengths she had gone to just to keep them alive. And though she had always insisted she was fine, that she was doing what she had to, Mareek couldn't erase the image of his sister, so young, so vulnerable, enduring something he would never wish on anyone.

It hurt him now more than ever to realize that his success had come at such a high cost, a cost he could never repay. Sara had sacrificed so much for him, and now she was still working tirelessly in that restaurant, despite all the fame and fortune he had amassed. He wanted to make things better for her, to take away the pain, but he knew it wasn't that simple.

The guilt of not being able to save her from those early years, from the things she had done out of desperation, gnawed at him. He wanted to forget it, to bury it in the past where it couldn't hurt him anymore, but he knew that wasn't possible. What his sister had done, the sacrifices she made, would haunt him for the rest of his life. And no matter how much success he achieved, no matter how many songs he released or how many people adored him, it would never be enough to undo the pain of those years.

Mareek closed his eyes, letting the memories wash over him, realizing just how much he owed to Sara. She had always been there, always protecting him, always shielding him from the worst of the world. And now, when he had everything, when he was at the peak of his fame, he couldn't help but wonder—did he truly deserve it? Did he deserve any of it, when all of it had come at the expense of his sister's innocence, her dignity, her strength?

As these thoughts lingered in his mind, Mareek couldn't help but feel that no amount of fame or wealth would ever fill the emptiness inside him. It would never be enough to make up for what Sara had endured, for the life she had lived in order to give him a chance.

The next morning, Mareek woke up with a clarity he hadn't felt in years. His thoughts from the night before had brewed into something more—an idea, a calling. For the first time since he'd taken the stage as a musician, he realized that he had never truly created something of his own. Everything he was known for, every chart-topping song, had come from Rakesh's genius. But now, he wanted something different. He needed to make something raw, something real, something that wasn't borrowed.

His first thought was of Sara. The sacrifices she had made, the pain she had endured—her story deserved to be told. It was more than just a way to honor her; it was a way to confront the parts of himself he had buried. It was time to create something honest, something that came from his soul.

As he sat with this idea, sipping his morning coffee and staring out of his window, there was a knock at the door. For a brief moment, Mareek smiled to himself. He had long since stopped being surprised when Max showed up unannounced. Somehow, Max always seemed to sense when he was needed, even without a phone or any connection to the outside world.

When Mareek opened the door, Max stood there, his familiar stoic expression softening just slightly.

"You look like you've had a revelation," Max said, stepping inside without waiting for an invitation.

"I have," Mareek replied. He wasted no time. "I've decided to write my first original song. Something that's mine. And it's going to be about Sara."

Max raised an eyebrow, his expression unreadable. "About Sara?"

"Yes," Mareek said, pacing the room as he spoke. "About her life, her struggles, everything she's done for me. I've spent so much of my career riding on Rakesh's legacy, pretending his songs were mine. But this—this will be different. It'll be my truth. My story. Our story."

Max watched him carefully, his arms crossed. "Are you sure you're ready for that? For something so personal? You've never been one to wear your heart on your sleeve."

Mareek paused, looking out of the window. "I don't know if I'm ready," he admitted. "But I have to do it. For her. For myself. I owe her that much."

Max nodded slowly, as if he could see the determination in Mareek's eyes. "It's about time," he said.

Encouraged by Max's response, Mareek began sketching out ideas for the song later that day. The memories of his childhood came flooding back in vivid detail—the cold nights, the empty stomachs, the way Sara had always been there to shield him from the worst of it. He remembered her quiet strength, her sacrifices, and the love that had carried them through the darkest of times.

The song began to take shape, its melody haunting and its lyrics raw with emotion. Mareek wanted it to be honest, unflinching, a reflection of the pain and resilience that had defined their lives.

As he worked, he glanced at Max, who sat quietly in the corner of the room. "You don't say much, do you?" Mareek said with a smirk. Max shrugged. "You're doing fine on your own."

For hours, Mareek poured himself into the song, and by evening, he had the foundation of something that felt real. It wasn't polished, but it was his.

"This is it," he said, looking at Max. "This is the start of something new."

Max nodded. "Make sure it's something you can live with. And don't forget who you're doing it for."

Mareek didn't need the reminder. This was for Sara—for the sister who had given him everything, and for the part of himself that needed to confront the truth. For the first time in his career, Mareek felt like an artist, not just a performer. And it felt good.

He didn't know how the world would receive this new side of him, but he didn't care. This wasn't about fame or money. It was about finally finding his own voice. And for Mareek, that was worth more than any amount of recognition.

fter weeks of relentless work, Mareek's song finally came together. He titled it "Sara's Love", a heartfelt tribute to the one person who had been his anchor through the storms of his life. It wasn't just a song—it was his story, his emotions, his way of acknowledging the sacrifices Sara had made to raise him.

Mareek decided on a special day for its release—Sufiya's birthday, November 10th. It felt fitting. Sufiya had been a guiding presence in his life recently, someone who reminded him to stay grounded, someone who helped him find clarity when he was lost.

The night before the release, Mareek couldn't sleep. He sat in his studio, the final version of the song playing softly in the background. It wasn't perfect, but it was raw, honest, and entirely his. As he listened to it, he thought about Sara—her struggles, her strength, and her unwavering love.

On the morning of November 10th, Mareek made his way to the NGO. He carried a small cake for Sufiya, something simple but thoughtful. When he arrived, the staff greeted him warmly, and Sufiya's smile lit up the room when she saw him.

"What's this?" she asked, eyeing the cake.

"Happy birthday," Mareek said with a rare, genuine smile.

"You remembered?" Sufiya looked genuinely touched.

"Of course," he replied. "But that's not all. I have something else for you."

As the staff gathered to celebrate, Mareek took out his phone and played "Sara's Love" for the first time. The room fell silent as the soulful melody filled the space. The lyrics flowed like a gentle stream, each word carrying the weight of his emotions:

"You gave your days, you gave your nights,
Fought our battles, hid your fights.
Through storm and fire, you stood tall,

For me, you'd sacrifice it all.
    Sara's love, unspoken, unseen,
The silent strength, the evergreen.
You broke your heart to build my own,
In your shadow, I've grown."
The melody swelled as his voice carried the chorus:
"The world turned cold, but you stayed warm,
My shelter, my light, in every storm.
Sara's love, a boundless sea,
Forever etched in the soul of me."
Sufiya listened, her eyes glistening with emotion. "It's beautiful, Mareek," she whispered when the song ended. "Absolutely beautiful."
He smiled, feeling a warmth he hadn't felt in a long time. "It's not just for Sara," he said. "It's for everyone who's ever been a light in someone's darkest times. People like Sara... and people like you."
Later that day, Mareek uploaded the song to all major streaming platforms. The response was overwhelming. Fans who had followed his career since the beginning were stunned by the shift in tone and depth. Critics praised it as his most personal and profound work yet.

The song quickly climbed the charts, not because it was flashy or trendy, but because it was real. It resonated with people in a way that none of his previous music had. For the first time, Mareek felt like he wasn't just riding on someone else's legacy. This was his voice, his story, and his moment.
And as the world celebrated "Sara's Love," Mareek found himself quietly celebrating something even greater—his growth, his journey, and the people who had helped him become who he was.
That evening, as Mareek sat in his studio reflecting on the overwhelming response to "Sara's Love," his phone rang. The screen lit up with a name he hadn't seen in a long time—Sara. His heart skipped a beat as he quickly answered, his voice trembling slightly. "Sara?" he said.
There was silence on the other end for a moment, and then he heard

her voice, warm and soft, but laced with emotion. "Mareek... I heard the song."

Mareek exhaled deeply, a mixture of relief and anticipation flooding him. "What... what did you think?"

"I don't even have the words," she replied, her voice breaking slightly. "It's like you put my entire life, my entire love for you, into music. Every word, every note—it's all true, Mareek. You've captured everything I've ever felt, everything I've ever done for you. And... you made it beautiful."

Mareek felt his chest tighten. For all the fame and accolades he'd received, this was the only validation that truly mattered. "I've been holding onto those feelings for years, Sara," he admitted. "I never said it out loud, but I've always known how much you sacrificed for me. I just... I wanted the world to know too."

There was a pause, and then Sara's voice came back, stronger this time. "You didn't have to do that for the world, Mareek. I didn't do any of it for recognition. I did it because I love you. You're my brother, my family. And hearing this song... it was worth every single sacrifice."

Mareek swallowed hard, his throat tight. "I should have said it sooner, Sara. I'm so sorry for everything you went through. For... everything you had to endure because of me. You deserved so much better."

"I don't regret a single thing," she replied firmly. "And seeing you now, hearing what you've become, it makes me proud. But Mareek..." She hesitated, and he could feel the weight of her words coming.

"What is it?" he asked gently.

"Promise me," Sara said. "Promise me you won't let this world take away your heart. You've always had this fire in you, but it's easy to lose yourself in fame, in success. Don't forget who you are."

Mareek closed his eyes, her words settling deep within him. "I promise," he said. "I'll never forget where I came from. Or who helped me get here."

For a moment, neither of them spoke, the silence filled with an unspoken connection that no words could describe.

"I love you, Mareek," Sara said finally.

"I love you too, Sara," Mareek replied, his voice soft but resolute.

As he hung up the phone, Mareek sat in the quiet of his studio, the weight of their conversation pressing against his chest. Sara's words lingered in his mind, grounding him in a way he hadn't felt in years. For the first time in a long time, he didn't feel like he was running from something. Instead, he felt like he was finally running toward something real—toward himself.

Mareek sat by the window of his office, staring out at the bustling city streets. It was late, the lights from passing cars creating streaks of motion against the darkened buildings. His thoughts were everywhere, scattered in a thousand different directions. The past few months had been a whirlwind. He had left his music career behind for the most part, stepping into something completely different, something more personal—working with the NGO, getting to know people who didn't care about his fame or reputation. People who didn't ask for anything except for his help, his time, and his honesty.

But there was one thing that hadn't changed, no matter how much he tried to bury it—the way he felt about Sufiya.

She had become an integral part of his life. Not just as a colleague at the NGO, but as someone he found himself confiding in, trusting, and in some strange way, depending on. From the moment they had first met, there had been an unspoken connection between them, something Mareek couldn't quite explain. She was different from the others. She didn't treat him like a famous DJ or a millionaire musician. She saw him—really saw him—and somehow, that was terrifying and comforting all at once.

Tonight, as he sat at his desk, going through paperwork that barely registered in his mind, Mareek found himself wondering why he hadn't confronted his feelings for Sufiya. It had been months since they'd started working together, and though they had grown close, nothing had ever gone beyond the surface. Their interactions were always kind, professional, even friendly, but there was a certain barrier between them—a line that neither had dared to cross.

Was it fear? Fear of what would happen if they crossed that line? Or was it simply that Mareek didn't know how to deal with feelings like these? He had always been more comfortable with music, with fame. He understood those worlds. But this, this was new. And new was always dangerous.

His phone buzzed on the desk, snapping him out of his reverie. It was a message from Sufiya.

Sufiya: "Are you still at the office?"

He glanced at the clock. It was nearly midnight. He hadn't expected to hear from her at this hour. He smiled despite himself and quickly typed out a response.

Mareek: "Yeah, just finishing up some work. Why? Something wrong?"

A few moments later, the reply came.

Sufiya: "I was thinking of grabbing some coffee. Want to join me? It's been a long day, and I could use some company."

He hesitated for only a second. Normally, he would have declined, citing exhaustion or the need to wake up early for work. But tonight felt different. He wasn't sure why, but he had an overwhelming urge to spend time with her, to talk to her more

Mareek: "Sure, I'm in. Meet you in 15?"

The message came through almost immediately.

Sufiya: "Perfect. See you soon."

When Mareek arrived at the small café where they usually met after work, Sufiya was already there, sitting at their usual corner table. She looked up as he approached, a smile spreading across her face as she noticed him. Her presence was always calming, the kind of quiet energy that seemed to fill the room without any effort at all.

"Hey," she said, standing up to greet him. "You look like you've been working all night."

Mareek shrugged, running a hand through his messy hair. "You know how it is. Always something to do."

They sat down, and Sufiya quickly signaled to the waiter to bring them their usual—black coffee for her, a cappuccino for him.

"So, how's everything at the NGO?" he asked, trying to steer the conversation to something light, something safe.

Sufiya hesitated before answering, her fingers tracing the rim of her cup absentmindedly. "It's been good," she said, though her voice was quieter than usual. "I've been thinking a lot about... everything, though."

Mareek leaned in slightly, sensing the shift in her tone. "Everything? What do you mean?"

Sufiya sighed, leaning back in her chair as she looked out the window. "I don't know... Sometimes, I wonder if I'm really doing enough. If I'm really making a difference. You know?"

Mareek understood that feeling all too well. There had been days when he felt like nothing he did was ever enough, no matter how hard he tried. The music, the fame—it all felt so hollow after a while. Helping people at the NGO had given him some sense of purpose, but even that didn't always seem to fill the void inside.

"I think you're doing more than you give yourself credit for," he said, his voice low and sincere. "You've changed lives already, Sufiya. You're making a difference every day."

She smiled faintly, but there was a sadness in her eyes that Mareek couldn't ignore. "I hope so," she said quietly. "I really do."

The waiter arrived with their drinks, and they both fell into a comfortable silence as they sipped their coffee. Mareek kept glancing at her, unable to shake the feeling that something was about to change. He had always been able to read people, but Sufiya was different. There was something about her, something that made him feel like he had known her for much longer than he actually had.

As the night wore on, they talked about the usual things—work, the challenges they faced, their hopes for the future. But Mareek couldn't ignore the way his heart seemed to race every time Sufiya looked at him, the way her laughter seemed to resonate in his chest. He hadn't felt this way in a long time.

When the conversation eventually drifted into silence, Sufiya looked at him with an expression Mareek couldn't quite decipher. It was a look that seemed to ask something without actually speaking it.

"Is there something on your mind?" Mareek asked, unable to resist any longer.

Sufiya took a deep breath and placed her cup down on the table. She met his gaze, her eyes serious, her voice soft but steady.

"Mareek," she began, her words deliberate. "I've been thinking about us. About everything. I don't know how to say this, but... I think I'm ready to be honest with myself. About what I want."

Mareek's heart skipped a beat. He had been expecting many things, but not this. He swallowed, suddenly unsure of what to say.

"I think I'm falling for you," she continued, her voice barely a whisper now. "And I've been scared to admit it, because I didn't want to complicate things. But I can't ignore it anymore. The way I feel when I'm with you—it's different. You make me feel like I'm not alone, like I'm actually seen for who I am. And I... I don't want to lose that."

Mareek felt a rush of emotions flood over him. He wasn't sure what to say. He had always kept his distance from people, always protected himself by building walls. But Sufiya had torn those walls down without even trying. He hadn't even realized how much he wanted to be with her until she said those words.

He took a deep breath and reached across the table, gently taking her hand in his. "Sufiya, I... I've never been good at this. At relationships, at letting people in. But I've never felt this way before. You make me feel... alive in a way I didn't know was possible."

A small smile tugged at the corners of her lips. "So, what does that mean?"

Mareek squeezed her hand, the decision made in his heart. "It means... I'm willing to take a chance on us. If you are."

For the first time in a long while, Mareek felt something shift inside him, something deep and undeniable. And as Sufiya's smile widened, he knew that this was just the beginning.

After leaving the office, Mareek's mind was racing. Sufiya's words replayed over and over in his head, like a song stuck on loop. She had confessed her feelings for him, something he hadn't expected—at least, not so directly. The weight of the conversation pressed down on him, and a strange feeling of both exhilaration and fear filled him.

He couldn't quite put his finger on what it was. But he knew one thing for sure: he needed to talk to someone. Not just anyone, though. He needed to talk to Max. Max had been his constant, the person who had always been there in the background of his life, guiding him, pushing him, whether Mareek wanted it or not. Max understood him better than anyone else, even when Mareek himself didn't fully understand what was going on inside his own head.

Mareek hurried out of the building, the cool night air brushing against his face, but his mind was too full to notice the chill. He could already see the conversation unfolding in his mind—the look on Max's face when he told him about Sufiya. Max, being Max, would probably give him some cryptic piece of advice, as always, but that was what Mareek needed. Max's perspective was always different. He didn't conform to the expectations of the world, and that made him the most reliable source of insight when Mareek found himself lost in his thoughts.

His steps quickened as he walked through the darkened streets, but then, as he approached the familiar turning where Max's apartment building stood, a thought struck him. He didn't know Max's address. In all their years of friendship, they had never needed to meet at Max's place—Max always came to him, or they met in places where the world didn't feel so heavy.

Frustrated, Mareek paused for a moment. Where was Max's apartment? He had always just shown up whenever Mareek needed him, never once asking for anything in return, never requiring an address or a place to meet. Max was the kind of person who transcended the physical space—his presence was the comfort, not the place.

Mareek stood still for a few moments, trying to shake the feeling of confusion that came over him. Finally, he sighed. He wasn't going to figure out where Max lived tonight. He couldn't waste any more time searching for a place that wasn't a place in the first place.

Instead, he turned on his heels and made his way home. His apartment, like the office, felt like a safe zone—his personal fortress where he could process everything without anyone interrupting. It wasn't the same as his house growing up, but it was his space, and for now, that was enough.

As he entered his apartment, Mareek kicked off his shoes, and, still lost in his thoughts, he flopped onto the couch. He leaned back, his mind still racing over everything that had happened earlier—Sufiya's confession, his inability to answer in a way that was certain, the nagging feeling that things were about to change in ways he couldn't control. The enormity of it all seemed to weigh down on him.

He looked at the clock—11:45 p.m. It had been a long day.

But the uncertainty of the moment made him restless. He grabbed his phone and scrolled through a few random notifications—nothing to distract him. No messages from Max, which wasn't surprising. Max didn't rely on technology, and Mareek didn't expect him to. Still, he felt the familiar ache of wanting to talk to someone, even if he didn't know exactly what to say.

After sitting in silence for a while, he reached over to his guitar, sitting neatly in the corner of the room. He picked it up, feeling the coolness of the strings against his fingertips. It had been a while since he last played—since he had focused on creating something that wasn't designed for fame or for anyone else's approval.

He strummed a few chords, letting the sound fill the space, feeling the tension in his shoulders slowly start to ease. His thoughts began to shift, and he let the music guide him into a kind of calmness that he hadn't felt in days. As the notes of the song he'd been working on for his sister, "Sara's Love," floated into the air, Mareek felt himself returning to a place of clarity. Music had always been his escape, his way of processing everything that didn't make sense.

But even as the melody played, his mind kept returning to Sufiya and her confession. He hadn't said anything in response. He didn't even know how to respond.

The doorbell rang, interrupting his thoughts.

Mareek froze for a second, unsure of who it could be. He didn't have many visitors, and at this time of night, it seemed strange. But as he got up and moved toward the door, his heart skipped when he saw who it was through the peephole.

Max.

He opened the door without hesitation, surprised by the sight of Max standing there, looking as composed as ever, wearing his usual neutral expression. Mareek had barely realized he was waiting for him, but now that Max was standing there, it made sense. He needed to talk. And, for some reason, he had known Max would be the one to show up.

Max didn't say anything at first. He just walked in, gave Mareek a quick look, and plopped down on the couch, his ever-present calmness filling the room. He didn't need to ask what was going on. He already knew.

Mareek sat down across from him, not sure where to start. After a few moments of silence, he finally spoke, his voice a little quieter than usual. "Max, something happened today. Sufiya... she, uh, she told me how she feels about me. And I—I didn't know what to say."

Max didn't flinch. He didn't seem surprised. Instead, he nodded slowly, as if this was exactly what he had expected to happen.

"Yeah?" Max said, his voice nonchalant. "What do you feel about her?"

Mareek stared at him, as if the question caught him off guard. "I—I don't know. I'm not sure. I don't... I've never really thought about it."

Max raised an eyebrow, leaning back into the couch. "Never thought about it? Come on, man. You know there's something there. Why do you think she feels that way?"

Mareek ran a hand through his hair, trying to gather his thoughts. "It's just... things are complicated. Everything's complicated. I've never been good at relationships, Max. You know that. And I'm not sure if I even want one. Not now. Not with everything going on."

Max gave him a small, knowing smile. "You're scared, Mareek. And that's okay. But you can't keep running from it. Sometimes, the only way to figure out what you want is to face it head-on."

Mareek sat there, processing his words. It wasn't a groundbreaking revelation. But somehow, hearing it from Max made it feel like it was.

"I don't know if I'm ready for this," Mareek admitted, his voice soft. "I don't know if I'm ready to let someone in again."

Max didn't say anything for a long moment. He just watched Mareek, his gaze steady and unwavering. "Maybe you're never ready," Max finally said. "But you have to take a chance, man. Otherwise, you'll never know."

For the first time in a long while, Mareek didn't feel alone. The weight of his confusion seemed a little lighter, and the uncertainty of the future felt less intimidating. Maybe Max was right. Maybe taking a chance was the only way forward.

And with that thought, Mareek made a decision. Tomorrow, he would talk to Sufiya. He didn't know what the outcome would be, but he would take the first step. He would stop running. And maybe, just maybe, he would find the answers he was looking for.

The next morning, Mareek woke up with an odd sense of calmness in his chest. The weight of his thoughts from the previous night had settled into something more manageable. His conversation with Max had shifted something inside him, and though he still felt unsure about the future, there was one thing he was certain of: he needed to talk to Sufiya.

He got ready quickly, his usual routine flowing smoothly as he tried not to overthink the situation. For the first time in a long while, he wasn't consumed by the noise of the world around him. His thoughts were focused on a singular thing—Sufiya.

By the time he finished his breakfast, it was already getting late. He grabbed his phone, stared at it for a moment, and then, as if something inside him clicked, he sent her a message: "Can we meet today? I need to talk to you."

There was a brief moment of hesitation before he put his phone down. Would she be free? Would she be open to talking? But then his phone buzzed with a response, and his heart skipped a beat.

"I'll be at the NGO office in an hour. See you then."

Mareek exhaled a breath he hadn't realized he was holding, grabbed his jacket, and made his way out the door. He drove quickly to the office, feeling like every second stretched longer than the last. His mind was still wrestling with everything that had happened—his growing feelings for Sufiya, the idea of commitment, the fear of opening up to someone in a way he never had before. But as he pulled up to the office, he took a deep breath and let it go. It was time to face what had been haunting him.

When he walked into the office, Sufiya was already there, sitting at one of the desks. Her face lit up when she saw him, a smile instantly spreading across her lips. It was a comfort, something familiar in a world that had felt increasingly uncertain.

Mareek walked toward her, feeling the weight of the moment settle over them both. As he stood in front of her, he opened his mouth to speak, but the words caught in his throat. He realized how much he had to say, and yet, none of it felt right.

Sufiya stood up and stepped toward him, her eyes warm, her presence grounding. "Mareek, you don't have to say anything," she said softly, reading the expression on his face. "I know that you're confused. I know that you need time. I don't want to pressure you."

Mareek's heart ached at the kindness in her voice. He reached for her hands, feeling the warmth of her skin against his, and for a moment, the world outside seemed to fade away. It was just the two of them.

"I'm not confused anymore," Mareek said, his voice low but steady. "I've been running from this, from you, and I'm tired of it. I don't know what the future holds, but I know that I don't want to lose you. I don't want to let fear stop me from being honest with myself."

Sufiya's eyes softened, and her lips parted in surprise, but there was no hint of doubt in her expression. "Mareek..."

"I care about you, Sufiya," he continued, his words now flowing more freely. "I don't know what love looks like for me, but I'm willing to find out with you. I want to be with you. I want us to be something real."

A smile broke across Sufiya's face, and her eyes shone with something more than just relief. It was understanding, a connection that neither of them had dared to speak aloud until this moment.

"Mareek," she whispered, squeezing his hands in hers, "I feel the same way. I've been waiting for you to figure it out, and I'm glad you finally have. I've never been more certain of anything."

In that moment, the world felt different. The fear, the hesitation—they all dissolved in the warmth of their connection. There was no need for grand gestures or elaborate promises. What mattered was this simple, unspoken truth: they had found each other, and that was enough.

"I love you, Sufiya," Mareek said, his voice barely above a whisper, but carrying all the weight of what he had been carrying for so long. Sufiya's smile widened, and she pulled him into a hug. "I love you too," she whispered back, holding him tightly as if the world outside could wait for them just a little longer.

They stood there for what felt like an eternity, wrapped in each other's arms, knowing that everything they had been through—every question, every fear—had led them to this moment. And while the future was still unknown, in that instant, Mareek knew he wasn't alone anymore. He had found someone who understood him, who saw him not for his fame or his past mistakes, but for who he truly was. And that was enough.

The office around them seemed to fade into the background, the noise of the outside world silenced by the steady rhythm of their hearts. It was just the two of them, together, with all the possibilities ahead of them.

And for the first time in a long while, Mareek didn't feel the need to run from anything. He had found his place.

The moment Mareek and Sufiya shared their first confession of love was timeless, suspended in the air like the breath before a storm. But, as with most things in the world of fame and scrutiny, their intimacy did not go unnoticed. The office, though quiet and intimate, had an audience. The door had been left ajar just enough for a curious eye, and the two of them, lost in the warmth of their newfound truth, hadn't noticed the hushed whispers or the subtle click of a camera phone.

The media, ever-present like shadows, had captured the rawness of the moment. As Mareek held Sufiya close, their faces illuminated by a rare moment of pure connection, the flashing lights from the street outside pierced through the blinds of the office. It was then, when they had finally let down their guards and spoken the words they had both long held back, that the world outside decided to take a closer look.

Minutes later, as the office began to settle, Sufiya and Mareek pulled away from their embrace, unaware of the unfolding consequences. Sufiya's smile was soft, a reflection of the vulnerability they had just shared. Mareek, too, felt lighter—like something heavy had been lifted off his chest.

But as they exchanged another quiet glance, the sound of hurried footsteps approached. The door to the office was flung open, and one of the NGO's volunteers, eyes wide, practically burst in.

"Uh, Mareek... Sufiya..." she began, her voice panicked. "You need to see this. The media is already outside. They've got the whole thing on tape!"

Mareek's heart skipped a beat. He immediately stood up, rushing to the window that overlooked the main street. Through the blinds, he could see the flashing lights of cameras, a crowd of reporters and photographers huddled together, anxiously awaiting a glimpse of him or Sufiya. The chaos had already started.

"No way," Mareek muttered under his breath, his mind racing. The last thing he wanted was for this personal moment, this first step in his relationship with Sufiya, to be plastered all over the news. The idea of it felt... wrong. It felt invasive.

Sufiya was standing behind him, staring at the scene unfolding outside. She looked back at Mareek, her face a mix of surprise and concern. "I knew the media would find out eventually... but not like this."

Mareek cursed under his breath, pacing back and forth. He knew how this worked. The press didn't care about the sincerity of the moment; they wanted the drama, the headlines, the story that would get the most clicks. And he and Sufiya were just the latest pawns in their game.

"Should we just leave?" Sufiya asked quietly, her voice barely above a whisper. "Slip away while we still can?"

Mareek shook his head, rubbing his temples in frustration. "No. If we leave now, it'll only make it worse. They'll follow us, chase us down. They'll want answers... They'll spin everything out of control."

But the tension in his voice was evident. He wanted nothing more than to escape—to go somewhere private, far away from prying eyes. The media, always hungry for a story, had taken a piece of their reality and turned it into a spectacle.

Sufiya's face softened, her expression filled with understanding. "We'll just have to face them. Together."

The words hung in the air between them for a moment, a promise, a decision made without fully knowing the consequences. It wasn't about avoiding the chaos, but about standing strong, side by side.

Taking a deep breath, Mareek turned to face Sufiya. "Alright. Let's do this."

They made their way to the front door of the NGO office. The moment they stepped out, the media snapped to attention. The camera flashes were blinding, the questions endless. Mareek's name echoed through the air, questions about his personal life, about the status of his relationship with Sufiya, and about his plans for the future.

Mareek and Sufiya stood in front of the swarm of reporters, and though the questions came at them like bullets, they stood firm. Mareek could feel the tension building inside him, but he didn't let it show. He kept his face calm, eyes steady.

"Sufiya," one reporter shouted, "are you and Mareek officially a couple now? Is this the start of something serious?"

Mareek shot a glance at Sufiya, who stood with her back straight, holding her ground. "Yes," she replied, her voice calm but clear. "We're together."

There was a brief pause as the reporters scribbled down their notes, and the flashes continued to go off like fireworks. But Mareek could see the shift in the media's tone. They had gotten what they wanted—the confirmation, the story they could sensationalize. They had captured the moment, and it would soon be all over the news.

Another reporter asked, "How do you feel about the public's reaction? Is this relationship going to affect your work with the NGO?"

Mareek took a breath before answering. "I've always believed in doing what's right. And I'm not here for the drama. I'm here because this work is important to me, and so is my relationship with Sufiya."

The reporters continued to shout questions, but Mareek could feel himself growing weary. This wasn't what he had imagined—this wasn't how he wanted his relationship with Sufiya to begin. Yet, here they were, being pulled into the spotlight once again.

Finally, Sufiya spoke up, her voice clear and strong. "We don't need to justify our relationship to anyone. What matters is that we're happy and committed to what we believe in. And if people can't understand that, that's their problem, not ours."

Her words hung in the air, and for a brief moment, everything went silent. The reporters seemed to respect her resolve, and though they didn't stop recording, they seemed to accept that they weren't going to get any more sensational soundbites.

Mareek glanced at Sufiya, a small smile tugging at the corner of his lips. She had handled the situation with more grace than he could have ever imagined. She had taken control of the narrative and had done it with strength and conviction.

They made their way past the reporters, walking into the NGO office once again, the door closing softly behind them. The outside world was loud, chaotic, and unrelenting. But in here, in this space, they could finally breathe.

As they sat down at a table in the corner, Mareek turned to Sufiya, his expression a mixture of relief and gratitude. "Thank you. I don't know what I would've done without you out there."

Sufiya smiled, her eyes warm. "You don't have to thank me. We're in this together, remember? We always will be."

Mareek reached for her hand, squeezing it gently. Despite the storm outside, he knew that with Sufiya by his side, he could face whatever came next. Together, they would navigate this world of fame, scrutiny, and uncertainty.

Apologies for the confusion! Let's pick up from the conversation between Max and Mareek, where Max had expressed his doubts about Sufiya's intentions. Here's how it could unfold:

Mareek sat in the plush chair of his living room, the dim light casting long shadows across the floor. His fingers drummed lightly on the armrest as his mind replayed the conversation he'd had with Sufiya earlier in the day. The vulnerability in her voice still echoed in his head, and yet, Max's words lingered like a dark cloud.

Max. The ever-cynical Max. Always the one to cut through the noise and give him a reality check. Mareek hadn't expected Max to be so blunt about it, but then again, maybe he should have. Max didn't care about the fame, the fame that Mareek had built his life around. Max cared about truth, about raw reality.

The doorbell rang, pulling Mareek out of his thoughts. He quickly stood up and made his way to the door, finding Max standing there, his usual casual demeanor in place.

"Max," Mareek greeted him, stepping aside to let him in. Max entered without a word, heading straight for the kitchen, the way he always did when he visited. He didn't even need to ask where anything was; he knew the place as well as Mareek did.

They sat at the kitchen table, silence hanging in the air between them. Mareek found himself lost in thought once again, but Max seemed unbothered, almost too casual, as he poured himself a drink.

Finally, Max broke the silence.

"So, how's the whole 'relationship' thing going?" His tone was light, but there was an edge to his voice.

Mareek glanced at him, surprised by the question. "It's fine," he said. "It's... good, actually. Sufiya's amazing. She cares about me. Not about the fame. Not about the media."

Max scoffed. "You really believe that?"

Mareek's eyes narrowed, sensing the challenge in his voice. "What do you mean by that?"

Max set his glass down with a slight clink and leaned back in his chair, folding his arms across his chest. "Look, Mareek. I'm not saying she's using you, but this whole thing—this 'perfect' image you've got going—it's dangerous. People, they change when they're in it. And people change for all sorts of reasons. Fame, money, power. They get swept up in it."

Mareek's gaze hardened. "You think that's what she's doing? Using me?"

Max shrugged, the casualness of his posture betraying the seriousness of his words. "I don't know, man. Maybe she's just doing what feels right at the moment. Maybe she's really into you, or maybe it's all about the audience. You can never really tell. What you need to understand is, people don't stay the same when all this media and fame is involved. Hell, look at you. You're a different person now than you were two years ago."

Mareek clenched his jaw, feeling the sting of Max's words. He didn't want to admit it, but Max was right. Fame had changed him. Changed the way people saw him, and how he saw himself. Everything had become about what he could give, about what the world expected from him.

"But that's not it," Mareek said, his voice growing more insistent. "I'm not trying to be someone I'm not. I want... I want something real with Sufiya."

Max met his eyes, his expression unreadable. "I get it, you want to believe it. You want to hold on to the idea that she's different. But sometimes, it's not about you, Mareek. It's about what people can gain from being close to someone like you. You can't ignore that. I'm not saying she's lying to you, but maybe you're not seeing the whole picture."

Mareek felt his pulse quicken. The words were starting to sink in, but they felt too close to home. "So, what should I do, Max? Should I just stop everything? Should I just... walk away?"

Max stared at him for a long moment before speaking again. "No. I'm not telling you to walk away. I'm telling you to be aware of the world you're in. Be aware of the people around you. Just because someone says they care about you doesn't mean they don't have their own motives. You need to keep your eyes open."

There was a long silence between them, the weight of Max's advice hanging thick in the air. Mareek leaned back in his chair, running a hand through his hair. He had never been the type to second-guess himself, to overanalyze things. But lately, with everything going on—his rise to fame, his relationship with Sufiya, the media frenzy—it felt impossible to ignore the nagging doubts.

He could hear Max's words echoing in his mind: People change. People change for all sorts of reasons.

But was that really the case with Sufiya? He couldn't imagine her using him, not when everything felt so real between them. He wanted to believe her. He wanted to believe that they had something genuine, something unaffected by the fame that surrounded him. But the doubt—Max's voice—kept creeping back into his thoughts.

"Thanks for the advice," Mareek finally said, breaking the silence. His voice was quiet, almost hesitant. He wasn't sure if he was ready to hear the truth that Max was giving him, but part of him knew he had to listen.

Max didn't respond immediately, but after a beat, he let out a small, almost imperceptible sigh. "I'm just trying to help, man. You're my friend, and I don't want you to get hurt."

Mareek nodded, though he didn't quite know how to respond. What was he supposed to do with the knowledge that everything he thought was real could just be a product of his own desires? Should he pull back from Sufiya? Should he distance himself, just to protect himself from the inevitable fallout?

He didn't have the answers. But one thing was clear—Max wasn't going to let him ignore the truth, no matter how hard it was to face.

As the night wore on, they talked more about music, about Mareek's next move in his career, and about the future. But the conversation kept circling back to the same topic: Sufiya. Mareek couldn't help it. She was always on his mind.

When Max left that evening, Mareek sat in the dim light of the living room, his thoughts swirling. He wasn't sure what the future held. He wasn't sure if he could fully trust Sufiya or if he should pull away from the relationship. But one thing was certain: the world around him was complicated. Nothing was ever as simple as it seemed.

And maybe that was the hardest part of all.

The next morning, Mareek, still wrestling with his feelings, went to Max. He found his old friend sitting calmly by the window, gazing out at the city. Without hesitation, Mareek poured out his heart, telling Max everything he had been feeling about Sufiya. The doubts, the fear of being used for fame, the uncertainty about her true intentions—everything that was weighing him down.

Max listened intently, his expression unreadable, but his silence spoke volumes. Finally, after a long pause, Max spoke in his usual calm, measured tone.

"You love her, Mareek," Max said, his words cutting through the tension. "For the sake of just that, be with her. Love her the way you can. Let her do whatever she wants, let her chase whatever she's chasing. It won't matter. I wasn't giving advice, Mareek. I was just warning you. Fame isn't something that can be trusted."

Mareek stood there, caught in the weight of Max's words. He had always known Max didn't care about fame or recognition, but hearing it in such a direct manner felt different.

Max continued, his gaze still fixed on the horizon, "You know, you can't control how things turn out. You'll never know what her intentions truly are, but you can choose how you react. And sometimes, that's the only thing that matters."

Mareek took a deep breath, processing the simplicity yet depth of Max's advice. For the first time in a long while, he wasn't sure what to say, but the lingering truth in Max's words stuck with him.

3

The night was cold and crisp, with a faint mist settling over the streets as Mareek drove home after his electrifying concert. The adrenaline of the performance was still coursing through his veins, but so was something else—a quiet emptiness that had begun to creep into his life more frequently these days. Fame, money, recognition—it all felt hollow.

As his car turned onto a narrow road near the city outskirts, Mareek saw a man standing by a parked motorcycle, waving his arms to flag him down. His helmet sat atop the bike, and he appeared calm, yet his posture suggested urgency. Mareek hesitated for a moment, unsure if he should stop. The road was deserted, and he didn't trust strangers easily. But there was something in the man's demeanor that disarmed him—composed yet commanding, a paradox Mareek couldn't ignore.

He pulled over and rolled down the window slightly. "Need something?" Mareek asked, his voice carrying a mixture of curiosity and wariness.

"Yeah, actually. My bike's acting up, and there's no one around this late. Any chance you could drop me off at the nearest bus stand?" The man's tone was polite yet self-assured, as though he was used to getting his way but preferred not to demand it.

Mareek studied him for a moment. The man was in his late twenties, sharply dressed in a tailored blazer and dark jeans, looking more like someone stepping out of a corporate meeting than someone stranded on a roadside.

"Get in," Mareek said, unlocking the door.

As the man slid into the passenger seat, Mareek couldn't help but notice his calm confidence. It was rare for him to meet someone who didn't immediately gush over his celebrity status or try to impress him.

"Thanks," the man said, extending a hand. "I'm **Sushant**."

"Mareek," he replied, not bothering with pleasantries. Most people knew who he was, and he assumed Sushant did too.

"I know," Sushant said with a slight smile. "I was at your concert tonight."

Mareek glanced at him, surprised. "Really? What were you doing stranded on a road, then?"

"Long story," Sushant said, leaning back into the seat. "Let's just say my motorcycle and I aren't on speaking terms tonight."

Mareek chuckled despite himself. There was something refreshing about Sushant's demeanor—unpretentious yet intriguing.

They drove in silence for a while, the hum of the car filling the space between them. Finally, Mareek couldn't resist asking, "So, what did you think of the show?"

Sushant tilted his head, as if carefully considering his answer. "You're talented. Your music is raw, emotional—hits right where it should. But..." He trailed off.

"But?" Mareek raised an eyebrow.

"It feels like you're holding something back," Sushant said, his tone measured but firm. "Like there's a part of you you're too afraid to put into your art."

Mareek frowned, gripping the steering wheel tighter. Who was this guy to psychoanalyze him after one concert? "And what makes you think that?" he asked, his voice edged with irritation.

"It's my job," Sushant replied simply. "I'm a psychiatrist."

That caught Mareek off guard. He glanced at Sushant again, his irritation giving way to curiosity. "A shrink, huh? What, you're here to analyze me now?"

"Not unless you want me to," Sushant said, smiling. "But I am a fan of your work. And as a fan, I think your music has the potential to be even more impactful if you're willing to dig a little deeper."

Mareek didn't respond immediately. Sushant's words struck a nerve, though he wasn't ready to admit it. They reached the bus stand, but instead of letting Sushant out, Mareek pulled over and turned off the engine.

"Alright, Doc," he said, turning to face him. "You've got my attention. What do you mean by 'dig deeper'?"

Sushant smiled again, this time with a hint of challenge. "You're an artist. Your job is to make people feel something. But to do that, you have to feel it first. Unapologetically. That takes courage—and sometimes help."

Mareek stared at him, unsure whether to feel intrigued or annoyed. Before he could decide, Sushant reached into his pocket and pulled out a sleek black card.

"Here," he said, handing it to Mareek. "If you ever want to talk—or just figure out what's holding you back—give me a call."

Mareek took the card reluctantly, glancing at it. "Dr. Sushant Malhotra," it read, followed by a phone number and the tagline, "Helping You Find Your Truth."

Without another word, Sushant opened the car door and stepped out. "Thanks for the ride," he said, giving Mareek a small wave before walking away.

As Mareek watched him disappear into the night, he couldn't shake the feeling that this wasn't the last time their paths would cross. He tucked the card into his pocket and drove off, his mind swirling with thoughts he couldn't quite articulate.

By the time he reached home, he had almost convinced himself to forget about the encounter. But the card in his pocket felt like a burning reminder that some truths, once uncovered, refuse to be ignored.

Mareek tossed Sushant's card onto his cluttered desk that night and promptly forgot about it. Or at least, he tried to. Something about the brief conversation stuck with him, as if Sushant's words had left an invisible imprint in his mind. He shook it off, burying himself in his usual routine—music, rehearsals, parties, and a sprinkling of NGO work when he felt up to it. The world around him demanded too much to allow room for introspection.

Meanwhile, Dr. Sushant Malhotra couldn't shake his own curiosity about the enigmatic artist he had encountered. Mareek's music had always intrigued him, but their roadside meeting had revealed something deeper—an emotional tension simmering beneath the surface. Sushant had a knack for reading people, and Mareek was no exception. There was pain there, hidden behind the glitz and glamour of fame, and Sushant wanted to understand it.

The next day, Sushant began his quiet investigation. Not in a nosy, obsessive way, but with the methodical curiosity of a man who had spent his career peeling back the layers of human complexity. He wasn't just a fan of Mareek's art; he was fascinated by the man behind it.

His first stop was the internet. Sushant scoured interviews, music videos, and articles, piecing together fragments of Mareek's life. He read about Mareek's meteoric rise to fame, his troubled childhood, and his enigmatic nature that left fans and critics alike guessing. The public narrative painted Mareek as a self-made artist with a tough exterior, but Sushant knew there was more to the story.

Next, he sought out people who had crossed paths with Mareek. Through some professional connections, Sushant managed to track down a few individuals—old college acquaintances, industry insiders, and even some NGO volunteers who worked alongside Mareek. Their stories varied, but one theme was consistent: Mareek was brilliant, driven, but also closed-off and deeply guarded.

One name kept coming up in these conversations: Max. Everyone seemed to agree that Max was the only person who truly knew Mareek. Sushant became increasingly curious about this elusive figure. But Max, as it turned out, was almost impossible to find. No phone, no social media, no public presence of any kind. It was as if he existed solely in Mareek's orbit, appearing and disappearing as needed.

Despite the dead ends, Sushant's curiosity didn't wane. Instead, it intensified. He began attending Mareek's concerts, blending into the crowd and observing the man on stage. Mareek was a performer unlike any other—dynamic, magnetic, but with a haunting edge that Sushant couldn't quite place. It was as if Mareek was pouring his soul into his music while keeping the rest of himself locked away.

One evening, after a particularly intense performance, Sushant lingered near the venue's exit. He wasn't there to approach Mareek again—he knew better than to force a connection. Instead, he wanted to observe, to see if the man behind the persona would reveal himself in quieter moments.

To his surprise, Mareek didn't leave in his usual entourage of assistants and bodyguards. Instead, he slipped out the back door alone, lighting a cigarette and leaning against the wall. For a moment, Mareek looked utterly human—tired, contemplative, and vulnerable.

Sushant stayed hidden, unwilling to intrude. But the sight of Mareek in that unguarded moment only deepened his resolve. Mareek was carrying something heavy, and Sushant, for reasons he couldn't fully explain, felt compelled to help him.

Back in his office, Sushant began piecing together a profile of Mareek—not as a celebrity, but as a person. He noted the themes in Mareek's music, the glimpses of pain in his lyrics, and the stories from those who knew him. Slowly, a picture began to emerge: Mareek was a man haunted by his past, driven by his need to prove himself, but deeply disconnected from his own emotions.

Sushant knew he couldn't force Mareek to open up, but he also knew that their paths had crossed for a reason. Sometimes, the people who need help the most are the ones least willing to accept it. And Sushant was nothing if not patient.

For now, he decided to wait. If Mareek ever chose to reach out, Sushant would be ready. Until then, he would continue to observe, to understand, and to hope that one day, Mareek would let someone in.

The dinner was planned at one of the city's most serene and private restaurants, the kind where the world seemed to melt away under dim lighting and soft music. Mareek had made sure it would be quiet, away from prying eyes and media frenzy, just for them. Sufiya arrived wearing a simple yet elegant black dress, her hair loosely tied back, which somehow made her look even more enchanting. Mareek, dressed casually yet sharp, stood up as she approached their table, pulling out her chair like a true gentleman.

"You didn't have to go to all this trouble," she said softly, settling into her seat.

"Well," Mareek replied, leaning forward with a smirk, "I thought you deserved a little break from all the NGO chaos."

As they began their meal, the conversation flowed naturally, sprinkled with laughter and moments of comfortable silence. Sufiya playfully teased him about how the media was obsessed with their supposed romance. "You know, they've already named us the power couple," she said, rolling her eyes.

Mareek laughed. "Oh, yeah? Should we give them something dramatic to write about? Maybe an engagement announcement?" He winked, making her chuckle.

"Let's not feed their fantasies," she replied, her cheeks slightly pink.

The night carried on like this, the food delicious but almost secondary to their connection. Mareek found himself studying her, the way her eyes lit up when she laughed, the way she nervously tucked a stray strand of hair behind her ear. He realized he wasn't just enjoying her company—he was cherishing it.

As they left the restaurant and got into Mareek's car, the air between them felt warm, almost magical. The city lights blurred into streaks as they drove through the quiet streets, the faint sound of music playing in the background. Sufiya leaned back in her seat, gazing out of the window. Then, out of nowhere, she asked softly, "If I die, will you love somebody else?"

The question caught Mareek off guard. He glanced at her briefly before focusing back on the road. "What kind of question is that?" he asked, half-laughing.

"Just answer," she insisted, her voice playful but her eyes searching.

Mareek shrugged. "No, I wouldn't. Simple as that."

She tilted her head, studying him. "What if someone else loved you?" she asked, her tone lighter now, almost teasing.

Without missing a beat, Mareek grinned and said, "Then I'd kill them."

Sufiya burst out laughing, shaking her head. "You're impossible, you know that?"

"Completely serious," Mareek replied with a mock-stern expression. "I'd be like, 'How dare you?'"

She smirked, looking at him. "So, what would you do if I actually died?"

His tone softened. "I'd live with your dead body," he said, half-joking but with an undertone of sincerity that made her pause.

"Promise?" she asked, raising an eyebrow, her lips curving into a mischievous smile.

"Promise," he replied with a small laugh, but deep down, the weight of the question lingered in his mind. The idea of losing her—though absurd and far from reality—felt unbearable.

They reached her place, and Mareek parked the car, turning to look at her. "Thanks for tonight," she said, her voice quieter now.

"No, thank you," he replied. "I needed this more than you know."

For a moment, they just sat there, the silence between them filled with everything unsaid. Then, with a soft goodbye, Sufiya got out of the car, leaving Mareek to sit there for a moment longer, the ghost of her words still swirling in his head.

When Mareek finished recounting the bizarre conversation he'd had with Sufiya earlier that evening, he looked up at Max, expecting ridicule or one of his usual sharp retorts. But to his surprise, Max was silent. He sat in the armchair, leaning back, his face serious for once, his fingers drumming on the armrest.

"So," Max finally said, breaking the silence, "she asked you to promise that you'd live with her dead body?"

Mareek nodded. "Yeah, and I said I would. I mean, I was joking... mostly."

Max tilted his head, his expression unreadable. "Why joking? Why not actually live with her dead body if she dies?"

Mareek blinked, taken aback. "What are you even saying?"

Max leaned forward, his elbows on his knees, his dark eyes locking onto Mareek's. "I'm saying you made a promise. And if you love her as much as you think you do, you should be ready to follow through."

"Max, that's insane," Mareek said, letting out a nervous laugh. "Nobody actually does that."

"Who cares what people do?" Max shot back. "You've spent your whole life being different. Look at your music career, your fame, your choices—they're all unconventional. So why not your love? If she means the world to you, then prove it. Even if it's ridiculous, even if the world calls you insane. Isn't that what love is supposed to be? Unconditional, no matter how absurd?"

Mareek opened his mouth to argue but found himself at a loss for words. Max's intensity was unsettling. He was usually sarcastic, dismissive, or even mocking, but now he seemed genuinely invested in this twisted idea.

"Listen," Max continued, his voice low and serious. "I'm not saying it's normal or sane. I'm saying it's love. And love doesn't care about normal or sane. If she ever dies—God forbid—you owe it to her to keep that promise. To live with her dead body, to remember her, to hold on to her in the way only you can."

Mareek stared at him, a lump forming in his throat. "You're not serious."

Max gave a small, crooked smile. "As serious as death itself. You told me you loved her. You told her you'd keep your promise. So do it. Don't be the kind of man who throws words around like they're nothing. Be the man she believes you are."

For a moment, the room fell into a heavy silence. Mareek felt the weight of Max's words pressing down on him, twisting his thoughts into knots.

Finally, he shook his head, forcing a laugh to cut through the tension. "You're out of your mind, Max. You know that, right?"

"Maybe," Max said, leaning back in his chair. "But if she ever dies, and you don't keep that promise, you'll regret it. Trust me."

Mareek sighed, rubbing his temples. "You're impossible."

"And you're predictable," Max retorted, his grin returning. "But hey, it's your life. Just don't come crying to me if you break her heart—alive or otherwise."

Max's words lingered long after he left, echoing in Mareek's mind as he tried to sleep. Somewhere deep down, he wondered if Max was right, if love really did mean going to the edge of reason and beyond. Or maybe Max was just messing with him, as he always did.

But the unsettling truth was that Mareek wasn't entirely sure. And that uncertainty clung to him like a shadow, even as he drifted into a restless sleep.

As Mareek lay in bed that night, Max's words swirled through his mind like an unwelcome storm. He tried to push them away, tried to find comfort in the darkness of his room, but sleep evaded him. The seriousness in Max's tone, the weight of the absurd promise to Sufiya, and his own doubts gnawed at his thoughts.

And then, like a bolt of lightning splitting the silence, he remembered another promise—one he'd made in jest but now seemed grotesquely intertwined with this entire mess.

"I'll kill anyone who loves me," he had said to Sufiya, laughing at the time, thinking nothing of it. But now, as the memory replayed itself in his head, the words didn't feel like a joke anymore.

Mareek sat up abruptly, his chest tightening. The thought horrified him. What kind of person makes a promise like that? What kind of person would even entertain it? He pressed his palms to his face, trying to steady his breathing.

It was all spiraling out of control—this strange, consuming love for Sufiya, the bizarre pact he'd made with her, and now the recollection of that dark, twisted jest.

"I was joking," he whispered to himself in the dim light of his bedroom. "It was just a joke."

But was it? Max's words about love being unconditional, about following through on promises no matter how absurd, echoed in his mind. Max had insisted he live with Sufiya's dead body if she ever died. What if someone else—someone foolish, someone brave, or someone insane—professed their love for him? Would he be bound by that careless, macabre oath?

He shuddered at the thought. It was absurd. Insane. And yet, he couldn't shake it.

The idea took hold of him like a parasite, feeding on his unease. He imagined scenarios, each more horrifying than the last. Someone declaring their love for him. His hand tightening around something sharp or heavy, almost as if on instinct. The flash of fear in their eyes as they realized what was happening.

"No," Mareek said aloud, his voice trembling. "That's not me. I'm not like that."

But his mind was relentless, dragging him deeper into the abyss. He thought of Sufiya again, her laughter, her teasing promise that he'd live with her dead body if she died. How had their love become so entangled in the morbid and the impossible? Was this what love did to people? Drove them to the brink of madness?

He stumbled out of bed and paced the room, his thoughts racing. He needed to talk to someone—anyone. Max? No, Max would probably make it worse, his twisted humor fanning the flames of Mareek's paranoia.

The promise felt like a curse now, binding him to a fate he hadn't chosen. Mareek clenched his fists, trying to force the thoughts away, but they clawed at him, whispering dark possibilities.

What if someone else did fall in love with him? Would he be able to resist the pull of that promise? Or would it consume him, turning him into something monstrous?

And worst of all, what would Sufiya think if she knew how deeply her playful words had scarred him? Would she laugh it off, or would she see the darkness it had unearthed in him?

The morning light filtered through the sheer curtains in Mareek's room as he sat, bleary-eyed, at the edge of his bed. The chaos of his thoughts had finally settled into a singular, burning question. He reached into the pocket of his jacket, hanging limply on the chair nearby, and pulled out the business card he'd almost forgotten about.

Dr. Sushant. Psychiatrist.

The polished card glimmered faintly in the sunlight, as though beckoning him to make the call. Mareek hesitated for a moment, his thumb tracing the embossed letters, before taking a deep breath and dialing the number.

The line rang only twice before a calm, professional voice answered. "Dr. Sushant speaking."

Mareek hesitated, suddenly unsure of what to say. His voice, when it finally emerged, was uncharacteristically soft. "Doc, it's Mareek."

A slight pause, followed by an almost amused chuckle. "Mareek? As in *the* Mareek? The DJ everyone's talking about these days? Didn't expect to hear from you this soon."

Mareek didn't respond to the levity. His tone was somber, almost pleading. "What is love, Doc?"

The question hung in the air, raw and unadorned, catching Sushant off guard. He paused, considering his reply. "That's... quite the question to ask first thing in the morning," Sushant said, his voice laced with curiosity.

Mareek leaned back against the wall, clutching the phone as if it were a lifeline. "I'm serious. What is it? People write songs about it, make promises over it, even destroy themselves for it. But what *is* it, really?"

Sushant's voice softened, sensing the weight behind Mareek's words. "Love," he began, "is many things. It's connection, vulnerability, a bridge between two souls. But it's also complicated—tied to our fears, our desires, our past. Why do you ask?"

Mareek exhaled sharply, his mind flashing back to Sufiya's playful questions, Max's cryptic warnings, and his own spiraling thoughts. "Because I think I'm losing myself to it. Or maybe... maybe I never understood it in the first place."

There was a long silence on the other end of the line before Sushant replied. "Losing yourself to love isn't uncommon, Mareek. It has a way of exposing parts of us we didn't even know existed. But it sounds like there's more to this than just... love. Something's bothering you. Am I right?"

Mareek's jaw tightened. He didn't want to spill everything—not over the phone, not to someone he'd just met. But he couldn't deny the truth. "It's complicated."

Sushant's tone remained steady. "Complications are my specialty. Why don't we meet? My office isn't far from where you live. We can talk in person."

Mareek hesitated, glancing at the card again. The thought of sitting across from someone and baring his soul felt daunting, but he also knew he couldn't carry this weight alone. "Alright," he said finally. "I'll come by this afternoon."

"Good," Sushant replied. "I'll be waiting."

As Mareek ended the call, he felt a strange mix of relief and apprehension. The idea of seeking help, of opening up to someone, was foreign to him. But something about Sushant's calm demeanor made him feel like he wasn't entirely alone in this battle.

He slid the card back into his pocket, grabbed his keys, and prepared to face whatever the day—and the conversation with Sushant—might bring.

Mareek paced around his sprawling living room, the floor-to-ceiling windows casting a glow of morning sunlight over his restless figure. The call to Dr. Sushant had been made, but now he was rethinking everything. Did he really want to lay it all bare? Did he want a stranger—no matter how skilled—to know the tangled mess of thoughts in his head?

No. He decided firmly. He would go, but he wouldn't bring up Sufiya. This was about him. About his confusion. He convinced himself that Sushant didn't need to know about her, not yet.

By the time he parked his car outside Sushant's minimalist office building, Mareek had rehearsed what he would say at least a dozen times. None of those rehearsals involved Sufiya's name.

The receptionist greeted him with polite curiosity—it wasn't every day a celebrity walked in unannounced. Moments later, Mareek found himself sitting across from Sushant in a room designed for calm: muted colors, soft lighting, and a sense of stillness that felt almost unnerving to him.

Sushant looked at him with a disarming smile. "Glad you came, Mareek. Let's talk."

Mareek leaned back, avoiding eye contact at first. He was a man who usually controlled every situation he was in, but now, sitting in this room, he felt stripped of that power. "I called because... I don't know what's happening to me."

Sushant nodded, encouraging him to continue.

"I've always been... detached," Mareek admitted, his voice steady but distant. "Never cared much for connections. I didn't need them. I've seen enough people betray each other for selfish reasons—fame, money, power." He paused, his hands gripping the armrests of the chair. "But lately, something's different. I feel like I'm not in control anymore."

Sushant leaned forward slightly, his eyes studying Mareek's face. "Not in control of what?"

Mareek hesitated. "Of myself. My thoughts. I keep questioning everything—my choices, my life. Even the promises I've made."

Sushant's eyebrows lifted slightly at the mention of promises. "Promises can weigh heavily on us, especially if we're not sure we can keep them. Are these promises tied to someone specific?"

Mareek stiffened. For a moment, Sufiya's face flashed in his mind—her playful smile, her voice teasing him with that morbid question about love after death. But he shook the thought away.

"No," he said firmly. "It's not about anyone. It's about... me. My life. My past."

Sushant didn't push further. He had dealt with enough guarded individuals to know when to give them space. "Alright," he said calmly. "Let's focus on you, then. You said you're questioning your choices. Which choices, specifically?"

Mareek looked out the window, his jaw tight. "Everything. My music, my fame, the way I got here. Sometimes I feel like I'm standing on the edge of a cliff, and the ground beneath me is crumbling."

Sushant studied him for a moment. "That's a powerful image. Do you feel like you're losing something? Or that you've already lost it?"

Mareek's throat tightened. His mind flickered briefly to Rakesh, to the songs he'd stolen, to the fame built on another man's genius. But he couldn't say it. He wouldn't. "I don't know," he said instead. "Maybe it's both."

Sushant leaned back, his expression thoughtful. "You've built a life that most people would envy. Fame, success, wealth. But sometimes, the things we achieve aren't enough to quiet the questions inside us. Maybe what you're feeling isn't about what you have or don't have—it's about who you are."

Mareek's lips pressed into a thin line. He hated how accurate those words felt. He hated how they seemed to scrape away the carefully constructed facade he'd worn for so long.

After a moment, he stood abruptly. "I need time to think," he said, his tone clipped.

Sushant didn't try to stop him. "Take all the time you need. But remember, Mareek, you don't have to carry it alone."

Mareek nodded stiffly and left without another word. As he drove home, the conversation played over and over in his mind. Sushant had seen through him too easily, and it unnerved him.

But more than that, it made him think. Not about Sufiya—not directly. But about himself. About the man he had become, the man he was trying to be, and the weight of the promises he had made to people who might not even need them.

As Mareek drove home, the weight of his conversation with Sushant lingered in the air like an echo he couldn't shake. Little did he know, Sushant was far from finished. The psychiatrist had been piecing together a puzzle—a puzzle with Mareek at its center.

Sushant, renowned for his ability to see past facades, had spent the last few days investigating the enigmatic artist. What began as a casual interest—born from admiration of Mareek's music—had slowly morphed into something deeper. His curiosity about Mareek's life was initially sparked by their coincidental meeting on the road, but the more he looked into the star's history, the more inconsistencies he found.

Through subtle inquiries and research, Sushant had unearthed fragments of Mareek's past. A mention of his humble beginnings. Rumors of a friend named Max who lived off the grid. The mysterious death of a fellow student, Rakesh, just before Mareek's rise to fame. And the whispered stories that Mareek's early songs bore an uncanny resemblance to Rakesh's unreleased work. The pieces were scattered, but Sushant's mind was trained to connect dots others might overlook.

Now, as he sat in his office after Mareek's abrupt departure, the blurry image he'd been piecing together was starting to take shape. He opened a folder on his desk—a collection of notes and articles he'd gathered. There were news clippings about Rakesh's tragic suicide, old interviews where Mareek spoke vaguely about his inspirations, and even grainy photographs from their university days that showed the two together.

Sushant tapped a pen against his desk, his brows furrowed in thought. Mareek's reluctance to open up during their session wasn't surprising, but it was telling. The way he avoided direct answers, the way he deflected from anything too personal—it all pointed to a man carrying a heavy burden.

But what burden? Sushant leaned back in his chair, staring at the ceiling. Was it guilt? Shame? Fear? He didn't know for sure, but one thing was clear: Mareek's success was built on a foundation that wasn't as solid as it seemed. And whatever secrets he was guarding, they were eating away at him.

Sushant's phone buzzed, pulling him out of his thoughts. It was a message from a contact at the university Mareek and Rakesh had attended. He'd reached out to them days ago, asking for any information about the two. The message was short: "Found something interesting. Call me."

He wasted no time dialing the number. The conversation that followed only deepened the mystery. His contact mentioned rumors that had circulated on campus after Rakesh's death, of Mareek's sudden possession of a room key that wasn't his. Nothing concrete, but enough to add another piece to the puzzle.

Sushant hung up and stared at the folder on his desk. The image in his mind was sharpening. Mareek wasn't just a man haunted by his past—he was a man running from it. But why? And for how long could he keep running?

For a moment, Sushant considered letting it go. Mareek was a client now, and there were ethical lines he couldn't cross. But something about the story nagged at him. It wasn't just professional curiosity—it was something deeper. A sense that Mareek's story, if uncovered, could help him heal. Or destroy him.

He glanced at the clock. It was late, but he knew he wouldn't sleep. Not with the questions swirling in his mind. He pulled out his notebook and began jotting down his thoughts, organizing the fragments of information he'd gathered. Somewhere in those pages, he believed, lay the truth about Mareek. And he was determined to find it.

Sushant was never one to give up easily. The next logical step in unraveling Mareek's story was to find the elusive Max—a figure who seemed to orbit Mareek's life like a ghost, always present in anecdotes but impossible to pin down.

Max was a mystery even to Sushant, a man trained to read between the lines. He had gathered scraps of information—whispers of someone who didn't own a phone, avoided technology, and lived far removed from the chaos of modern life. It was an odd profile for someone so integral to

Mareek's world, and it intrigued Sushant even more.

After a few days of searching, Sushant managed to track down a possible lead. A vague mention in an old interview Mareek had given hinted at Max living somewhere in the countryside. It wasn't much, but it was a start. With a map spread across his desk and the determination that had earned him the title of the country's best psychiatrist, Sushant charted out potential places Max might be.

Sushant, though sharp and meticulous, was met with an unusual dead end in his quest for Max. The countryside, where he assumed Max might reside based on Mareek's vague mentions in interviews, turned out to be a place of no answers. No one had even the faintest clue of someone by that name or description.

He wandered through quiet villages, speaking with locals, shopkeepers, and passersby. Each encounter yielded nothing but confused shrugs or polite dismissals. Max's name was like a ghost—uttered but never seen, a presence that seemed more myth than man. Sushant began to feel a growing sense of futility, as though chasing Max was like trying to grasp mist in his hands.

"Who is this Max?" he muttered to himself, sitting in his car after yet another fruitless inquiry at a roadside tea stall. The world outside his windshield was serene, bathed in the golden hues of the setting sun, but inside his mind was a storm of questions. For someone so central to Mareek's life, Max left no footprint, no evidence of existence.

It was perplexing. In an age where everyone left a digital trail—pictures, messages, social media posts—Max seemed to have none of it. No one even spoke of him with familiarity. The lack of any tangible lead was unnatural. Sushant leaned back in his seat, his fingers drumming on the steering wheel. Could Max even be real? Or was he a fragment of Mareek's psyche, an embodiment of something deeper?

The psychiatrist in Sushant wouldn't allow him to dismiss Max as a figment of imagination. Mareek's interactions, the way he spoke about Max, were too vivid, too consistent to be fabricated. But that didn't make the man any easier to find. Max seemed to be a person who existed outside the boundaries of the world others lived in—untouchable and unseen unless he chose to show himself.

After a long drive back to the city, Sushant found himself sitting in his office, staring at his notes on Mareek. Every line he'd written about Max felt like a dead-end. There was no address, no mutual connections, no photos—nothing. It was as if Max had been erased from existence, leaving only whispers behind.

But the oddest part of it all was how this lack of evidence didn't surprise Sushant. It fit with the elusive, enigmatic character Max seemed to be. The more he thought about it, the more he realized that finding Max wasn't a task that could be accomplished through conventional means.

Perhaps Max was one of those rare people who didn't want to be found—and, more importantly, didn't need to be. Sushant wondered if Max's apparent invisibility was intentional, a safeguard not just for himself but for Mareek as well. If that were the case, then Sushant knew one thing for certain: Max would only appear when he wanted to.

"Maybe Max isn't meant to be found," Sushant murmured to himself, leaning back in his chair. A wry smile tugged at his lips. "Maybe he finds you."

The thought was oddly comforting, and it brought Sushant back to his central focus: Mareek. If Max was as loyal and significant to Mareek as he seemed, then he would show up when Mareek needed him most. All Sushant could do was wait—and keep digging into Mareek's complex world.

But as he closed his notes for the night, Sushant couldn't shake the feeling that Max was watching from somewhere, silently aware of his every move.

One quiet evening, Mareek and Sufiya found themselves sitting on the terrace of her modest apartment, the city lights twinkling below them. Mareek had just finished a long day at the NGO, and Sufiya had prepared a simple dinner that they had shared under the stars. The air was calm, but there was a heaviness in Sufiya's demeanor that Mareek couldn't ignore.

As they leaned back on the old, weathered chairs, Mareek noticed her gaze fixed on a distant point in the cityscape. She seemed lost in thought, her usual warmth replaced by a strange sadness.

"What's on your mind, Sufi?" Mareek asked softly, breaking the silence.

She looked at him, her expression unreadable. Then she sighed, tucking a strand of hair behind her ear. "It's about a student I used to teach," she began. Her voice was calm, but there was a trace of guilt in it. "His name was **Anuj**."

Mareek tilted his head, sensing there was more to the story. "What about him?"

Sufiya hesitated for a moment, her fingers fidgeting with the hem of her scarf. "He was... difficult," she said finally. "He was one of those kids who always seemed to be carrying the weight of the world on his shoulders. Quiet, withdrawn. His grades were poor, and he hardly participated in class. It wasn't that he wasn't capable—he was just... lost."

Mareek listened intently, his dark eyes fixed on hers.

"One day," she continued, her voice quieter now, "he didn't complete his homework. It wasn't the first time, but I was frustrated. I was juggling so much back then, trying to balance teaching and the NGO. I let my frustration get the better of me, and I scolded him. Harshly. Maybe too harshly."

"What did you say?" Mareek asked, his tone gentle.

"I told him he needed to stop making excuses and take responsibility for his life," she admitted, her voice barely above a whisper. "And when he didn't respond, I... I slapped him. Just once, but it was enough."

Mareek raised an eyebrow, surprised. "You? Sufi, you're the kindest person I know."

Sufiya shook her head, a rueful smile on her lips. "Even kind people have their breaking points, Mareek. I didn't mean to hurt him. I just wanted him to realize that he had to try, that life wouldn't always be forgiving. But instead of helping him, I think I pushed him further away."

"Did you talk to him afterward?" Mareek asked.

"I tried," she said, her eyes glistening with unshed tears. "But he avoided me. He stopped coming to class. Eventually, he transferred to another school. I heard he'd had some trouble at home, but I never found out the details. It's one of my biggest regrets, Mareek. I don't know what became of him. I just hope he's okay."

Mareek reached out and took her hand, his grip firm yet comforting. "You were trying to help him, Sufi. Sometimes, no matter what we do, people have their own battles to fight."

She nodded, but her expression remained troubled. "I know, but... I can't shake the feeling that I failed him."

They sat in silence for a while, the weight of her confession hanging in the air. Mareek didn't press her further, sensing that she needed time to process her own emotions. Yet, in the back of his mind, he couldn't help but wonder about the boy she had mentioned. Anuj. A name that now seemed to linger in the air like an unspoken question.

As they sat there, the stars above them unchanging, neither of them could have known the dark turn their lives would soon take—or how the past would come crashing into the present in ways neither of them could have imagined.

When Mareek returned home that night, his mind was clouded with Sufiya's story about the boy, Anuj. The way her voice had trembled when she spoke of her regret lingered in his ears. It wasn't like Sufiya to carry guilt so visibly, and the sadness in her eyes had shaken him. Needing someone to talk to, he instinctively thought of Max. And, as always, when Mareek needed him, Max showed up—seemingly out of nowhere.

Mareek found Max seated on the couch in the dimly lit living room, his legs crossed and his eyes scanning a tattered paperback he must have picked up somewhere along the way. Mareek didn't bother asking how Max had come in; he had stopped questioning those things years ago.

"You always appear when I need you," Mareek said with a tired smile as he plopped down on the chair opposite Max.

Max didn't look up. "It's a talent," he replied dryly, turning a page.

Mareek exhaled deeply and leaned back, staring at the ceiling. For a moment, he wasn't sure where to start. Finally, he said, "Sufiya told me something today. About a kid she used to teach."

Max lowered the book slightly and glanced at him, sensing the weight behind Mareek's words. "Go on."

"She told me about this boy, Anuj," Mareek began. "She said she scolded him harshly once for not doing his homework. Even slapped him. And after that, he withdrew from her, stopped coming to class, and eventually transferred schools. She thinks she failed him."

Max's expression remained neutral, but his eyes sharpened. "Interesting."

"That's it?" Mareek said, frowning. "It was a big deal to her, Max. She's carrying a lot of guilt over it."

Max closed the book, resting it on his lap. "And what's bothering you about it, Mareek? Because I can tell there's more."

Mareek hesitated, choosing his words carefully. "I don't know. The way she talked about him, it felt... ominous. Like something wasn't quite right. She doesn't know what happened to him after he left her class."

Max leaned back, studying Mareek. "And that's eating at you?"

Mareek shrugged, then nodded. "A little, yeah."

Max tapped his fingers thoughtfully on the book's cover, his eyes narrowing. "You said the kid's name was Anuj?"

"Yeah."

Max tilted his head, as if connecting invisible dots in his mind. "Think about it, Mareek. A kid like that, already carrying the weight of the world, getting scolded and slapped by someone he might have looked up to... That kind of thing leaves scars. Maybe he's moved on. Or maybe he hasn't."

Mareek frowned. "What are you getting at?"

Max's voice lowered, his tone almost conspiratorial. "Sometimes, people don't let go of their past. Especially the parts that hurt them the most. They carry it, let it fester. It shapes them in ways you can't predict."

Mareek felt a chill run down his spine. "You think—"

"I'm not saying anything definitive," Max interrupted, his eyes narrowing further. "But if this kid—Anuj—never got past what happened, he might've taken a darker path. People who feel wronged sometimes spend their whole lives waiting for a moment of reckoning."

"That's... a lot of assumption, Max," Mareek said, though his unease was growing.

"Maybe," Max admitted. "But you know I'm usually right about these things. It's worth keeping in mind."

Mareek rubbed his temples, trying to push away the disturbing thought. "I don't know, Max. I don't think Sufiya would have told me the story if she thought he might hold a grudge against her."

"Maybe she doesn't think that," Max said, standing up and placing the book on the table. "But people aren't always aware of what they've left behind. Guilt has a way of clouding judgment."

Mareek stared at the floor, Max's words settling heavily in his mind. He wanted to dismiss it as one of Max's cryptic warnings, but something about the way Max had said it made him feel otherwise.

As Max grabbed his coat to leave, he turned back to Mareek and added, "Just be careful. You've got a lot going on already. Don't let your emotions blind you to possibilities."

Mareek looked up at him, the unease still gnawing at him. "You're always so dramatic."

Max smirked faintly. "And you're always so trusting. Try not to let it get you killed."

With that, Max left the room, leaving Mareek alone with his thoughts. For the rest of the night, Mareek couldn't shake the feeling that Max's warning, as vague as it was, might hold more truth than he wanted to admit.

Mareek spent the rest of the night wrestling with his thoughts, Max's cryptic words echoing in his mind. The mention of Anuj had stirred something in him, an uneasy feeling that he couldn't quite name. It wasn't fear exactly, but a gnawing sense of foreboding that clung to him as he sat alone in his dimly lit living room.

He ran his fingers through his hair, frustrated at his inability to shake the heaviness of the conversation. Max always had a way of planting seeds of doubt, and once they were there, they grew uncontrollably. Mareek knew he could be overly trusting at times, but he also didn't want to live in a constant state of suspicion, especially about someone like Sufiya. She was the only light in his chaotic, fame-filled life, and thinking of her in danger was unbearable.

As the hours passed and the house fell silent, Mareek suddenly remembered something. Sushant. He hadn't mentioned him to Max at all. In all the chaos of discussing Sufiya and Anuj, Sushant had completely slipped his mind.

Mareek sighed, leaning back against the couch and closing his eyes. Maybe it was for the best that he hadn't brought it up. Max already had enough suspicions about everything. If Mareek had told him about Sushant—a sharp, inquisitive psychiatrist who seemed overly interested in him—Max might have made even wilder predictions. And right now, Mareek wasn't sure he could handle another lecture on trust, fame, or how the world worked.

Sushant sat at his desk, flipping through the file he had been building on Mareek. The layers of his life intrigued him—his sudden rise to fame, the mysterious bond with an unseen friend named Max, and his connection to Sufiya. It was a tangled web, and Sushant was intent on unraveling it. Yet, something was missing. A key piece that would bring the blurry image into sharp focus.

As he mulled over the details, his gaze fell on the notes he had jotted about Mareek's work at the NGO. A name had come up repeatedly: Raj. A former Stanford roommate and one of the key figures in the NGO. Sushant smirked, the edges of a plan forming in his mind. If Mareek was careful around him, perhaps he could reach Mareek indirectly—through Raj.

With calculated ease, Sushant reached out to Raj. It wasn't difficult; Raj was active on social media, frequently posting about his NGO's work. Sushant sent a message, pitching himself as a fan of Raj's initiatives and an admirer of his vision. Within a day, Raj responded, delighted to reconnect with his old Stanford roommate. They exchanged pleasantries, reminiscing about their time at university, and Sushant subtly hinted at wanting to support the NGO's cause.

"You've always been the altruist, Raj," Sushant said during their first phone call. "Your work is inspiring. I'd love to contribute in any way I can."

Raj, ever eager to expand the NGO's network, welcomed Sushant with open arms. "Why don't you visit? We could always use someone with your expertise, especially someone who understands human behavior as deeply as you do."

Sushant didn't hesitate. "I'd be honored."

Within a week, Sushant found himself walking into the NGO, his polished appearance and effortless charm making an immediate impression on the staff. Raj greeted him warmly, introducing him to the team and showing him around the facility.

As they walked through the building, Raj mentioned Mareek casually, unaware of Sushant's true intentions. "You'll probably run into Mareek soon. He's been working with us for a while now, and his involvement has really brought attention to our cause."

Sushant smiled, masking his anticipation. "I've heard of him, of course. Quite the talent. It's great to see someone using their platform for good."

When Mareek arrived at the NGO, he immediately noticed an air of familiarity that he hadn't felt in weeks. The bustling activity of the volunteers was the same, yet something about the day felt unusual. As he walked in, Raj greeted him with a wide smile.

"Mareek! Long time, my friend. I just got back from my holiday," Raj said enthusiastically, pulling Mareek into a quick hug.

"Raj, welcome back," Mareek said, masking his underlying tension with a polite smile. His mind was still swirling with thoughts of Max's predictions, Sufiya's troubling conversation, and the chaos his life seemed to invite at every corner.

But then Raj's tone shifted slightly. "Oh, and by the way," he added, gesturing toward the far end of the room, "you'll never believe who's here. Dr. Sushant Malhotra. I've known him since college. We reconnected a while ago, and he's been really interested in the work we're doing here. I thought you two might want to catch up."

Mareek's heart skipped a beat. Sushant. Again. What was he doing here, mingling with the NGO staff? He glanced toward the corner where Raj had motioned and saw Sushant standing there, casually conversing with a group of volunteers. As if sensing Mareek's gaze, Sushant turned and locked eyes with him. A faint smile played on his lips, and he nodded slightly.

Raj continued, oblivious to the tension Mareek was feeling. "Come, let me introduce you properly," he said, leading Mareek toward Sushant.

But as they approached, Sushant spoke first, his tone calm and knowing. "Mareek, it's good to see you again," he said, extending his hand. "Fate seems to keep crossing our paths, doesn't it?"

Mareek took his hand reluctantly, shaking it while trying to maintain his composure. "Dr. Sushant," he said, his voice steady but distant. "You've been around quite a bit lately."

Sushant chuckled lightly. "I could say the same about you. But it's always a pleasure, Mareek. I've heard some fascinating things about the work you've been doing here."

Before Mareek could respond, Raj chimed in, oblivious to the undercurrent of tension between the two. "Sushant has been looking into expanding his own initiatives, maybe even partnering with NGOs like ours. I thought he could bring some valuable insight."

Mareek nodded, forcing a polite smile. "That sounds great. I'm sure your expertise could be a big help here."

Sushant's eyes lingered on Mareek for a moment, his smile not quite reaching his eyes. "I'd certainly hope so. After all, it's important to understand the people you work with, don't you think?"

Mareek caught the subtle edge in his words, but he didn't let it show. "Absolutely," he replied, keeping his tone neutral. "Understanding is key."

The conversation moved on, with Raj taking over to share updates about the NGO's recent projects. Mareek stayed quiet, his thoughts churning as he watched Sushant interact with Raj and the volunteers. There was something about Sushant's presence that felt calculated, almost as if he were gathering pieces of a puzzle that only he could see.

As the day went on, Mareek kept his distance, choosing instead to focus on his usual tasks. But he couldn't shake the feeling that Sushant was watching him, studying him, waiting for the right moment to strike.

When the day finally ended, Mareek left the NGO with a heavy heart. His encounters with Sushant were becoming more frequent and more unsettling. It was clear that Sushant wasn't just passing through—he had a purpose, and Mareek was at the center of it.

Whatever game Sushant was playing, Mareek knew he needed to be ready. Because this wasn't just a coincidence anymore—it was a confrontation waiting to happen.

Sushant's curiosity about Mareek was gnawing at him, and despite his best efforts to appear casual, he could feel his focus narrowing. The room he was sitting in at the NGO had a tranquil vibe, the soft hum of the fluorescent lights filling the otherwise silent space. But Sushant's mind was far from quiet. He had to know more about Mareek—and more specifically, the elusive Max, a figure who seemed to exist like a shadow, always in the background but never fully seen.

After an hour of aimless wandering around the building, Sushant finally found his opportunity. He was walking past Mareek's room when he noticed the door slightly ajar. Without hesitation, he stepped inside, making his presence known with a light knock.

Mareek, who had been sitting at his desk, looked up briefly and gave a nod of acknowledgment. "Dr. Sushant, right? What brings you here?"

Sushant smiled politely, slipping into the room with an air of nonchalance. "Just wanted to check in. Raj mentioned you were around today, so I thought I'd say hello."

Mareek leaned back in his chair, his arms crossed as he gave Sushant a small, guarded smile. "Hello. I wasn't expecting you here today."

Sushant glanced around, observing the room with a quick sweep. It was modest but comfortably furnished, with a few personal touches that gave it a lived-in feeling. Nothing too extravagant—just enough to feel like a space where someone would spend their time working.

He let the silence stretch for a moment before he casually brought up the subject that had been on his mind. "I've been hearing quite a bit about you, Mareek. You've made quite an impact, not just with your music but with your work here too. Impressive, really. But there's something I'm curious about."

Mareek looked up from his desk, sensing a shift in the conversation. His instincts told him to be cautious. "Curious about what?"

Sushant's eyes twinkled with feigned innocence as he took a step closer. "Well, Raj told me about your past. Your early days, your rise to fame, the music... It's a lot to carry for anyone. But what's interesting is how often people mention a certain name. Max."

Mareek's posture stiffened almost imperceptibly. "Max?" His voice was neutral, but something in his eyes betrayed a flicker of emotion.

Sushant's smile remained in place, though it was more like a mask now, covering his deeper intentions. "Yes. Max. He's been around in the background of a lot of your success, hasn't he? From what I hear, you two have quite the bond. I'm curious about him.

He's not someone I've heard much about, yet everyone who talks about you mentions him."

Before Mareek could respond, his phone buzzed on the desk. He glanced down at it, his expression unreadable, before he let out a soft sigh. "Sorry, Sushant, I need to take this."

Sushant nodded understandingly, his smile never faltering. "Of course. I'll let you get back to work. I just wanted to check in and make sure everything's going well with your projects here. I'll leave you to it."

Mareek, already distracted by the phone call, simply nodded as he picked up the device. "Thanks for stopping by."

With that, Sushant left the room, but his mind was still racing. He hadn't gotten the answers he was hoping for, but the seeds had been planted. He knew Mareek had just given him a glimpse of something far deeper than he had anticipated. The way Mareek had reacted when Max's name was brought up—subtle but telling—was enough to fuel Sushant's curiosity for days to come.

As Sushant walked down the hallway, he found himself reflecting on what had just transpired. He had pressed, but not enough. Not yet. There was more to Mareek than he let on, and Sushant was certain that understanding Max's role in his life was the key to unlocking the rest of the story.

But as he moved toward the door, he received a message from Raj. It was about some paperwork that needed his immediate attention, a request that couldn't wait. Sushant made his way toward Raj's office, where the mundane task would pull him away from his investigation.

By the time he finished helping Raj with the necessary paperwork, the day was winding down. Sushant knew he had to head home—there was little left to gain from further digging for the moment. But as he stepped out of the NGO, he couldn't shake the feeling that he was slowly uncovering something monumental. Mareek had his walls up, but Sushant was patient. He would get to the bottom of it all, sooner or later.

And what's more, he had the perfect way to do it—by slowly weaving his influence into Mareek's life, gaining his trust, and gathering every shred of information he could about the man who seemed to be surrounded by so much mystery.

Back at the NGO, Mareek sat in his room, reflecting on the brief encounter with Sushant. The psychiatrist's probing questions had unsettled him, but he wasn't ready to confront them yet. He knew he had bigger things to deal with, not just in his own mind, but in the world of people he was entangled with.

But the shadow of Sushant's visit lingered in his thoughts. Would he ever be able to hide the truth from someone so perceptive? Would Max's secrets, and his own, remain buried in the silence that had long protected them? The questions gnawed at Mareek as the evening wore on, but he pushed them aside, knowing he couldn't afford to be distracted.

The days ahead would demand his focus, especially as the lines between truth and illusion continued to blur.

And somewhere in the background, Sushant was still watching, waiting for the moment when the last piece of the puzzle would finally fall into place.

That night, as Sufiya lay in bed, her phone pressed to her ear, her voice carried a soft weariness. "Mareek, I'm tired today," she murmured.

"You've been pushing yourself too much," Mareek replied gently. "Between the school, the NGO, and everything else, you need a break, Sufiya. You're not invincible."

She smiled faintly, though he couldn't see it. "Says the man who juggles fame, music, and the same NGO. You're one to talk."

There was a pause on the line, the silence filled only by the faint hum of static.

"Sufiya…" Mareek's voice softened further, almost hesitant. "If you ever feel like it's all too much… you can lean on me, you know? I'm here. Always."

Her heart ached at the sincerity in his words. "You're too good to me, Mareek," she whispered. "But I don't want to be a burden."

"You're not a burden," he said firmly. "You never could be."

The quiet between them grew deeper, more comfortable this time. Then she broke it with a sudden laugh, light but tinged with exhaustion.

"Do you ever think about the future, Mareek?" she asked.

"Not much," he admitted. "But if you're in it, it doesn't scare me."

Her laughter softened into something more tender. "You say the strangest things sometimes."

"Strange, but true," he countered.

She didn't reply immediately, letting his words sink in. Finally, she yawned and said, "I think I'll sleep now. Goodnight, Mareek."

"Goodnight, Sufiya," he replied. "Take care."

The quiet of Sufiya's apartment was broken by the soft creak of her bedroom door opening. In the faint glow of the nightlight, a shadow loomed—small and hesitant, yet charged with a dark intent.

Anuj stood there, clutching the pillow tightly in his hands. His eyes darted to the sleeping figure of his teacher, the one who had humiliated him, made him feel worthless in front of his peers. Her scolding voice still echoed in his ears, blending with the voices of his own insecurities.

His breaths were shallow as he stepped closer to her bed, his bare feet making no sound against the cold floor.

She stirred slightly but didn't wake. His hands trembled as he lifted the pillow. "I'll show you," he whispered, though the words were meant more for himself than for her. "I'll show you I'm not weak."

With a sudden burst of desperation, he pressed the pillow over her face. Sufiya woke with a start, her body jerking as she tried to push him off. Her muffled cries filled the room as she clawed at his arms, but his grip only tightened.

Her struggles grew weaker, her movements slower. The faint light caught the tears streaming down her face as her body finally went still.

Anuj staggered back, dropping the pillow as if it burned his hands. He stared at her motionless body, his chest heaving, his mind racing. He hadn't thought this far ahead.

He turned and bolted, his heart pounding as he fled down the stairs. The building's watchman, sitting at his post, saw the boy sprinting toward the gate.

"Hey! Stop right there!" the watchman shouted, grabbing his flashlight and running after him.

Anuj didn't stop. He pushed open the gate and darted onto the street. The watchman, realizing the boy wasn't going to listen, drew his pistol—a rare necessity for the quiet neighborhood.

"Stop, or I'll shoot!" he yelled again, his voice echoing in the empty street.

But Anuj didn't even glance back.

The watchman fired a warning shot into the air, but the boy kept running. A second shot rang out, this one aimed lower, striking Anuj in the leg. The boy cried out, collapsing onto the asphalt. Blood seeped through his pants as he writhed in pain, clutching his wounded leg.

The watchman approached cautiously, his flashlight trembling in his hand. "What the hell were you running for?" he muttered, his eyes narrowing. "What did you do?"

Anuj didn't answer. He just stared at the ground, his face pale and wet with tears, as the sound of sirens began to grow in the distance.

As the first rays of dawn pierced through the curtains, Mareek's phone buzzed loudly on the nightstand. Still half-asleep, he reached for it and answered groggily.

"Hello?"

"Mareek, it's Raj." The urgency in Raj's voice jolted him awake.

"What happened?" Mareek sat upright, the sheets slipping off him.

"It's Sufiya…" Raj's voice cracked, and Mareek felt a sinking pit form in his stomach.

"What about her?" he asked, his voice rising, heart pounding against his ribcage.

"She's… gone."

Mareek froze, gripping the phone tighter as if the world had stopped spinning. "Gone? What do you mean, gone?"

"She was murdered last night," Raj said, his tone heavy and grim. "A boy from the school, Anuj… he broke into her room and…" Raj took a deep breath, trying to steady himself. "He killed her."

Mareek's mouth went dry, his thoughts racing and colliding. "No," he whispered. "No, you're lying. This can't be real…"

"It's real," Raj said, his voice breaking again. "The watchman heard noises, came in time to see the boy trying to escape, and shot him. Anuj's in the hospital now, barely alive."

Mareek felt his chest tighten, his breath coming in shallow gasps. "Where… where is she?"

"They've taken her body to the city morgue. If you can, come here. You need to see this, Mareek."

His hands shook as he ended the call, the phone slipping from his grasp onto the bed. For a long moment, he sat there, unable to move, the weight of Raj's words crashing over him like waves in a storm.

The image of Sufiya's gentle smile, her voice from their call the night before, and her laugh—it all replayed in his mind, a cruel echo of what he'd just lost.

Finally, he forced himself to get dressed, each movement slow and mechanical as if his body had disconnected from his mind. He grabbed his car keys and headed for the morgue, his heart heavy with dread and disbelief.

Mareek parked his car near the morgue, his hands trembling as he stepped out. The cold morning air bit into his skin, but he hardly noticed. His mind was clouded with images of Sufiya—her smile, her laughter, her scolding him for silly things, and the last conversation they'd shared.

As he entered the morgue, Raj greeted him with a solemn nod. The atmosphere was heavy with silence, interrupted only by the faint hum of machinery.

"She's in there," Raj said quietly, gesturing toward the metal table where Sufiya's lifeless body lay under a white sheet. "I'll give you a moment."

Mareek nodded numbly. Raj hesitated for a second, as if wanting to say something more, but then he turned and left, leaving Mareek alone with her.

For a long moment, Mareek just stood there, unable to approach. Finally, he took a shaky step forward, then another, until he was standing beside her. Slowly, he reached out and pulled back the sheet.

Her face was peaceful, almost as if she were just sleeping. But the stillness—the unnerving, unnatural stillness—shattered the illusion. His chest tightened, and he let out a ragged breath.

"Sufiya..." he whispered, his voice breaking. "Why...?"

Suddenly, he heard footsteps behind him. He turned quickly, startled, and there stood Max.

Max, as always, appeared calm, but his presence in the morgue was unexpected, almost surreal. Mareek stared at him, disbelief mixing with grief.

"What... what are you doing here?" Mareek managed to ask, his voice hoarse.

Max stepped closer, his gaze steady. "I came because I knew you'd need me."

Mareek turned away, unable to face him. "She's gone, Max. She's... I can't believe it."

Max stood beside him, silent for a moment. Then, he said softly, "You remember your promise, don't you?"

Mareek froze. His promise—the one he'd made in jest, the one Sufiya had made him seal with a laugh.

"If she ever dies, you'd live with her dead body," Max continued, his voice eerily calm. "You promised."

Mareek's head snapped toward Max, his eyes wide with horror. "You can't be serious, Max! That was... it was just a joke! She didn't mean it!"

Max tilted his head slightly, his expression unreadable. "But a promise is a promise, Mareek. And you don't break promises, do you?"

Mareek felt his legs weaken, the weight of Max's words pressing down on him. He looked back at Sufiya's lifeless face, his heart breaking all over again.

"This isn't right, Max. This isn't... I can't do this."

Max stepped closer, his voice dropping to a whisper. "You don't have to decide now. But think about it, Mareek. Think about what she meant to you, what you meant to her. And think about what you promised."

With that, Max turned and walked out of the room, leaving Mareek alone with his thoughts—and the unbearable weight of his grief.

Mareek stood in the morgue, staring at Sufiya's still face. Max's words lingered in his mind, echoing like a haunting melody: "A promise is a promise." His chest tightened, and a storm brewed within him—a mix of denial, grief, and something far darker, more consuming. He couldn't let her go.

The idea, absurd as it seemed, began to root itself in his mind. The memory of Sufiya's playful tone when she had asked him if he'd live with her dead body now felt like a twisted prophecy. A promise made in jest now felt like an unbreakable chain.

Raj hadn't returned. The morgue was eerily silent. Mareek's fingers trembled as he reached for her hand under the sheet. It was cold, lifeless, but it was her. His Sufiya.

His breathing grew shallow, and before he realized it, he was dialing his driver.

"Bring the van to the back of the morgue. Don't ask questions. Just do it," Mareek said, his voice unsteady but firm.

The driver, loyal and accustomed to Mareek's eccentricities, complied without hesitation. Mareek moved swiftly, covering

Sufiya's body with the sheet. He carefully lifted her into his arms, her weight heavier than he'd imagined, both physically and emotionally.

When the van arrived, Mareek loaded her body into the back himself, dismissing the driver. "I'll drive," he said curtly.

The drive home was surreal. The city lights blurred as Mareek sped through the streets, his hands gripping the wheel so tightly his knuckles turned white. His mind raced with memories of Sufiya—her laugh, her voice, her touch. He couldn't let her fade into nothingness.

By the time he reached his mansion, the sun was beginning to rise, casting a pale light over the sprawling estate. He parked in the garage and carried her inside, careful not to let anyone see. The staff wouldn't arrive for hours.

In his private quarters, Mareek laid her gently on a chaise lounge. He stepped back, staring at her as if expecting her to wake up. But she didn't. She couldn't.

The mansion, once a symbol of his success and fame, now felt like a tomb. Mareek closed the curtains, shutting out the world. He sat beside her, his head in his hands, as the reality of what he had done began to sink in.

Days turned into weeks. Mareek's world shrank to the confines of his home. He had Sufiya's body preserved, sparing no expense. He dressed her in the clothes she loved, talked to her as if she could hear him, played the music she adored. The outside world became a distant memory.

Max stood silently in the dimly lit room, gazing at Sufiya's lifeless body draped in one of her favorite dresses. The room smelled faintly of the flowers Mareek had brought in daily, as if to keep the air filled with the presence of life. Mareek sat on the floor beside the chaise lounge, his eyes hollow but resolute, holding Sufiya's hand as if she might squeeze it back.

Max crouched beside him, studying Mareek with a peculiar look—not judgmental, not pitying, but something closer to understanding.

"You've really done it, haven't you?" Max said quietly.

Mareek looked at him with a distant expression, as though Max's voice had to travel miles to reach him. "I made a promise," he whispered. "And you told me to keep it."

Max tilted his head, a faint smile tugging at the corners of his lips. "I did, didn't I?" He leaned back, settling into the room's heavy stillness. "And I meant it. People like us, Mareek, we don't live by the world's rules. We live by our own. If this is what you need, then so be it."

Mareek turned to Max, his eyes searching for reassurance. "I can't let her go, Max. I feel like if I let her go, I'll lose myself too."

Max nodded slowly. "You won't hear me say you're wrong. The world would call this insanity, sure. But the world doesn't understand love the way we do."

Mareek's brow furrowed. "It's not just love, Max. It's... it's her. She was the only thing that made sense. The only thing that made this chaos of fame and life bearable."

Max chuckled softly, shaking his head. "You're preaching to the choir, brother. I'm not here to tell you to stop. I'm here to remind you that the promise wasn't just for her. It was for you, too. If this is what keeps you anchored, then let the world think what it wants."

Mareek's grip on Sufiya's hand tightened. "But what if they find out? What if someone takes her away?"

Max's expression hardened, his voice low and firm. "Then you fight, Mareek. You fight like hell. If anyone tries to take this away from you, I'll stand beside you. Let them call it madness, let them try to interfere. We'll remind them that we don't owe them anything."

For the first time in weeks, a flicker of something close to relief crossed Mareek's face. Max's unwavering support steadied him, gave him the strength to continue down the path he had chosen.

As the evening stretched on, Max stayed with Mareek, sitting quietly, occasionally muttering words of encouragement or cracking a dark, sardonic joke to lighten the oppressive atmosphere. The two of them shared a bond deeper than friendship, an unspoken understanding of each other's brokenness.

Before he left, Max stood over Sufiya's body and looked at her with an odd mix of respect and amusement. "Well, Sufiya," he said, as if she could hear him, "you've made your mark on him, haven't you? Don't worry—I'll make sure he keeps his promise."

He glanced at Mareek one last time, his voice softer now. "You do what you have to, Mareek. And when it feels too heavy to carry, you know where to find me."

Mareek nodded, his gaze locked on Sufiya. "Thank you, Max. For understanding."

Max smirked as he walked toward the door. "Understanding? Nah. I'm just as messed up as you are."

And with that, he disappeared into the night, leaving Mareek alone with Sufiya once more. But Mareek didn't feel alone—not with her there, and not with Max's words still echoing in his mind. For now, that was enough.

4

The world moves fast, and in its endless pace, people forget. For a few months, Mareek's disappearance made headlines. A sensation, a mystery, a story to feed the insatiable appetite of media and fans. Where had the famous DJ gone? Why did he vanish? Speculation ranged from a quiet retirement to conspiracies of a tragic accident. But as time rolled on, other stories replaced his. The world forgot.

Months turned into years, and Mareek's name became a whisper in the industry he once dominated. No one knew where he was, not even the ones closest to him—because, truthfully, there were no "closest ones." Sara had given up after countless unanswered calls. The NGO carried on its work without him, though Raj sometimes wondered if he'd ever hear from Mareek again.

But one person hadn't forgotten: Dr. Sushant Malhotra.

Sushant couldn't let it go. The image of Mareek, his enigmatic demeanor and broken brilliance, haunted him. Something had never felt quite right. The man Sushant had met during that fateful concert was more than just an artist. He was a storm, a fractured soul hiding behind a mask of music and fame. And then there was Max—a ghost in Mareek's life that no one seemed to know or even confirm existed.

Sushant spent years piecing together clues, revisiting conversations, and tracing fragments of Mareek's past. He wasn't doing it for the public or even for Mareek's fans. He wasn't sure why he was doing it at all—maybe it was the puzzle, the inexplicable pull toward understanding Mareek's mind. Or maybe it was the hope that, somehow, he could help.

Meanwhile, Mareek was trapped in a world of his own making. The house he lived in had become a tomb, both for Sufiya's body and for himself. He'd sealed himself off from everything, cutting all ties with the outside world. The once-vibrant mansion, which had echoed with music and life, now stood in eerie silence.

Mareek had kept his promise. Sufiya's body lay preserved, carefully tended to by Mareek as if she were still alive. Her favorite perfume lingered in the air, and he spoke to her as if she could hear him, sharing his thoughts, his fears, and even his music—songs he never released but wrote just for her.

At first, he'd tried to keep some semblance of normalcy. He'd wake up, cook, and care for the house. But over time, the lines between reality and illusion blurred. Days bled into nights, and seasons changed outside his window without him noticing. His beard grew wild, his once-polished appearance now a shadow of the man he used to be.

Max, as always, was there—though no one else ever saw him. Mareek's only companion in this isolation, Max never judged or questioned. He simply existed, offering his cryptic wisdom and dark humor.

One evening, as Mareek sat by Sufiya's side, Max leaned against the wall, his arms crossed. "You've really outdone yourself, Mareek. Three years. Most people would've cracked by now."

Mareek didn't look up. "Maybe I have cracked. Maybe that's what love does to you."

Max chuckled softly. "Love? Or obsession? Or guilt? They all look the same after a while."

Mareek ignored him, gently brushing a strand of hair from Sufiya's face. "She's all I have, Max. She's the only one who never left me."

Max's smile faded, and for a moment, he looked almost... sad. "And what happens when you stop being enough for yourself, Mareek? What happens then?"

Mareek didn't answer.

Outside, the world carried on. Inside, time stood still.

But Sushant wasn't done. He'd tracked down Mareek's mansion, though he hadn't dared approach it yet. Something told him he wasn't ready for what he'd find inside. For now, he waited, watching from afar, piecing together the final parts of the puzzle.

The world may have forgotten Mareek, but Sushant hadn't. And he was determined to uncover the truth—no matter how dark it might be.

One evening, as Mareek sat in the dimly lit room beside Sufiya's still form, Max spoke up, his tone more pressing than usual.

"You've been hiding here for years, Mareek," Max began, leaning casually against the doorframe. "You can't live like this forever. Not even I can keep you company forever."

Mareek didn't look at him, his fingers running over the strings of his acoustic guitar as he softly played a tune he had written just for Sufiya. "This is all I need, Max. She's all I need. I made a promise."

Max shook his head and stepped closer, his boots clicking softly against the wooden floor. "You've fulfilled that promise, Mareek. You've lived with her, kept her close. But she wouldn't have wanted this. You know that. She loved life, and she loved you because of the life you had."

Mareek's fingers stilled, and he finally glanced up at Max, his eyes hollow but searching. "What are you saying?"

Max sat down across from him, leaning forward with an intensity that Mareek rarely saw. "You're a creator, Mareek. You were born to pour your soul into music. That's why she fell for you in the first place. You can honor her in a way the world will remember—through your music. It's time to do a concert. One big, unforgettable show. For her."

The idea hit Mareek like a wave, both thrilling and terrifying. A concert? After all these years? He had abandoned the stage, cut himself off from the world. Could he even face an audience again?

"I can't do that," Mareek whispered, his voice trembling. "The media, the questions... they'll never understand."

Max smirked, his dark eyes gleaming with a mix of challenge and encouragement. "Let them ask. Let them wonder. They'll see the truth in your music. And maybe, just maybe, it'll set you free."

The thought lingered in Mareek's mind long after Max left the room. That night, he sat beside Sufiya's body, speaking softly to her as though she could hear him. "Do you think I should do it, Sufiya? Would you want me to?" His voice cracked, and for the first time in years, tears welled in his eyes.

The night Mareek finally decided to go through with the concert, he sat alone in the dimly lit room, staring at the space where Sufiya's body had once rested. The room, once filled with an overwhelming sense of grief and loss, now felt oddly still, as though time itself was holding its breath. It was Max's words that echoed in his mind: "You can't live like this forever. You have to let her go. Not in the way you think, but through your music. Do it for her. Do it for yourself."

Mareek's hands trembled as they rested on the guitar in his lap. He had spent years hiding away, locked in the shadows of his grief. But now, after Max's blunt insistence, he realized he couldn't keep running. He needed to take a step forward, not for fame, but to pay tribute to the woman he had loved.

He hadn't spoken to Max in days, but somehow, he could feel his presence in the back of his mind, urging him to do this. He could never have imagined this day would come, but it was time. He was ready.

The decision was made.

The next morning, Mareek reached out to his manager, explaining that he was ready to perform again. The news was met with a mix of disbelief and excitement. His manager scrambled to get everything in order—booking a venue, sorting out the logistics, and handling the media. Mareek didn't care about any of that. He had no interest in the spectacle; all he cared about was the music and the message he needed to convey.

Max wasn't involved in the details. He never was. Mareek didn't want him to be. Max had always been more about supporting from a distance, offering the occasional blunt advice, or pushing Mareek to face his fears, but never getting involved in the practical stuff. Mareek was grateful for that. This was his journey now, and he needed to walk it on his own terms.

The night of the concert arrived. The venue was small, intimate, and filled with a mixture of fans, reporters, and a few old friends from Mareek's past. The audience buzzed with anticipation, eager to witness the return of the reclusive artist. The moment Mareek stepped onto the stage, the crowd went silent, as if holding its collective breath.

Mareek didn't look out into the audience. He didn't need to. His focus was on the guitar in his hands, the microphone in front of him, and the music that was about to pour from his soul. The first few notes rang out, and as his voice joined them, a shiver ran through the room.

He sang of love, loss, and promises. He sang of Sufiya. Every song carried with it a piece of his heart, a fragment of the years he had spent hiding away, and the hope that somehow, through his music, he could find some form of peace. He didn't need words for the audience to understand. The emotions were there, in the melodies, the lyrics, and in the rawness of his voice.

The crowd was enraptured. They could feel it too. The pain, the rawness, the beauty of it. There were no theatrics, no grand displays—just Mareek, his guitar, and his truth.

As the final notes of the last song lingered in the air, the room was utterly silent for a moment. Then, as if on cue, the audience erupted into applause. Some stood; some remained seated, stunned by the intensity of the performance.

Mareek bowed his head, overwhelmed with emotion. For the first time in years, he felt as though he had shared a part of himself again, something pure and untainted. The applause was no longer for the fame he had once enjoyed, but for the music, for the honesty, for the vulnerability that poured from him onto that stage.

Backstage, after the concert, Mareek stood alone for a moment, trying to collect his thoughts. He wasn't sure what to do next, but he knew one thing—he had taken a step forward. He had done what he set out to do, and it had felt right.

Max wasn't there to offer his usual post-concert critique. Mareek didn't expect him to be. Max had his own way of showing support. He had planted the seed, and now it was up to Mareek to water it, to nurture it, to let it grow.

As Mareek walked out of the venue and into the cool night air, he felt a strange peace settle over him. The world hadn't stopped turning, and neither had his pain, but for the first time, he felt as though he was moving forward. He could still honor Sufiya. He could still carry her with him. And maybe, just maybe, he could start living again.

Mareek was walking back home, his steps slow and deliberate after the whirlwind of the concert. The streets were empty, the city quiet under the cool night sky. Lost in his thoughts, he barely noticed a figure approaching him until she spoke.

"Excuse me, Mareek?"

He stopped and turned, a bit surprised to see a young woman standing a few feet away. She looked familiar but he couldn't place her immediately. She was bundled in a thick coat, with a stethoscope hanging loosely around her neck.

"Yeah?" he responded, his tone neutral.

"I'm **Aruna**," she said, her voice a little shaky but filled with excitement. "I'm an animal doctor. I just wanted to say... I'm a huge fan of your music."

Mareek nodded curtly, not particularly in the mood for a conversation, but he didn't want to be rude either. "Thanks," he said. "Appreciate it."

Aruna hesitated before continuing, her hands nervously clasping together. "I've been following your work for a while. I... I don't know if this is weird, but... I think you're amazing. I— I actually... love you."

Mareek froze for a moment, the words hitting him with an unexpected weight. He blinked, trying to process what she'd just said.

"I... I didn't mean to make it awkward," Aruna quickly added, her face flushing red. "I just thought... maybe you'd like to know. I've always admired you."

Mareek's expression didn't change, but his gut twisted. He wasn't sure why, but hearing those words from her made him feel uncomfortable, like something was out of place.

Without saying another word, he turned on his heel and started walking away. His pace quickened as he tried to shake off the feeling of unease that had settled in his chest.

"Wait, Mareek!" Aruna called after him, but he didn't stop. He didn't turn around.

He didn't owe her an explanation. He didn't know how to respond anyway. The last thing he needed was to deal with this now, when his life felt so tangled up in other things.

When Mareek arrived at home, the weight of the encounter with Aruna still lingered in his mind. He felt unsettled, but it wasn't just her words. As usual, Max was there when Mareek needed him most, though in his own silent, unspoken way.

Max had always been there—though he never called or showed up with any warning. Mareek could count on him, just like always. He knew Max's presence would help him make sense of things, even if he didn't exactly know what to make of this particular situation.

As he walked into his living room, Mareek saw Max sitting in the corner, looking calm, as if nothing had changed.

"Hey," Mareek muttered, dropping onto the couch beside him.

Max looked at him silently, then spoke, his voice low and clear. "What's bothering you?"

Mareek rubbed his temples, trying to make sense of his thoughts. "I... I met a fan today. She said she loves me."

Max, who had been standing there silently, finally broke the silence. "You made a promise to Sufiya," he said, his voice low but clear. "You promised to kill anyone who loves you."

Mareek's heart skipped a beat. He hadn't been thinking about that promise at all, caught up in the whirlwind of everything else. But now, Max's words hit him like a slap to the face. He had made that promise—to Sufiya.

"Shit," Mareek muttered under his breath. He had always managed to forget about the weight of that promise, pretending it was something that didn't matter anymore. But now, it was staring him right in the face.

Max didn't say much more. He didn't need to. He just stared at Mareek, waiting for him to process the truth. Mareek was silent for a long moment, then finally exhaled sharply, as if he had just been hit with an overwhelming realization.

"Aruna," he said softly, as if saying the name made it more real. "She loves me."

Max didn't respond at first. He just stood there, his gaze piercing, as if he knew exactly what Mareek was thinking.

Finally, Max spoke. "You have to do it, Mareek. You promised. A promise is a promise."

Mareek closed his eyes, his thoughts swirling in a chaotic storm. He had never wanted to be caught in situations like this. Promises. Death. Love. All these things that he had tried to avoid for so long were now cornering him, forcing him to face them head-on.

He had made a promise to Sufiya, and now the consequences were unfolding. Would he really go through with it? Would he kill Aruna, someone who had been nothing but kind to him, simply because she loved him?

"I didn't want any of this," Mareek whispered, more to himself than to Max. "I never wanted to be this person."

Max, as always, was unfazed. "It doesn't matter what you wanted, Mareek. You've already made your choice. Now you have to live with it."

The weight of his promise bore down on Mareek, crushing him in ways he couldn't even explain. He looked down at his hands, as if they were capable of answering all the questions in his head. But there were no answers. No easy way out.

After a long silence, Mareek finally looked up at Max. "What do I do now?"

Max's eyes were cold, unwavering. "You know what you have to do."

Mareek didn't say anything more. He didn't have to. The reality of the situation was sinking in. And there was no escaping it.

Mareek's voice was low, almost drowned by the heaviness in the room. "I have to do this."

Max nodded, his expression unreadable. "You made a promise. Now it's time to fulfill it."

The words hung in the air, thick with the weight of inevitability. Mareek stood still, a tightness in his chest threatening to crush him. He had said it out loud, admitted the truth to himself, but it didn't make it any easier. Killing someone who loved him wasn't just a task. It wasn't something he could simply check off a list. It was a betrayal of every ounce of humanity that he had left.

But the promise—Sufiya's final words, her wish, her plea—echoed in his mind, and he knew there was no turning back. No matter how much it tore him apart, he had made that promise. It had been sealed with her blood, and the universe, in its twisted sense of justice, had brought this moment to him.

"I don't want to do this," Mareek muttered, almost to himself, his gaze fixed on the floor. "But... I have no choice, do I?"

Max didn't answer immediately. Instead, he let the silence stretch between them, allowing Mareek to confront the reality of what was to come. Finally, Max spoke.

"No, you don't," he said quietly. "You made your choice the moment you promised her. And now you live with it."

Mareek's hands clenched into fists at his sides. Every muscle in his body felt tense, like a coiled spring, ready to snap. The thought of taking Aruna's life, the very thought of ending someone who had shown him kindness, crushed him. She had no idea of the storm brewing inside him. She was just someone who had gotten too close to the dark truth of his existence.

"What do I even say to her?" Mareek asked, his voice cracking as the weight of his situation became unbearable. "How do I explain this? That I promised someone who's dead that I'd kill anyone who loves me?"

Max didn't offer sympathy. "You don't explain. You just do what you need to do. There's no room for talking in this."

Mareek's mind raced, searching for any possible escape. He wanted to scream, to throw everything away, to find a way out of this twisted nightmare. But he knew deep down, as much as he hated it, that there was no escape.

"I've always tried to run from this," Mareek whispered, his voice barely audible. "From the consequences of my choices. But now it's here. And I can't hide from it anymore."

Max didn't offer any words of comfort. He didn't need to. Mareek knew that he was alone in this, just as he had always been.

"Tomorrow," Mareek finally said, his voice determined. "I'll do it tomorrow. I'll... make the call. And end it."

Max nodded, as if everything had already been decided. "Good. There's no turning back now."

As Mareek walked out of the room, the weight of the promise settled deeper into his soul, a shadow that would haunt him forever. He didn't know how he would be able to carry out the act. He didn't know what it would feel like to take another life, especially someone who had never done anything wrong. But he had no choice. The promise had been made. And it was his to fulfill.

The next day, he would carry out what had to be done. And there would be no coming back from it.

As Mareek left his house in the morning of 10th of november, the words echoed in his mind, like a haunting whisper. "Happy birthday, my love." He had said them to Sufiya's dead body before leaving for the promise fulfillment of love.

He walked briskly through the empty streets, the weight of the promise and the events that led him to this moment hanging over him. His mind was numb, the fog of his emotions thick and suffocating. It was a path he had chosen, a path he couldn't turn back from, no matter how much he wanted to.

He didn't think of Aruna much as he walked, but the image of her had haunted him. She had admired him, a simple fan. She had loved him, and yet she had unknowingly walked into the web he had spun. His promise to Sufiya was clear, and now, he would make sure to fulfill it.

He arrived at her clinic in the early morning, the sun barely rising in the distance. He found the address using his contacts. The quiet street was still, save for the soft hum of distant traffic. The clinic's sign hung above the door, a symbol of her dedication to animals, to life itself. He stopped just outside for a moment, breathing in the cool air. He pushed open the door to the clinic, the chime above the door ringing softly as he stepped inside. The smell of antiseptic and the faint scent of animal care filled the air.

Aruna was in the back, busy with her work, unaware that the man she admired was about to destroy everything she had built, everything she had worked for.

Mareek walked quietly through the clinic, the silence amplifying every step. He reached the back, where Aruna was attending to a patient, a small dog lying on the table.

"Aruna," Mareek's voice cut through the air, low and steady.

She turned, startled at his sudden appearance but quickly masking it with a warm smile. "Mareek! You?" she asked with nervousness, her eyes brightening. "I didn't expect you to come. How are you? Everything good?"

He stood still, watching her for a moment. He saw her innocence, her genuine concern, her unknowing affection. It all felt so far away now. He had promised Sufiya, and this was the price he had to pay.

"I came to say goodbye, Aruna," he said coldly. The words felt alien as they left his mouth, but they were true. This would be the last time she ever spoke.

Aruna's brow furrowed, confused. "Goodbye? What do you mean?"

Mareek didn't answer immediately. He stepped closer, and in one swift motion, he grabbed the tools from the nearby medical tray. The needle was the first thing he reached for—a sedative, something quick to numb her, something to make this process easier.

"What are you—" Aruna began, but before she could finish, Mareek pressed the needle into her neck, injecting the sedative into her bloodstream. She froze for a moment, her body trembling slightly before she collapsed onto the table, unconscious.

His heart pounded in his chest, but there was no turning back. Mareek carefully moved her body into a more comfortable position, his hands trembling as he prepared to do what he had set out to do. The clinic was silent except for the soft sounds of his movements.

"Please forgive me," Mareek whispered, more to himself than to her. He didn't know if he could believe the words, but he said them anyway.

But there was no time for regret, no time to wonder. This was his fate now, sealed by the promises he made and the twisted love that had guided him to this point.

When it was over, when he had taken what he needed, Mareek stood over her, his heart empty. He looked at Aruna's lifeless body, and for a brief moment, the weight of everything hit him all at once.

He turned away, his breath shaky, his body tense. Mareek walked out of the clinic, the door clicking shut behind him as he carried out the final act. He had fulfilled his promise.

Mareek entered his house, his steps heavy but steady. The stillness of his mansion felt suffocating as he moved through the halls, the weight of his actions bearing down on him. There were no cameras in the clinic, no records of his visit, no fingerprints left behind to trace him. He had been meticulous, careful, and now, he was free—free from any connection to Aruna's death.

As he passed through the empty house, the silence felt almost comforting, like an old friend. He reached the room where Sufiya's body lay, as it always had, resting in the same position, her stillness a constant reminder of the promise he had made to her.

He stood there for a moment, staring at her lifeless form. The memories of their time together flooded back to him—the laughter, the love, the moments that had once felt so real. Now, they were nothing more than distant echoes.

Mareek walked slowly toward her, his eyes tracing the contours of her face. He gently brushed a lock of hair away from her face, as if trying to erase the pain that lingered in his heart. He had promised her that he would always be with her, that he would never let go. And now, in a twisted way, he was keeping that promise.

He kneeled beside her, his breath shaky as he spoke the words that had been lingering in his mind ever since he left the clinic.

"This is your birthday gift, my love," he whispered, his voice trembling. It was meant to be a tribute, a way to show her that he had done what she had asked of him, that he had fulfilled his promise. But deep down, he knew that this gift—this act—would never bring her back. It would never make things right.

Mareek's gaze lingered on her for a moment longer before he stood, his hands shaking as he slowly moved away from her body. He didn't know how much longer he could continue living this lie, this twisted existence. But for now, all he could do was keep moving forward, one step at a time.

He glanced back at Sufiya's body one last time, the weight of everything crashing down on him. This was the life he had chosen—one of solitude, of promises kept at any cost. The thought of it all left him hollow, but he knew there was no turning back.

He left the room and closed the door behind him. The house was silent again, and Mareek was alone—alone with the ghosts of his promises, with the remnants of a love that had led him down a dark path.

For now, he could only wait and wonder what the future would hold. Would he ever find peace? Or would he remain trapped in this self-imposed prison, forever bound by the promises he made? Only time would tell.

But as he sat down in the quiet of his home, his mind still reeling from everything that had happened, he couldn't shake the feeling that his journey—his story—was far from over.

Mareek had become something far darker than he ever imagined. The years had warped him into a person who no longer recognized the man he once was. His emotions, once fragile and real, had been crushed under the weight of his own promises, and now, they were but distant memories. What remained was an empty shell—a psychopath who could no longer distinguish love from obsession.

He had promised Sufiya that he would never let her go. And he hadn't. He had kept her by his side, but at what cost? His soul was gone. His heart was numb, replaced with a cold, mechanical drive to fulfill the promises he had made. The desire to never be alone, the fear of abandonment, had pushed him into a world where only death and preservation could hold his grasp.

His actions had no remorse. Each step he took, whether it was killing Aruna or preserving Sufiya's body, was a calculated move to maintain control over his broken, twisted version of love. He felt no guilt as he looked at the lifeless bodies around him. The once romantic idea of love had deteriorated into a sickening need to dominate, to possess, to keep people close—even in death.

The murder of Aruna hadn't fazed him. It was simply another task to cross off, another step to follow through on his promise. He had become so numb to everything that the world around him faded into nothingness. He lived only for the moments when he could prove to himself that he had not failed—when he could still hold onto the illusion of control.

Each time he looked at Sufiya's body, the face of the woman who had once been full of life, he found solace in knowing that she wasn't going anywhere. She wouldn't leave him, because she couldn't. She was his—forever. But in the depths of his mind, a part of him understood the tragedy of it all. He had reduced their love to this sick display of possession, of suffocating dependence.

And then there was Max. Max, who had been the only person to truly understand him, or so Mareek had thought. But even Max's support had become twisted in Mareek's mind. What was once encouragement had now transformed into the very thing that kept him trapped in his cycle. He had followed Max's advice blindly, without thinking of the consequences. Max had told him to live with Sufiya's body, to carry out his promises. But the words had lost their meaning, and Mareek now lived in a haze of detached madness, unable to comprehend the enormity of what he had become.

It was no longer about love, or even loss. It was about control. It was about holding on to something, anything, that gave his life meaning. He had no reason to care about the people around him, no empathy for those who had once been close to him. In his mind, they were all just pawns in his game—his existence no longer defined by human connections but by the need to perpetuate his own twisted idea of loyalty.

Mareek had lost all semblance of humanity. He was no longer the boy who had once been shaped by the cruelty of his father's abuse and his sister's sacrifices. He was no longer the young man who had dreams of music and fame. All of that was gone, replaced by a cold, calculating psychopath who measured his worth by the things he could possess and control.

As the days passed, Mareek continued his life in isolation. His mansion was a tomb—a cold, lifeless place where he and Sufiya's body coexisted, locked in a macabre dance of death and preservation. The world outside had forgotten about him. His fame, his music, everything that had once defined him was now irrelevant. He had no purpose beyond his promise. He had no ambition beyond the walls of his home.

And as time bled into years, Mareek became a shell of the person he had once been. He wandered through his days with the same blank expression, feeding his twisted desires and avoiding any confrontation with the reality of his actions. His only connection to the outside world was the occasional visit from Max, who had long stopped questioning his actions. Max simply watched, silently supporting his decisions, as if resigned to the inevitable outcome.

It wasn't until the end of those years, when everything had already fallen apart, that Mareek began to question if this was really what he wanted. But even as he asked himself that question, deep down, he knew there was no going back. There was nothing left for him to return to. The darkness he had embraced had consumed him entirely.

Mareek was a psychopath, but perhaps that had always been his fate. The trauma of his past, the brokenness of his heart, had all led him here—to a place where love no longer mattered, where death was the only constant. And in the hollow silence of his home, with only Sufiya's dead body as company, Mareek waited. He waited for something—anything—to remind him of the world that he had left behind.

But it never came.

And so, he remained. A broken man, a twisted love, and a lifetime of promises fulfilled in the most horrifying way imaginable.

As Mareek sat alone in his mansion, the silence weighed heavily on him. He had long since become accustomed to it—this emptiness that filled every corner of his home, every crack in his mind. But even in the quiet, his thoughts often spiraled, repeating the same promises he had made, the same horrifying choices he had carried out.

He had killed for love, for obsession, for possession. He had done everything he could to fulfill the twisted promise he had made to Sufiya—never to let her go. And now, he lived in the aftermath of that promise, alone with her dead body, and no one to remind him of the life he had once had.

But today, something changed.

Max walked into the room.

Max was there, standing in the doorway, watching Mareek with that same unreadable expression he always wore.

For a moment, Mareek didn't know what to say. Max didn't need to speak—he never did—but Mareek could feel the weight of the unspoken words, the reminder of all the promises he had made.

Finally, Max spoke. His voice was calm, almost detached, but the words cut through the silence like a knife.

"You haven't forgotten, have you?" Max asked.

Mareek blinked, his eyes flicking to the body lying on the table nearby. His hand involuntarily clenched into a fist. He knew what Max was talking about. He knew that every step he had taken had led him here—this life of death, isolation, and twisted love.

"I remember," Mareek said, his voice hoarse. "But it's... it's different now. I have her. I fulfilled my promise."

Max's lips curled into a smirk. "You think you're done? You think this is all over?"

Mareek frowned, confusion clouding his mind. "What do you mean?"

Max stepped forward, his presence suffocating in its intensity. He looked down at the body of Sufiya, then back at Mareek, his gaze unwavering.

"You made a promise," Max said, his voice colder now. "A promise to kill anyone who loves you. Not just her."

Mareek's heart skipped a beat. "What are you saying?"

Max's gaze never wavered. "You still have that promise to fulfill, Mareek. You promised to kill anyone who loves you. Including your sister."

Mareek's blood ran cold. He felt a chill settle deep in his bones. He had never truly considered it before, but the truth of Max's words hit him like a slap to the face.

Sara.

His sister.

The one person who had been there for him when no one else had. The one person who had cared for him, loved him, when he was nothing more than a broken, lost soul. She had always loved him, even when he didn't deserve it. She had taken care of him when their father had abused them both, when their mother had died.

But now, Max was reminding him of the promise. The promise that had started with Sufiya, but had never been truly fulfilled.

Mareek's mind raced, the weight of his past, his promises, crashing down on him.

Max's voice broke through the chaos of his thoughts. "You know what you have to do."

Mareek stood frozen. He couldn't move. The thought of killing Sara—of killing the one person who had always stood by him—was incomprehensible. But the promise... the promise he had made to Sufiya, to himself, to Max...

It haunted him.

"Do you love her, Mareek?" Max asked, his tone eerily calm. "Because if you do, you know what you have to do. If you don't, you'll betray your own word. Your own life will be a lie."

Mareek's head throbbed as the weight of the decision pressed down on him. He looked at Max, at the lifeless body of Sufiya, and he felt a wave of nausea crash over him. What had he become? Was there still a part of him that cared about Sara? Or had he become so consumed by his own twisted love and promises that he could no longer feel anything?

"I... I don't know anymore," Mareek whispered.

Max's cold gaze softened just slightly, but it was still filled with the same quiet, unyielding intensity. "You've made your choices. Now, you live with them. No one escapes the consequences of their promises, Mareek."

The room seemed to close in on him as Max's words lingered in the air. He had killed before. He had killed for love, for possession, for control. But could he really kill the one person who had been there for him all his life? Could he really fulfill this final promise?

Max was right. He had promised. He had promised to kill anyone who loved him.

But as Mareek stood there, his mind a swirl of confusion and torment, he knew that the cost of breaking that promise was something far worse than death. To betray his own word would mean to lose everything he had ever been—his humanity, his soul, his reason for living.

And so, the choice was made.

Mareek's heart shattered as he knew what had to be done.

The life he had once known, the family he had once loved, had all been sacrificed for the sake of his promises. And now, even Sara—the only person left who truly cared for him—would pay the ultimate price for his obsession.

The madness had consumed him.

And now, Mareek knew there was no way back.

Mareek stood motionless, holding the phone to his ear, his breath shallow. It had been years since he'd last spoken to Sara, years since their paths had diverged so drastically. He could barely recall the last time they had seen each other, the last time they had even spoken. But now, the weight of everything he had done—every choice, every sacrifice—pressed on him. The memories of his sister, of the warmth she had offered when their world was nothing but darkness, surged back. But they also brought with them the shadow of what he had become.

He swallowed hard, trying to steady his racing heart, before he pressed the call button.

The phone rang three times before Sara's voice came through, her tone hesitant but warm. "Hello? Mareek?"

The sound of her voice hit him like a wave, and for a moment, he didn't know what to say. He had promised to kill anyone who loved him, and now he was faced with her, the one person who had never stopped loving him.

"Sara," he finally said, his voice rough, a mix of guilt and longing. "It's... been a while."

There was a long pause on the other end of the line, as though Sara was trying to process the unexpected call. "Mareek? I... I didn't think I'd hear from you again."

"I know," he said, the words coming out strained. "I... I've been away, lost in my own world. But I want to see you. I want to meet, like old times."

"Where?" she asked, her voice wary but tinged with hope.

"I was thinking the old house," Mareek said, his voice barely above a whisper. "We can meet there, just like we used to, when everything was different."

The silence stretched between them, thick and heavy. For a moment, Mareek wondered if she would refuse. If she had moved on, if the pain of their broken past had been too much for her to bear. But then she spoke again, her voice soft, almost uncertain.

"Okay. I'll come. Tomorrow, then?"

"Tomorrow," he echoed, his grip tightening on the phone. "I'll be waiting."

He ended the call, the weight of what was about to happen settling heavily on him. As the day passed, Mareek couldn't shake the feeling of dread that hung over him. The promise, the obligation, the love he had felt for his sister—all of it twisted together in his mind, creating a knot of confusion and fear.

The night dragged on, but eventually, the sun rose. Mareek drove to the old house, his hands shaking as he gripped the steering wheel. He hadn't been here in so long, and the memories came rushing back—of the house they had grown up in, of their childhood, their shared laughter, their shared pain.

When he arrived, the house was just as it had been—quiet, abandoned, as if it had been waiting for them to return. He stood in front of it for a moment, his eyes scanning the familiar surroundings, before he went inside.

He set everything up. The chairs, the table, the empty space that had once been filled with their lives. But nothing seemed right anymore. The house felt like a shell, a mockery of what it had once been. He couldn't shake the feeling that something was wrong, that everything was wrong.

The night was still, almost eerily so. Mareek stood in the dim light of his room, the weight of his actions pressing down on him like a suffocating cloud. His hand trembled as he reached for his phone, the screen glowing softly in the dark. He opened the music player and scrolled to the song that had once been an ode to his sister's love—the very same song that had come from the depths of his own heart. "Sara's Love."

He hit play.

The soft melody filled the room, the sound of the guitar resonating like a hollow echo in the silence. The lyrics—the words that once had meant everything to him—now felt like a distant memory. His eyes locked on the screen, the voice of his past haunting him. This was the moment he had feared, the moment he had known would come.

"Sara's Love" played, and as the music swirled around him, Mareek stood frozen for a moment, feeling the cold grip of regret and sorrow seep into his very bones. He closed his eyes, trying to block out the guilt, but it was too strong, too overwhelming. The promise he had made to her, the love they had shared, was now shattered beyond repair.

He couldn't go back. He had already gone too far, and he had to follow through.

With each note of the song, he was reminded of everything he had lost—his sister, the love they once shared, and the life that could have been. But there was no turning back now. He had to finish what he had started.

The doorbell rang.

Mareek didn't move. The song continued to play softly, almost as if it were urging him to act. His heart raced as he heard the sound of Sara's footsteps approaching. She was here, unaware of the nightmare that was about to unfold.

When she entered the room, her face lit up with a smile, as if she hadn't a care in the world. But that smile quickly faded as she saw Mareek's somber expression. "Mareek?" she asked gently, her voice tinged with concern. "What's wrong? What is this all about?"

He didn't respond. Instead, his gaze remained fixed on the screen, the song still playing, now seeming to echo louder in the silence between them.

Sara took a cautious step forward, unsure of what was happening. "Mareek, please, talk to me."

He slowly turned to face her, the weight of his promise crushing him. "I'm sorry, Sara," he whispered, his voice low and distant. "I can't do this anymore. You shouldn't have loved me. You shouldn't have come here."

Before she could react, Mareek moved swiftly, his body a blur of motion. The pain of the past, the twisted promises he had made, and the insanity that had overtaken him all seemed to converge in one brutal, final act.

The moment was swift, brutal, and filled with a terrible finality. Mareek used the same method that had brought him peace in his deranged mind—the promise he had kept to kill anyone who loved him. He moved with terrifying precision, suffocating her, not leaving a trace, ensuring that she would be just another ghost in his broken world.

Sara's body fell limp, the smile on her face frozen in time, as the song continued to play in the background—a haunting reminder of what could have been.

Mareek didn't look back. He couldn't. He knew that the world outside would never understand. The world would never know the torment he had endured, the promises he had made, and the path he had taken. And as he stood there, alone with her body, the reality of what he had just done hit him like a wave.

But the emptiness inside him was even greater now. There was no relief. No sense of closure. Only the hollow feeling of what he had just destroyed.

The song continued to play.

"Sara's Love" echoed through the room, the melody now taking on a chilling quality. And Mareek, in his madness, was left with nothing but the haunting knowledge that he had lost everything—his sister, his humanity, and the very soul he had once possessed.

He had kept his promise.

And now, he was completely and utterly alone.

Sushant Malhotra had been watching Mareek for longer than he could count. His obsession with the enigmatic, twisted figure had grown steadily since their first meeting. Sushant had always been drawn to people with dark pasts—people who hid their true selves behind a veil of normalcy. But Mareek... he was different. There was an almost unnatural calmness about him, an absence of guilt or remorse that fascinated Sushant more than anything.

The psychiatrist had known about Mareek's bloody history long before Mareek had even begun to notice him. His investigation started slowly, like peeling back the layers of an onion, revealing the chilling truths hidden beneath. He had discovered the murders, the promises, the twisted logic that governed Mareek's life. And yet, it was never just about the killings for Sushant. It was the psychology, the mind behind the chaos, that gripped him.

He had followed Mareek's every move, piecing together fragments of his life, all while maintaining the guise of a simple psychiatrist. But deep down, Sushant was more than just an observer. He was a participant in this twisted game, playing his own role, looking for the answers to questions that had no clear answers.

The latest murder—the brutal killing of Sara—had hit something deep inside Sushant. He had followed Mareek to the abandoned house, the old family home, knowing that something would happen. He was certain. His instincts, honed from years of dealing with the disturbed minds of others, told him that Mareek would kill again. But what he hadn't expected was the sheer coldness of it. The lack of hesitation, the finality in Mareek's actions, it sent a shiver down Sushant's spine.

Sushant's mind raced as he replayed the scene in his head. He had watched, not from a distance but up close, hidden in the shadows, waiting for the moment to reveal itself. It was almost as if he had predicted it. He had known that Mareek's promises—his twisted, dark promises—would come to fruition. He had studied the patterns, understood the mind of the killer better than anyone. But nothing could have prepared him for this.

As Mareek finished, as he disposed of the body with methodical precision, Sushant stood there, frozen in place. The cold, calculating efficiency with which Mareek moved—it was as though he had done this a thousand times before. There was no remorse, no hesitation, no sign of human emotion. Just a man with a job to do, and doing it.

Sushant's hand tightened around the notebook he had been carrying. His heart pounded in his chest as he processed everything.

He had always been drawn to dark minds, to people who lived on the edge of sanity. But Mareek was something else entirely. He was a force, an entity, a psychopath with a twisted sense of morality. And now, after everything Sushant had learned, he knew that Mareek would keep killing. He would keep fulfilling the promises he had made, no matter the cost.

Sushant's thoughts were interrupted as he saw Mareek leave the scene, disappearing into the night with the lifeless body of his sister in tow. A sick, twisted sense of satisfaction crept through Sushant's veins. This was his work now. Mareek was his creation, a subject to be studied, analyzed, and ultimately understood.

But something gnawed at the back of Sushant's mind. He had been so focused on Mareek, so obsessed with unraveling the mysteries behind his actions, that he had almost missed something important. The promises. The rules Mareek had set for himself. The killing wasn't random. It was deliberate, methodical. And each murder had a reason behind it.

Sushant smiled to himself. He had always known that Mareek was a man who lived by his own rules. And now, it seemed that those rules were beginning to close in on him.

Sushant knew that Mareek couldn't keep running from his promises forever. Eventually, the walls would close in. The darkness would consume him, and there would be no escaping it. But until then, Sushant would be there, watching, waiting. He wasn't done with Mareek yet. Not by a long shot.

The psychiatrist's mind raced as he made his way back to his office, already thinking of the next steps. He had seen something in Mareek that no one else had—something dangerous, something almost supernatural. And it fascinated him. It consumed him.

The game wasn't over. It was just beginning.

Sushant paused, looking out the window of his office as he considered **Javed**'s question. The room was quiet, save for the soft hum of the city in the background. The assistant stood expectantly, his expression betraying a mix of confusion and frustration. Sushant had been unusually distant lately, lost in his thoughts, and

Javed was starting to worry.

"Why aren't we complaining against him, sir?" Javed repeated, his voice rising slightly.

Sushant slowly turned, his eyes narrowing as he fixed his gaze on his assistant. There was a moment of silence before he spoke, his tone calm but laced with an unspoken intensity.

"Because," Sushant began, his voice quiet but firm, "we don't understand him. Not yet."

Javed frowned, unsure whether Sushant was talking about Mareek or something deeper. "But, sir... we know what he's doing. He's murdering people. That's... that's wrong, isn't it? Why are we letting him get away with it?"

Sushant gave a small, almost imperceptible smile. It was a smile that didn't reach his eyes, a smile that carried with it a cold, unsettling understanding.

"You see," Sushant continued, "what's happening with Mareek isn't as simple as 'right' and 'wrong.' It's not about complaining or seeking justice. It's about understanding the pattern, the mind behind the actions. Mareek isn't just another murderer. He's a case study. A subject of the highest interest to me."

Javed stared at him, still trying to grasp the depth of what Sushant was saying. "But... he's killing people. How can you justify that? How can we—"

Sushant held up a hand, silencing him. "I'm not justifying anything, Javed. What Mareek is doing is... horrifying. But it's a means to an end for him. He has rules, a philosophy that drives him. You can't just approach this like any other criminal investigation. You have to understand him on a deeper level. To truly understand his motivations, we need to see it through. We need to watch how he plays out his promises, how he handles the consequences of his actions."

Javed was silent for a moment, digesting the words. "So... you're saying we just watch him? We let him kill?

Sushant's smile faltered for a second, his eyes glinting with something darker. "Not just watch, Javed. We learn. We learn everything we can about him. About the way he thinks, the way he justifies his actions. Because the moment we understand him fully, we can predict what he'll do next. And when that happens, we'll be ready."

Javed's stomach churned at the thought. "Ready for what, sir? To stop him?"

Sushant leaned back in his chair, his gaze turning thoughtful. "To guide him, Javed. To make him our own. Mareek is not just a monster. He's an opportunity. An opportunity to study the darkest corners of the human mind. And if we play our cards right, he could be the key to something far bigger than either of us could imagine."

The assistant was stunned into silence, his mind racing as he tried to process what Sushant was implying. He had always known that his boss had a somewhat... unconventional approach to his work, but this? This felt different. This felt dangerous.

"You're saying we control him?" Javed asked, his voice barely above a whisper.

Sushant nodded slowly, his gaze unwavering. "Yes. We understand him. We let him play his part. And when the time comes, we step in. We use him. He'll be our perfect subject, Javed. And once we have him, we can do whatever we want."

The silence between them stretched on, and Javed's mind swirled with confusion and unease. He had signed on for strange cases and unusual patients, but this... this was something else entirely. Sushant's obsession with Mareek was becoming more and more apparent, and it was starting to feel like the psychiatrist's moral compass had completely gone off course.

Finally, Javed spoke, his voice hesitant. "But... what if Mareek realizes what we're doing? What if he turns on us?"

Sushant's eyes darkened, his expression growing serious. "If he does, Javed, then we adapt. We evolve. We are the ones in control. Understand that, and you'll see the bigger picture."

Javed swallowed hard, a sense of foreboding settling in his chest. He had followed Sushant into this darkness willingly, but now, as the psychiatrist's true intentions became clearer, he wasn't sure how far he was willing to go.

Javed couldn't shake the feeling that they were both walking a fine line—one that would lead them into depths from which there would be no return. And he had no idea just how much he was about to lose in the process.

"but sir...., what if police caught us and arrest us thinking we are involved too", Javed asked.

Sushant's gaze hardened at the question, his expression cold and calculating. He didn't immediately respond, instead taking a moment to carefully consider Javed's concern. Finally, his lips curled into a small, almost imperceptible smile.

"Javed," he began, his voice low and measured, "you're thinking too small."

Javed looked confused, waiting for the psychiatrist to continue.

"The police," Sushant said slowly, "are not our problem. Not yet. What they don't know, they can't catch us for." He paused for a moment, his eyes glinting with a dangerous spark. "And by the time they start sniffing around, we'll be too far ahead of them. We won't leave a trace."

Javed nodded hesitantly, but the unease didn't leave him. "But... what if they get suspicious? What if they find out we're connected to Mareek?"

Sushant leaned forward in his chair, locking eyes with Javed. His voice was calm, but there was an edge to it. "We won't give them anything to find. No connections. No evidence. Do you understand? Mareek may be leaving bodies behind, but we won't leave anything behind, Javed. We're smarter than that. We'll keep our hands clean."

Javed swallowed, still not fully convinced. "But if they suspect us—"

"If they suspect us," Sushant interrupted, "it's too late for them. They'll be chasing shadows while we already have control. We are playing a different game, Javed. A much larger game. We don't let small things like the police get in our way. We anticipate their every move."

Sushant's tone was final, and Javed was left with no more room for doubt or argument. Sushant was right, in a sense—he had always been right. The man had a way of thinking that saw beyond the immediate threats, focusing instead on the bigger picture.

"But the most important thing," Sushant continued, his voice growing even softer, "is that we keep moving forward. We keep learning. Every step Mareek takes, we take with him. And when we finally have him, when we understand what makes him tick, we'll be the ones pulling the strings."

Javed's mind raced with the implications of that last statement. He had been with Sushant long enough to know that the psychiatrist was always several steps ahead of everyone else. But now, it felt like they were stepping into territory that could no longer be controlled.

"What if... what if Mareek does realize what we're doing?" Javed asked, his voice barely above a whisper.

Sushant's eyes flashed with cold amusement. "That's the beauty of it. If he realizes it, it'll be too late for him. We won't let him see the trap we're setting until it's already sprung. You see, Javed, the key is not just in understanding Mareek. It's in controlling him. And that's exactly what we're going to do."

Javed stood there, his heart pounding in his chest. A part of him wanted to walk away, to leave this dangerous game behind. But another part of him—one that had been slowly corrupted by Sushant's influence—felt the pull to stay, to see it through to the end.

"We're in this together," Sushant added, his tone almost reassuring now. "No one can touch us. Not the police. Not Mareek. Not anyone."

Javed nodded, though doubt still lingered in his mind. Sushant had a way of making things seem so simple, so controlled, but Javed couldn't shake the feeling that they were playing with fire—fire that could consume them both if they weren't careful.

Sushant smiled again, but this time it was different. It was a smile that spoke of victory already achieved, of a future where everything was already in place. "We just need to be patient, Javed. Patience is the key. In time, Mareek will be ours. And when that happens, we will be untouchable."

With that, Sushant turned back to his desk, signaling that the conversation was over. Javed stood there for a moment, lost in thought. The weight of Sushant's words settled on him like a heavy cloak. He had known that the psychiatrist was obsessed with Mareek, but now it felt like something much darker was at play. The stakes were higher than ever, and Javed had no idea just how far Sushant was willing to go—or how much he himself was willing to sacrifice.

The door clicked shut behind him as he left, but the unease remained.

Sushant's plan to manipulate and control Mareek emerged from a pathological obsession with psychological dominance, fueled by his need to assert intellectual superiority. As one of the country's most esteemed psychiatrists, Sushant saw Mareek not as a mere patient, but as a fascinating, complex specimen whose deep-rooted emotional wounds and fractured psyche could serve as the perfect canvas for his manipulative experiment. His approach was cold, calculating, and devoid of empathy. Sushant's intentions were not to heal, but to dominate, twist, and ultimately destroy Mareek's perception of reality.

By orchestrating the series of murders surrounding Mareek, Sushant sought to gradually erode his sense of self, distorting his understanding of love, loyalty, and morality. He didn't just want to control Mareek's actions; he wanted to shatter his identity, turning him into a mindless puppet in an experiment of psychological annihilation. This was not just about psychological manipulation but about proving his supremacy over human emotions and relationships.

Sushant viewed Mareek's distorted relationships as a means to an end—a test of his power. He sought to exploit Mareek's deep-rooted vulnerabilities: his promise to kill anyone who loved him, his internalized guilt, and his overwhelming need for control. By manipulating these aspects, Sushant aimed to induce a sense of helplessness in Mareek, forcing him to adhere to the warped ideals Sushant instilled within him.

Sushant, driven by an insatiable thirst for academic acclaim, sought to use Mareek as the centerpiece of a grotesque psychological experiment for his thesis. He viewed Mareek's fractured psyche as an invaluable subject, a canvas upon which he could demonstrate the malleability of human emotions and behavior. Sushant meticulously manipulated Mareek's mental vulnerabilities, intending to publish a groundbreaking, albeit unethical, thesis that would solidify his dominance within the psychiatric field.

Sushant, blinded by his ambition and intellectual vanity, meticulously crafted a labyrinthine web of psychological manipulation, using Mareek as the perfect subject for his thesis. He viewed Mareek's profound psychological deterioration as a rare, raw opportunity to explore the limits of human morality, identity, and madness. By pushing Mareek to commit atrocities, Sushant aimed to dissect the complexities of the human psyche, cementing his place in the annals of psychological science, regardless of the ethical ramifications.

Mareek had become something of a legend, not in the way he had once hoped, but as a figure surrounded by darkness. After the deaths of those who loved him, his heart had grown colder, a void that only seemed to expand. He had kept his promises, each one marking a soul lost in the wake of his own twisted sense of justice.

The night after he killed Aruna, Mareek stood in his mansion, the silence of the empty rooms pressing against him like a heavy weight. He no longer found solace in his music. It was a hollow tool he used to drown out the incessant whispers in his mind. The crowd, the media, the endless applause had become meaningless. His entire existence was reduced to an endless cycle of death, his actions fueled by an unquenchable desire to fulfill the promises he had made.

Max, his confidante, was a constant presence in his life, but even his presence was beginning to feel like a distant echo. He had once been the guiding voice in Mareek's descent, now he was more of a reminder of the man Mareek used to be—a man who still held some semblance of humanity.

One evening, as Mareek sat by the window, watching the city lights flicker below, a thought struck him. It had been months since he had killed anyone. But the burning desire to continue had not dimmed. His promises were unfulfilled, a gnawing ache that wouldn't leave him. And so, he set out again.

The first target was a girl from his high school. He had never truly noticed her back then, but she had a significant role in his life—a fleeting moment in the hallway, a rejection that had haunted her for years. She had loved him, but he never returned the feelings. Mareek had been indifferent, brushing her off as if she were nothing. But in his twisted mind, he now saw her love as a liability, a threat to his existence.

He stalked her for days, watching her live a life so different from his own. It was as if she were another version of what he could have been—an ordinary person, unaware of the horrors lurking within him. She went to work, met friends, and lived a life filled with simple joys. But none of that mattered to Mareek. She had once loved him, and for that, she had to die.

Mareek approached her one evening after her shift. He had watched her walk home alone every night, knowing this was the perfect time. She didn't recognize him at first, her face clouded with confusion when he stepped in front of her. He smiled, a cold, empty grin. "Remember me?"

She nodded, her expression shifting from curiosity to unease as she recalled their past. "You... You're Mareek."

"Yes," he said, his voice a soft whisper, "I remember you too."

Before she could speak further, he silenced her with his hand, cold and firm against her lips. The knife he had been concealing was suddenly in his grip. Her eyes widened with fear as Mareek drove the blade into her chest, her body crumpling to the ground like a ragdoll.

He stood over her for a moment, feeling nothing. There was no satisfaction in her death, no relief from the torment that constantly gnawed at him. It was simply a necessity. A promise fulfilled.

The next morning, Mareek washed the blood from his hands, his heart steady in its rhythm, as though nothing had happened. The world outside continued to turn, oblivious to the darkness that had unfolded. He had done what he needed to do.

It wasn't long before he chose his next victim. An elderly woman who had once thanked him for a loan he had given her. She had been nothing more than a blip in his life, a passerby. But her gratitude, her innocent expression as she wished him well and told him she loved him, was too much for him to bear. She had loved him, and for that, she had to be erased.

Mareek's encounter with her was as cold and calculated as his previous ones. He had no connection to her, no emotional tie. But he couldn't leave anyone alive who loved him. That was the rule.

He arrived at her small apartment, his heart beating in his chest like a drum. She greeted him with a warm smile, completely unaware of what was about to unfold. "Thank you so much, Mareek," she said, her voice filled with the warmth of a life well-lived. "I'll never forget what you did for me. You're a good person."

The words echoed in his mind as he stepped forward, a blade in hand. She didn't see it coming. Before she could speak another word, the blade was at her throat, silencing her forever. Her body fell limp in his arms, and he stood there, breathing heavily, feeling nothing but the coldness of his actions.

It had become a routine—killing those who had once shown affection, killing those who had once loved him. Each death was a step closer to the emptiness he sought to fill. But it wasn't enough. No matter how many he killed, it was never enough.

Max's voice echoed in his mind, a reminder of the promise he had made. He had to kill them all. Everyone who had ever loved him. The weight of his actions was starting to crush him, but he could not stop. He couldn't break his own rules. He was trapped in a cycle of death, and there was no way out.

Days passed, and Mareek's life continued to spiral. He lived in isolation, his connection to the world fading more and more each day. The media had long forgotten him, his fame a distant memory. His mansion was his prison, and the bodies of those he had killed were his companions. He no longer cared about the world outside. All that mattered was fulfilling his promises.

But even in the darkness, there was a flicker of light. A single voice in his head that refused to fade. Max's words were no longer comforting. They were haunting. "Do it," Max would say. "Kill them all. That's the only way you'll be free."

And Mareek continued. He had no choice. The promises were his only tether to the world, and he couldn't break them, not now, not ever. Each death was a step toward his own freedom, or so he believed. But in the end, there would be no freedom for him. Only the cold, empty darkness of his own mind.

As the years passed, Mareek's name became synonymous with fear and death. He was a ghost, a shadow haunting the world, leaving nothing but destruction in his wake. And through it all, Max remained by his side, a silent accomplice, a reminder of the promise that had driven him to madness.

But in the end, it was all for nothing. The promises were unfulfilled, and Mareek was lost. The world had moved on without him, and he was left to wander through the wreckage of his own making.

Mareek had become a figure larger than life. His fame and success in the music industry shielded him from suspicion, and the public's obsession with his talent allowed him to operate in the shadows without anyone raising an eyebrow. Behind his charming smile and the glitzy facade of his concerts, a darkness simmered—a darkness that was not only tolerated but worshipped by the public.

He had now killed ten people, each one more meticulously executed than the last. From the girl who had once proposed to him in high school to the elderly woman who had thanked him for a simple loan, Mareek had carefully eradicated anyone who had once loved him. Each death was methodical, clean—no trace left behind. His popularity and wealth shielded him from the scrutiny that should have beenfalling him. He had learned, through careful observation, how to remove every trace of himself from the crime scene, leaving behind nothing but the body and the silence.

No one suspected Mareek, not even the police. His fame had provided him with the perfect cover. The authorities, caught up in the media frenzy surrounding his success, turned a blind eye to any strange occurrences surrounding his life. The bodies that turned up—each one a casualty of unrequited love—were dismissed as random acts of violence, nothing more. The police had no solid leads, no motive, no suspects. They were too preoccupied with the shining star that was Mareek.

But there was one person who knew. Dr. Sushant Malhotra, the psychiatrist who had been investigating Mareek for his thesis on psychopathy, had uncovered the pattern. He had followed Mareek from the shadows, piecing together the puzzle of his increasingly erratic behavior. Along with his assistant, Javed, Sushant had been the only one to truly understand the depths of Mareek's descent into madness.

Sushant had spent months observing Mareek's actions. The psychiatrist knew more than anyone about Mareek's promises—the promises he had made to kill anyone who loved him. And Sushant had come to the conclusion that Mareek was not merely fulfilling these promises out of some twisted sense of duty. He was feeding into his own psychological addiction to power, to control, to dominance over the lives of those who had once held affection for him.

Sushant knew that Mareek's crimes were not just about love; they were about control. Mareek had made the promise, and each murder was a way of asserting his power over those who had shown vulnerability, affection, or even simple gratitude. To Mareek, these people had been threats, weaknesses that needed to be eliminated to maintain his control over his own world. Each time he took a life, he believed he was only fulfilling his promise to Sufiya, and that kept him grounded in his twisted rationale.

Javed, Sushant's assistant, had been a reluctant accomplice in all of this. He had helped with the investigation but never fully understood the depths of Sushant's obsession with Mareek. Javed had seen the murders as a series of unfortunate events, yet he couldn't shake the nagging feeling that something more sinister was at play. Sushant had been determined to continue his investigation into Mareek, even when Javed began questioning the ethics of being involved in something so morally corrupt.

While the police remained oblivious, Mareek's actions became more erratic. He had no clear motive other than to eliminate anyone who dared to love him. The people he murdered had not wronged him in any way, but in Mareek's mind, their affection was a form of weakness that he couldn't tolerate. To him, love was a trap—an emotional snare that could bind him to people and their expectations. It was easier to kill them than to face the complex emotions love brought.

Sushant, however, saw Mareek's actions through a different lens. The psychiatrist did not see Mareek as a mere killer; he saw him as a subject of study. To Sushant, Mareek was a living experiment—a case study in psychopathy, a complex maze of violence, mental illness, and warped morality. Sushant knew that Mareek's motivations were not entirely clear-cut, but there was a pattern: each death was a confirmation of Mareek's need for power, for control, and for the freedom to operate without anyone questioning him.

The ten bodies were not just statistics to Sushant—they were pieces of evidence, parts of a larger puzzle that Sushant was determined to piece together. Yet, Sushant remained an outsider to the true horror of Mareek's existence. The psychiatrist had never been invited into the dark recesses of Mareek's mind, and his investigation had only revealed fragments of the monster within.

Javed's role in this investigation had become increasingly uncomfortable. He had been privy to too much information, and though he had initially agreed to work with Sushant out of professional curiosity, the reality of Mareek's murders was beginning to weigh heavily on him. Javed could no longer justify being a passive participant in Sushant's pursuit of the truth. As much as he was fascinated by the psychological aspect of Mareek's actions, he also felt that he was complicit in something far darker than he had anticipated.

Meanwhile, Mareek continued his spiral. His popularity remained intact, his name revered by fans who had no idea of the blood on his hands. The media continued to fawn over him, praising his artistry, his talent, and his mysterious, brooding nature. Mareek's fame provided him with an impenetrable barrier against suspicion. No one would ever connect him to the bodies that were found in abandoned apartments or secluded spots. The police were too wrapped up in their investigation of mundane crimes to notice the pattern. No one even suspected the quiet, reclusive man who played music and lived in his mansion.

But Sushant knew. He was the only one who understood the true depth of Mareek's depravity. He continued his investigation, following the twisted trail that Mareek had left behind. Mareek had become an enigma—a figure whose charm and allure hid the grotesque truth that only a few knew. And Sushant had vowed to unravel that truth, no matter the cost.

As Mareek's actions became more frequent, more extreme, the pressure on Sushant to act began to build. He knew that Mareek was getting closer to his breaking point. And while the police remained clueless, Sushant couldn't shake the feeling that it was only a matter of time before Mareek's world would collapse, and when it did, there would be no way to stop the chaos that would follow.

And so, the clock ticked. Mareek, lost in his world of death and isolation, was blind to the storm that was about to engulf him. His fame shielded him from suspicion, but it would not protect him from the truth. And Sushant, the only one who truly knew the depth of his darkness, was waiting, patiently, for the inevitable.

Mareek sat in his dimly lit living room, the flickering glow of a single lamp casting long shadows against the walls. The silence was suffocating, broken only by the occasional creak of the wooden floorboards as he shifted in his seat. Sufiya's lifeless body lay nearby, carefully preserved and draped in her favorite silk dress, her presence both a source of comfort and a reminder of the promises he had made. But tonight, something stirred within him—something that was neither bound by promises nor tethered to the memory of Sufiya. It was anger, raw and unfiltered, aimed at a ghost from his past: his father.

He hadn't thought of his father in years. The man had been a phantom of his childhood, a specter that haunted the darkest corners of his mind. Mareek could still recall the sharp sting of his father's belt, the cold, cruel words that tore through his and Sara's young hearts like daggers. His father had been a tyrant, a man who ruled with fists and fear, and then one day, he had vanished—gone without a trace, leaving them to fend for themselves.

But now, as the memories resurfaced, they brought with them an overwhelming desire for retribution. Mareek clenched his fists, his nails digging into his palms as the familiar sting of anger burned in his chest. This wasn't about Sufiya or the promise he had made to her. This was personal. His father had been the architect of his pain, the man who had scarred him and his sister in ways that no one else could understand. And Mareek wanted to make him pay.

For the first time, Mareek's thoughts of murder were not tied to the cold logic of fulfilling his promise but to the fiery rage of vengeance. It felt different—messier, uncontrolled, but oddly exhilarating. The thought of finding the man who had destroyed his childhood and ending his life sent a shiver down his spine. This wasn't about love or promises; it was about justice—or at least, what Mareek saw as justice.

He stood and paced the room, his mind racing. Where could his father be? Had he remarried? Did he have other children? Was he even still alive? The questions only fueled his anger, the uncertainty gnawing at him like a relentless beast. Mareek's mind was a whirlwind of plans and possibilities, each one darker than the last. He imagined finding his father in some rundown apartment, a shadow of the man he once was. He imagined confronting him, watching the realization dawn in his father's eyes as he understood who Mareek was and why he had come.

But there was one problem: Mareek didn't know where to start. His father had disappeared years ago, leaving no trail, no clue as to where he might have gone. Mareek would need to dig, to search, to unearth the man who had caused him so much pain. And for that, he would need help.

The thought of involving someone else made him uneasy. He had always operated alone, his crimes meticulously planned and executed without leaving a trace. Bringing someone else into his world, even for a task as personal as this, felt like a risk. But Mareek knew he couldn't do this alone.

As he sat back down, his mind drifted to Max. Max, who had always been the voice of reason—or rather, the voice of chaos disguised as reason. Max would understand. Max would help. Mareek could already hear Max's voice in his head, urging him to take the plunge, to hunt down his father and make him pay for everything he had done.

The room grew colder as the night stretched on, but Mareek's resolve only hardened. For the first time, he felt a sense of purpose that wasn't tied to Sufiya or her memory. This was about him, about his pain, his scars, his need for closure. And as the first light of dawn crept through the curtains, Mareek made up his mind. He would find his father, no matter how long it took. And when he did, he would make sure the man who had caused him so much suffering would never hurt anyone again.

With this decision, a new chapter in Mareek's life began—a chapter driven not by love or promises but by vengeance. And as he stared at Sufiya's lifeless face, he whispered, "This one's for me."

As the sun climbed higher, bathing the room in a faint morning glow, Mareek sat motionless, lost in the tangled web of his thoughts. The stillness was broken by the unmistakable sound of footsteps—heavy, deliberate, and familiar. Max had arrived, as he always did, uninvited yet always present at the most critical junctures of Mareek's life.

Max entered the room with his usual air of nonchalance, his piercing eyes scanning the cluttered space. He smirked, gesturing toward Mareek, who seemed unusually still. "You look like you've seen a ghost," Max remarked, settling into the chair across from him.

Mareek's gaze remained fixed on the floor, his fists clenched. "I need your help," he said, his voice low but resolute.

Max raised an eyebrow, leaning forward slightly. "Help with what? Writing another song? Hiding another body? What now?"

Mareek finally looked up, his eyes burning with a mix of anger and desperation. "I want to find him. My father."

The smirk disappeared from Max's face, replaced by a rare look of surprise. He leaned back in his chair, folding his arms. "Your father?" he repeated. "Why?"

Mareek's jaw tightened. "He destroyed us. Me, Sara... He left us to rot. I need to find him, Max. I need to make him pay for everything he did."

Max studied Mareek for a moment, his expression unreadable. Then he shook his head. "No. I can't help you with this."

Mareek's eyes narrowed. "Why not?"

Max sighed, leaning forward again. "Because this isn't about Sufiya or your promise. This is personal. And personal means messy. You've managed to keep everything clean so far—no traces, no suspicions. But this? This will drag you into chaos."

"I don't care," Mareek snapped. "This isn't about keeping things clean. This is about closure."

Max shook his head again. "You're not thinking straight. If you want to find your father, you need to involve someone who isn't... well, *me*. Someone who doesn't know what you've done, someone you can feed a simple story to."

Mareek frowned. "What do you mean?"

Max leaned back, gesturing vaguely. "Find an old friend, someone who knew you back in the day but doesn't know the real you now. Tell them you've been wanting to reconnect with your father, that you're looking for closure. Make it sound normal, sentimental even. They'll believe it because they don't know the truth."

"And you think that'll work?" Mareek asked, skepticism evident in his tone.

"It's your best shot," Max replied. "But listen, Mareek. Once you find him, you're on your own. Don't expect me to clean up the mess when things go south."

Mareek nodded slowly, his mind already racing. Max's advice made sense, even if it left a bitter taste in his mouth. He didn't like relying on others, especially outsiders, but if it was the only way to find his father, so be it.

Max stood, brushing imaginary dust off his jacket. "One last thing," he said, his voice serious. "Think long and hard before you do this. Once you open this door, there's no closing it."

Mareek didn't respond. He didn't need to. His mind was made up. As Max left the room, Mareek sat back in his chair, staring at the ceiling. The path ahead was uncertain, but one thing was clear: he would find his father, no matter what it took. And when he did, the man who had haunted his nightmares would finally pay for his sins.

After days of deliberation, Mareek found himself seated at his dining table, staring at Sushant's business card. It rested in his hand, the edges worn from the countless times he had turned it over, questioning his decision. Max's words echoed in his mind: *"Find someone outside who knows less about you."*

Sushant Malhotra was perfect for the task. Mareek had intentionally kept their conversations on a superficial level, withholding all details about his private life. Sushant was persistent but hadn't pushed too hard, always circling the boundaries with curiosity but never crossing them. The man had an air of confidence, a sense of control that both irritated and intrigued Mareek. If anyone could help locate his father without raising suspicion, it was Sushant.

The following morning, Mareek picked up his phone and dialed the number on the card. The line clicked, and Sushant's smooth, professional voice answered, "Dr. Sushant Malhotra speaking."

"It's Mareek," he said, his tone curt.

"Ah, Mareek," Sushant replied, his voice brightening with interest. "To what do I owe the pleasure?"

"I need to meet you," Mareek said. "It's personal."

There was a brief pause. "Of course," Sushant replied. "When and where?"

Mareek arranged for them to meet at a small café downtown—neutral ground where prying eyes would be fewer. When the day arrived, Mareek felt a rare twinge of nervousness as he spotted Sushant sitting by the window, sipping coffee and scrolling through his phone.

Sushant stood as Mareek approached, greeting him with a warm handshake and a measured smile. "You look tense," Sushant observed, gesturing for Mareek to take a seat.

Mareek wasted no time. "I need your help," he said, leaning forward. "I'm looking for someone. My father."

Sushant's eyebrows raised slightly, the only visible sign of his surprise. "Your father?" he repeated. "That's... unexpected. May I ask why?"

Mareek hesitated. He had rehearsed this part in his mind, crafting a plausible story. "I've been carrying this weight for years," he began. "There are... unresolved things between us. I just need to find him, to confront him. For closure."

Sushant studied him carefully, his sharp eyes scanning Mareek's face for any sign of deceit. Finally, he nodded. "I can see how that would be important to you. And you think I can help?"

"You're resourceful," Mareek replied. "Connected. I figured you might have ways to track someone down."

Sushant leaned back in his chair, his fingers tapping thoughtfully against the table. "I can certainly try. But you'll need to be honest with me, Mareek. If I'm going to help, I need to know what I'm walking into."

Mareek's jaw tightened. "I've told you all you need to know."

Sushant didn't press further, sensing the boundaries Mareek had set. Instead, he nodded. "Fair enough. Give me any information you have—his name, last known location, anything that might help. I'll see what I can do."

Mareek provided the details in a detached tone, recounting what little he knew about his father without betraying the storm of emotions underneath. As he spoke, Sushant listened intently, his mind already formulating a plan.

When they parted ways, Mareek felt a strange mix of relief and unease. He had taken a step closer to his goal, but involving Sushant added a layer of uncertainty. What if the psychiatrist dug too deep? What if he uncovered more than Mareek intended to share?

As he walked away from the café, Mareek's thoughts were a whirlwind. Max's words echoed once more: "Think long and hard before you do this. Once you open this door, there's no closing it."

But Mareek had already opened it, and there was no turning back.

Sushant leaned back in his chair, watching Mareek leave the café. His lips curved into a faint, knowing smile. Everything was falling into place, just as he had predicted. Mareek's request was no mere cry for closure—it was a carefully veiled glimpse into the unraveling psyche of a man consumed by his past.

Sushant had been piecing together the puzzle of Mareek's life for months. The pattern of disappearances, the carefully sanitized trails, and Mareek's descent into isolation were all too telling for someone with Sushant's expertise. And now, this sudden desire to find his estranged father? It wasn't hard to deduce where this path was headed.

He sipped his coffee, his mind already calculating the next steps. Mareek's request for help wasn't a surprise—it was an inevitability. The singer had become a living experiment, a study in obsession and moral disintegration. Sushant wasn't just watching; he was orchestrating, subtly steering Mareek toward choices that revealed his fractured humanity.

"Fascinating," Sushant muttered under his breath. The request to find his father was an escalation, a predictable but crucial piece of Mareek's narrative. Sushant knew this wasn't about closure or reconciliation. It was vengeance. The kind of vengeance that would push Mareek further into the abyss of his own psyche.

The psychiatrist's mind raced through scenarios, weighing the implications of each move. He would find Mareek's father, of course—doing so would be easy enough. But the real intrigue lay in observing what Mareek would do once he had him. Would he hesitate? Would the rage that simmered beneath his composed exterior finally boil over?

Sushant's ultimate goal wasn't to stop Mareek or save him. It was to understand him—to explore the boundaries of morality, love, and madness. Mareek wasn't just a client or a subject; he was a living thesis, a masterpiece in progress.

As Sushant left the café, he was already composing the next chapter in his mental notes. He knew exactly what was going to happen. And he couldn't wait to see it unfold.

Mareek sat in his dimly lit studio that night, replaying the conversation with Sushant in his mind. He felt an odd mix of relief and unease. The idea of reconnecting with his father stirred memories he had buried long ago—the bruises, the shouting, the abandonment. But more than anything, it fueled a dark desire that he could no longer suppress.

As he stared at the piano in front of him, Mareek's hands trembled. His music had always been a refuge, a way to channel emotions he couldn't articulate. But now, even the melodies seemed hollow. His mind wasn't on his art; it was consumed by the prospect of confronting the man who had scarred his childhood.

Across the city, Sushant was already at work. Using the connections he had cultivated over the years, he began tracing Mareek's father. It wasn't difficult. A few calls, some subtle probing, and he had a name and location. The man was living in a rundown apartment on the outskirts of town, working odd jobs to make ends meet.

Sushant didn't rush to tell Mareek. He wanted to observe how the singer's anticipation would manifest, how the wait would gnaw at him. Over the next week, Mareek grew restless. He hardly slept, and when he did, his dreams were filled with fragmented images of his father's face, twisted in anger and regret.

When Sushant finally gave Mareek the address, he did so with calculated indifference. "I found him," he said, sliding a piece of paper across the table during one of their meetings. "He's not far. But are you sure this is what you want?"

Mareek didn't hesitate. "I need to see him," he replied, his voice cold and resolute.

The drive to his father's apartment was suffocating. Every mile felt heavier than the last. When Mareek finally arrived, he sat in his car for what felt like an eternity, staring at the flickering light outside the building. This wasn't just a meeting. It was a reckoning.

He climbed the stairs slowly, each step echoing in the silence of the dilapidated building. When he reached the door, he hesitated for a moment before knocking. The sound was sharp and hollow.

The man who opened the door looked nothing like the tyrant Mareek remembered. He was older, thinner, and his eyes carried a weariness that spoke of a life lived in regret. For a moment, neither of them spoke.

"Dad," Mareek finally said, the word feeling foreign on his tongue.

The man's eyes widened in shock. "Mareek?" he whispered, as if saying the name aloud would make it real.

They sat in the cramped living room, the tension between them palpable. Mareek's father tried to explain himself, stumbling over apologies and excuses. He spoke of his own pain, his failures, and the guilt that had haunted him every day since he left.

But Mareek wasn't listening. His mind was elsewhere, calculating, planning. This wasn't about forgiveness. It wasn't even about closure. It was about fulfilling a need—a dark, insatiable need that had taken root in him the day he made that promise to Sufiya.

Later that night, as Mareek walked away from the apartment, his hands were steady, and his face was calm. He left no trace, no evidence. He had become a master of his craft, a ghost that haunted the lives of those who crossed him.

Sushant watched from a distance, his suspicions confirmed. He didn't intervene. This was all part of the experiment, part of the narrative he was carefully constructing. As Mareek disappeared into the shadows, Sushant smiled to himself. The singer was spiraling deeper into his own darkness, and Sushant was there to document every moment of it.

Back in his studio, Mareek sat before Sufiya's body, as he always did after each act of violence. He placed a small token—a memento from his father's apartment—beside her. "This was for you," he whispered, his voice thick with emotion. "Everything I do is for you."

In his mind, Mareek wasn't a murderer. He was a lover, a man bound by a promise, fulfilling the ultimate expression of devotion. But to Sushant, he was something far more intriguing—a living paradox, a man whose love and madness were indistinguishably intertwined. And the story was far from over.

Sushant's fascination with Mareek's enigmatic life only deepened when he started piecing together the shadowy figure of Max. In all his meticulous observations and inquiries, Max remained an unsolvable puzzle. Sushant was certain of one thing: Max was no ordinary friend, and his influence on Mareek was pivotal.

Sitting in his study late one evening, Sushant reviewed his notes. Every critical moment in Mareek's spiral seemed to involve Max in some intangible way—words of advice, subtle nudges, and uncanny timing. Yet, Max existed as a ghost, a name without a face, a presence without proof.

"Who are you, Max?" Sushant muttered to himself. The frustration was beginning to gnaw at him. He had questioned shopkeepers, neighbors, and even people from Mareek's NGO, but none could recall ever seeing Max. There were no photographs, no records, no witnesses. It was as if Max was a figment of Mareek's imagination—a manifestation of his fractured psyche.

But Sushant wasn't one to jump to conclusions. "If he's real," he thought, "he's the key. If he's not, then Max is the most profound insight into Mareek's mind."

The psychiatrist's interest in Max wasn't purely academic. He recognized that Max might be the fulcrum of Mareek's descent—the quiet voice that encouraged his darkest instincts. If Sushant could unravel the mystery of Max, he could unlock the final piece of the puzzle that was Mareek.

"What if Max is a projection?" Sushant speculated to Javed during one of their late-night strategy sessions. "A mental construct, a coping mechanism to externalize his inner turmoil?"

Javed looked skeptical. "But, sir, if Max isn't real, how does Mareek act on such precise advice? It's almost like Max anticipates outcomes perfectly."

Sushant leaned back in his chair, his fingers steepled. "That's exactly what makes this so fascinating. Either Max is a phantom of Mareek's mind, or he's the most elusive manipulator I've ever encountered. Either way, Max holds the answers we need."

For Sushant, Max wasn't just a mystery to solve; he was the axis on which Mareek's entire descent revolved. To uncover the truth about Max was to understand the full depth of Mareek's psyche—and that was a challenge Sushant couldn't resist.

The office was silent, save for the ticking of an ornate clock on the wall. Sushant sat at his desk, staring at the notes scattered across its surface. Years of research, observations, and deductions all led to this moment. His pen tapped rhythmically against the table as he mulled over his next step.

Javed had left hours ago after yet another round of questions and protests. But Sushant was resolute now. The experiment had to reach its final act.

"This is the tipping point," he muttered to himself, leaning back in his chair. His mind was a whirl of possibilities. Mareek's descent was spiraling faster than even he had anticipated. But there was one piece still missing, one variable he needed to observe up close—Max.

He picked up his phone, dialing Mareek's number with deliberate precision. The line rang twice before Mareek answered.

"Sushant," Mareek's voice came through, curt and uninterested.

Sushant smiled faintly, leaning forward. "Mareek, I hope I'm not disturbing you."

"What do you want?" Mareek asked flatly.

"I've been thinking," Sushant said smoothly, "about Max. You've mentioned him a few times. He seems... important to you. I'd like to meet him."

There was a pause on the other end. Then Mareek's voice came, edged with suspicion. "Why?"

"I'm curious," Sushant replied, his tone unchanging. "He seems like a significant figure in your life, and I'd like to understand you better. Call it professional interest."

Mareek let out a short, derisive laugh. "I'll ask him. If he wants to meet you, fine. But don't hold your breath."

"Fair enough," Sushant said, the faintest trace of amusement in his voice. "I'll wait for your word."

As the call ended, Sushant placed the phone back on his desk and leaned back, staring at the ceiling. A small smile played on his lips as he murmured to himself, "This will be the last chapter."

Javed barged into Sushant's office, looking like he'd just seen a ghost—or worse, missed his morning tea. Sushant, reclining in his chair with the calmness of a cat who owns the house, glanced up lazily.

"Ah, Javed. You look like you've discovered a new form of stress. What's troubling you now? Forgot to feed the office fish?"

"Sir," Javed began, ignoring the jibe, "I've been thinking... What if Max refuses to meet you? Or worse, what if Mareek doesn't even tell him? What then? Do we... improvise?"

Sushant gave a theatrical sigh, as if the mere thought of improvisation exhausted him. "Oh, Javed. You're worrying about the wrong things again. If Max refuses, then we've learned something new about him—if he even exists."

Javed's jaw dropped. "Wait, *if* he exists? Sir, we've been talking about Max for months, and now you're doubting he's real? You sound like a conspiracy theorist!"

Sushant smirked, spinning his chair slowly. "Every great discovery begins with a little doubt, Javed. Besides, don't you think it's a tad odd that no one has ever seen Max? Not even a blurry CCTV photo? He's like Bigfoot but with a better PR team."

Javed groaned, pinching the bridge of his nose. "Sir, you're playing with fire here. Mareek has killed *ten people*! What if he realizes you're... you know, meddling?"

"Meddling?" Sushant echoed, feigning offense. "Javed, I'm not meddling. I'm observing. There's a difference. Meddling is what you do when you insist on reheating fish curry in the office microwave."

Javed ignored the jab. "And if he comes after us? What then? Do we just smile and say, 'Oh, sorry for studying you like a science project'?"

Sushant leaned forward, a mischievous glint in his eyes. "Javed, if Mareek turns on us, it'll be the ultimate test of my thesis. Besides, I've already prepared a contingency plan. You're on it."

"Me?!" Javed yelped, taking a step back. "I didn't sign up to be bait, sir! I just wanted a stable job! You didn't say anything about psycho pop stars and imaginary friends!"

"Relax, Javed," Sushant said, waving a hand dismissively. "You're overthinking it. If Max doesn't show, we pivot. If Mareek gets suspicious, we pivot. If Mareek tries to kill us, well..." He shrugged. "We pivot harder."

Javed threw his hands in the air. "Pivot, pivot, pivot! Sir, this isn't a dance class! You're going to get us killed!"

Sushant chuckled, standing and clapping Javed on the shoulder. "Oh, Javed. If I wanted safe, I'd have studied plants. But where's the fun in that?"

As Javed stormed out muttering about updating his résumé, Sushant sat back, smiling to himself. Whatever came next, it was going to be... entertaining.

The following day, Mareek sat across from Max, who was leaning against the wall with his usual nonchalant demeanor. Mareek was quiet for a moment before he spoke, his voice laced with something akin to desperation.

"I asked you to meet him. Sushant... He's been asking about you, and I think it's time to clear the air."

Max's eyes flickered toward Mareek, but he didn't move from his spot. His voice was calm, but there was a certain edge to it.

"No. I won't meet him," Max said, his response sharp. "It's a bad idea, Mareek. You want him to see you as some... experiment? That's exactly what he'll think, and then you'll lose control of this situation faster than you can handle it."

Mareek leaned forward, his eyes intense. "You don't understand. Sushant's not here to judge. He's trying to understand everything about me, about us. He's the only person who knows anything real, anything deeper. And now I need him to meet you. I need him to see that there's more than just me."

Max shook his head slowly. "It's not about you. It's about me. You don't get it. I don't want to be in his game. He's too sharp, too focused. And if I meet him, it just makes it worse. You won't like what happens after that."

Mareek stared at him for a long moment, trying to read between the lines of Max's refusal. There was something behind Max's words, but Mareek couldn't quite place it.

"You don't want to meet him because you don't trust him?" Mareek asked quietly. "Or is it something else?"

Max was silent for a while, his gaze distant. Finally, he spoke, his voice low and almost contemplative.

"I don't trust him. But more than that... I don't trust how much of you he's going to take when he starts asking questions."

Mareek felt a pang of something—frustration, perhaps. He wasn't sure. But he needed to follow through with this. He needed Sushant to meet Max, no matter the risks.

"Fine," Mareek said, standing up. "I'll tell him myself."

Max's eyes narrowed, but he didn't stop him. As Mareek left the room, Max called out quietly.

"Be careful, Mareek. You're diving into something that has no end. And once it's out there... you won't be able to control it."

But Mareek didn't turn back. He already knew what needed to be done. Sushant had to know the truth, and so did Max.

After Mareek hung up with Sushant, a heavy silence filled the room. His thoughts were jumbled, each piece of information spinning in his mind, but nothing seemed to make sense anymore. Max, his constant companion, had refused to meet Sushant—something that had never happened before. Sushant's request to meet him was too strange, too personal, and yet, it felt like everything in his life was unraveling.

But Sushant, ever the professional, had remained calm. He didn't seem shaken by Mareek's refusal to let him meet Max, instead, his voice had held a quiet, almost detached certainty. It was then, in the lingering silence, that Sushant's voice echoed in his mind once more: *Max might not even exist*.

Sushant was a psychiatrist, after all. His mind was trained to observe, to analyze, and to deduce, and what Mareek hadn't realized until now was that Sushant had likely been observing him for far longer than he'd known. The pieces of his life—Max, his promises, his compulsion to kill anyone who loved him—all seemed to fit together in a chilling pattern. Could it be that Max was merely an imaginary figure, created in the depths of Mareek's loneliness, a coping mechanism from his childhood to help him deal with the pain of abandonment and betrayal?

Mareek's breath caught in his throat. The thought had never crossed his mind. He wanted to dismiss it, to convince himself it wasn't true, but the more he thought about it, the more plausible it seemed. His relationship with Max had always been strange, detached from reality in a way he couldn't quite explain. Max was never a person anyone else saw, never a figure who interacted with the outside world. But in Mareek's mind, Max had been there, always present, always offering advice, always there to protect him from the dark thoughts and emotions that consumed him.

"Javed," Sushant called out to his assistant, who had been waiting quietly in the corner of the room. "We need to go to Mareek's village."

Javed raised an eyebrow, surprised by the sudden change of direction. "Sir? To the village? But why?"

Sushant didn't answer immediately. Instead, he grabbed his coat and placed it over his arm, his face impassive. "I need to find out more. There's something about his past that's critical to understanding what's happening now. I want to see the environment where all of this began. Maybe I'll find the answers we need."

Javed didn't question him further. He had learned long ago that when Sushant set his mind on something, there was no stopping him. "Understood," he said. He gathered his things, and the two of them left, heading toward the place that had shaped Mareek into the person he had become.

Sushant knew the truth was hidden somewhere in Mareek's childhood. Everything he had witnessed, every small detail he had picked up over their interactions, pointed to the same thing: Mareek was a man caught between reality and the world of his own creation. He didn't know if he could help Mareek find the peace he needed, but he knew that he had to try.

It was time to confront the past. Time to uncover the truth about Max.

5

The sun had barely risen when Sushant and Javed arrived at the small village on the outskirts of town. The air was thick with the scent of early morning dew and the earthy undertones of a place that had seen little change over the years. Sushant looked out the window of the car, his eyes tracing the winding roads, the rustic houses, and the fields that stretched on endlessly. The village was a world unto itself—isolated, forgotten by the bustling cities that lay far beyond the hills.

They passed a few people as they drove down the narrow, dusty roads, all of them familiar faces, but to Sushant, they were just pieces of a puzzle he didn't quite understand yet. The whole place felt suspended in time, as though nothing had happened here in years.

It was almost as if Mareek had never left.

Their car pulled to a stop in front of an old, creaking house—Mareek's childhood home. The wooden structure, though worn down by time, still stood with an air of quiet dignity, as if guarding the secrets of the past. The front door was slightly ajar, and the windows were dim, their glass reflecting only the faintest light.

"Here we are," Sushant murmured, his voice barely audible over the sound of the engine ticking.

Javed stepped out first, stretching his arms. "This place is... something else. Feels like time has forgotten it."

Sushant nodded, his thoughts heavy. "Everything Mareek is now, every piece of this tragedy, has roots here. We need to understand his past, Javed. If we're going to help him, we need to know what shaped him."

The two of them approached the house. The door creaked loudly as Sushant pushed it open, the sound reverberating through the empty rooms. The interior was dim, with dust settled on the furniture and old photographs hanging crookedly on the walls. It smelled like forgotten memories—stale air and something heavier beneath it, something Sushant couldn't yet place.

They walked slowly through the house, each step echoing in the stillness. The hallway led to a small living room, and Sushant paused before the faded portraits on the wall. They were all of Mareek—pictures from his childhood, his teenage years. In each one, he seemed to grow more isolated, more withdrawn, as though the world around him had become too much to bear.

Sushant's heart sank as he studied the pictures. He could feel it—the loneliness. It clung to the very walls of this house, soaking into the floorboards. No matter how far Mareek had come in life, this place had never let him go.

"Do you think Mareek will be okay?" Javed asked, his voice suddenly small in the silence.

Sushant turned to face him, his expression grim. "He was never okay, Javed. This place—this house—has a dark hold on him. The person he became... it all started here."

They continued their search through the house, and soon enough, they encountered an elderly neighbor sitting on a weathered bench outside her cottage. She greeted them with a smile, but it faded slightly as Sushant introduced himself.

"We're here about Mareek," Sushant explained. "We're trying to understand his past."

The neighbor's expression softened, her eyes reflecting a lifetime of memories. "Ah, Mareek... I remember him well. A quiet boy, kept to himself mostly. But there were things he used to do, you know? Odd things. He'd talk to someone who wasn't there."

Sushant's brow furrowed. "Someone?"

The neighbor nodded slowly. "He'd sit outside for hours, talking to the air. At first, we thought he was just imagining things, but he used to argue with that... someone. He'd shout at the sky, at the trees, like there was someone standing right there beside him."

Javed blinked, confused. "Who was he talking to?"

The neighbor shook her head. "He used to call him... Max. Always Max. He'd tell him to leave him alone, that he couldn't trust anyone else but Max. I don't know what happened to him, but... after his father left, it got worse. Mareek never really had friends, but Max was always there. I heard him talking to Max for years. Never saw anyone else, though."

Sushant's chest tightened, a cold realization creeping up his spine. He turned away from the neighbor, trying to process the gravity of what he'd just learned.

"Max," he whispered under his breath. "Max wasn't just an imaginary friend. Max was his survival mechanism. His mind created him to shield him from the abuse... the isolation. And now... Max is still with him, in some form."

Javed's voice broke through the tension. "But that means—"

"That means Max is more than a figment of Mareek's mind," Sushant continued, his voice low, almost to himself. "Max is a part of Mareek. A part of his psychosis. A part that he can't shake off, no matter how much he tries. And I think that part... that part is still calling the shots."

They left the neighbor and made their way deeper into the village, toward the small, forgotten places where Mareek had spent his childhood. They found themselves standing at the edge of the village, where the fields stretched out in all directions. The wind picked up, rustling the leaves, and Sushant stood there, staring out over the land that had witnessed Mareek's solitude.

"This is where it all started," Sushant said softly. "This is where Mareek's mind fractured. And it's also where we can help him heal. But first... he has to confront the truth. Max... Max is his demon, and if we're ever going to save him, we need to help him face that truth."

Javed looked at Sushant, his face drawn with concern. "And what if he can't face it? What if he refuses?"

Sushant's eyes hardened, determination settling in. "Then we have no choice but to make him."

They stood in silence, the weight of their words sinking in, as the village around them seemed to hold its breath. The past was never truly gone. It lingered in the air, in the shadows, waiting to be confronted.

Sushant knew one thing for sure: the journey ahead would be difficult, but Mareek's salvation depended on facing the darkest corners of his mind. Only then could he ever hope to be free of Max—and, in turn, free of the violence and torment that had defined his life for so long.

And if it meant going to the very heart of his madness to drag him back... then that's exactly what Sushant would do.

As the police continued their investigation, a new lead surfaced, and the thread of the mysterious killings began to unravel, inching closer to Mareek. Among the ten victims, two stood out for reasons that had not been initially apparent. The first was Mareek's estranged father, a man who had left his family years ago under dark circumstances. The second was his sister, Sara, a woman Mareek had not been in contact with for years, but whose brutal murder still haunted those who knew her.

Sushant, ever the keen observer, saw this new development as a crucial turning point. For him, Mareek was no more than an experiment, a case study to delve into the intricacies of the human mind. The fact that the murders had escalated to the point of involving Mareek's own blood relatives only added complexity to his hypothesis. It was no longer just about a mind breaking down or succumbing to its darker urges; it was about understanding how far that breakdown could go.

Sushant observed the police's reaction to the two murders. Their suspicions had shifted towards Mareek now, though they had yet to gather concrete evidence. It was a game of cat and mouse, where the true killer had done everything possible to leave no trace, and Mareek's fame and popularity had shielded him from suspicion for so long. But now, with his father and sister dead, the authorities were circling closer. They had begun to piece together the connections between the victims, and the fact that Mareek had once been close to them made him a prime suspect.

Sushant couldn't help but feel a sense of satisfaction at this new turn of events. As much as he had watched Mareek spiral deeper into his delusions and compulsions, this was precisely the outcome he had been waiting for. The question that lingered in his mind now was whether Mareek would ever acknowledge the weight of his actions or continue down the path of self-destruction.

Javed, too, had noticed the shift in the investigation. "They're getting closer," he remarked one evening as they sat in Sushant's office, going over the latest reports.

Sushant's eyes remained focused on the file in front of him. "It doesn't matter. Mareek will either slip away or face the consequences. But I'm not interested in the police. I'm interested in him."

Javed frowned. "You're treating this like it's all just a game to you. People are dying, and Mareek—he's not just some lab rat."

Sushant's expression hardened. "He's not a lab rat. He's the culmination of a theory—a theory about the human psyche, about how far someone can go when their identity fractures. Mareek is not the monster I feared he would become. He's a symptom, Javed. A living, breathing illustration of the consequences of isolation, neglect, and trauma. And now, as his world unravels, we'll see if he can face the truth of what he's done."

Javed shook his head, a slight edge of unease in his voice. "But what if he can't? What if he's too far gone?"

Sushant paused, letting the question hang in the air for a moment. "Then we'll see how deep the rabbit hole goes. And if he's truly lost... then I will be there to understand it, to witness it. This experiment... it's more important than anything else."

Meanwhile, the police were beginning to close in. The murder of his father, a man who had been both abusive and absent, along with the brutal killing of his sister, who had once tried to reach out to him, painted a troubling picture. As the investigators looked into Mareek's past, they began to connect the dots. His history of violence, his mental health struggles, and the strange circumstances surrounding his family's demise all pointed toward one conclusion: Mareek was the prime suspect.

But what the police didn't know was that, in the shadows, Sushant had already begun to plant seeds of doubt in their investigation. He had purposefully kept Mareek's proximity to the murders a secret, subtly steering their focus elsewhere, for he had an even bigger plan unfolding in his mind. The deaths of Mareek's father and sister, in Sushant's eyes, were merely the beginning of a larger psychological breakdown that would play out in ways the police could never understand.

As Mareek continued to spiral, isolated and unaware of the full extent of the forces at play around him, Sushant's experiment was edging closer to its final phase. The question was no longer whether Mareek would confess, but whether he could even recognize the full depth of his crimes—whether he could grasp the consequences of his actions or simply continue down the path of madness he had chosen.

The investigation was intensifying, and Mareek was beginning to feel the pressure. His every move was under scrutiny, but it wasn't the police he feared—it was the creeping awareness of his own brokenness. And as the walls closed in, Sushant could only watch with clinical detachment, waiting for the inevitable unraveling of Mareek's mind.

For Sushant, the experiment was nearing its conclusion. For Mareek, the nightmare had only just begun.

The police had been circling Mareek for months. The investigation had grown more intense, and with every passing day, the suspicion surrounding him seemed to mount. The deaths of his father and sister were the final straw that brought the authorities to his doorstep. The mounting pressure from the public, the detectives working tirelessly to unravel the mystery of the killings, and the nagging doubts about his involvement—everything had led them to believe that Mareek was no longer just a victim of circumstance. He was a suspect.

It had been late in the evening when the call came in—tip-offs from informants who had been tracking Mareek's movements, those who were convinced that something wasn't right in his mansion. The police had their doubts, but they had also gathered enough evidence to act. They couldn't let another day go by with the murderer still at large. The raid was set into motion. They would break down the doors if they had to.

As the SWAT team geared up, the tension in the air was palpable. Sushant, in his quiet corner, had been keeping track of everything. He had known this day would come—the unraveling of Mareek's carefully constructed facade. But even he couldn't have predicted how the police would uncover the chilling truth.

At Mareek's mansion, the police stormed the house with military precision. The once-immaculate home now felt more like a tomb than a place of residence. The lights were dim, casting eerie shadows against the walls. The officers moved through the rooms systematically, each one more tense than the last. But it wasn't until they reached the master bedroom that everything changed.

The room was eerily still. The air, thick with the faint scent of decay, made it clear that something was terribly wrong. One officer moved the curtains aside, revealing the lifeless body of Sufiya, preserved in a way that spoke of prolonged neglect. The body lay on the bed, as if Mareek had been keeping it there, a twisted shrine to his lost love.

Sufiya, who had once been so vibrant and full of life, was now nothing more than a macabre reminder of Mareek's descent into madness. The officers stood frozen for a moment, processing the sight before them. The crime scene was more horrifying than anyone had imagined. Mareek had been hiding her death in plain sight, and yet no one had suspected the truth.

"Found it," one officer muttered under his breath, his voice barely audible in the thick silence. "The body. It's her."

As the full weight of the discovery sank in, Mareek, who had been nowhere to be found in the house, was swiftly arrested. His face was pale, his eyes wide with an eerie calm as they read him his rights.

The officers moved quickly, shackling him as they escorted him out of his home, the weight of his crimes now exposed for the world to see.

Outside, the flashing lights of the police cars reflected off the walls of the mansion, casting an unsettling glow over the entire scene. News cameras were already gathering, and soon, the world would know the truth about the man who had once been hailed as a prodigy—a star on the rise, only to descend into darkness.

As Mareek was driven away in the back of a police car, his mind seemed strangely blank. The weight of everything he had done was only just beginning to seep through. But even as he was taken to the station, the one thing that still lingered in his mind was Sufiya—her face, her memory, and the twisted love he had for her. He had kept her with him for all these years, preserving her in his mind as if she were still alive. But now, the world knew the truth. And as the realization hit him, Mareek felt an emptiness he had never known before.

Back at the police station, Sushant sat in his office, watching the news unfold on the television screen. He wasn't surprised by what had happened. In fact, he had expected it. Mareek's descent into madness had been inevitable, a result of the toxic mix of isolation, trauma, and the warped promises he had made.

But even as Sushant processed the outcome, a dark sense of satisfaction crept into his thoughts. Mareek had been his experiment, and now, with everything exposed, the final chapter of his twisted study had been written. The monster, once an enigma, was now fully known to the world.

And yet, in the pit of Sushant's stomach, there remained a question that he could never quite shake: Was Mareek truly the villain of his own story, or was he just another victim of a system too broken to save him?

As the days went on and the media frenzy over Mareek's arrest escalated, Sushant found himself increasingly detached from the narrative. The case had become more about the spectacle than the truth. Mareek was a symbol of something much larger than himself, a reflection of a world filled with broken people and shattered minds.

In the end, it wasn't just about Mareek anymore. It was about the people who had been left in his wake—the ones who had suffered because of his madness. It was about the deeper, more unsettling truths that no one had wanted to acknowledge. And as Sushant watched the unfolding story, he couldn't help but wonder: What kind of world had Mareek been born into, and what kind of man had he become as a result?

Sushant had been expecting it, but still, when the call came, it struck him like a sharp blow. The police needed his expertise. Mareek's mental state, his twisted psyche, the unexplained motivations behind his murders—all of it had to be assessed. He was the best in the country for such cases, renowned for his sharp mind and deep understanding of the criminal mind.

The voice on the other end of the line was curt, professional. "Dr. Malhotra, we need you to assist us. We have to determine whether Mareek is fit to stand trial. Your insight into his mental condition is crucial."

Sushant paused for a moment, his mind calculating the implications. This was more than just another case for him—it was the final piece of the puzzle he had been working on for so long. Mareek, the experiment, the monster, the mystery. Now, he was about to dive deeper than ever before into the darkness of his mind. "I understand. I'll be there shortly," Sushant replied, his tone unwavering.

Hanging up, he leaned back in his chair, thinking for a moment. This was no longer about studying a subject for his thesis. This was about understanding the twisted culmination of everything Mareek had become. He had followed him from the shadows for so long—now it was time to confront the truth head-on.

But even as he prepared to meet Mareek in the cold, sterile walls of the prison, a sense of unease settled over him. What would he find in Mareek's mind? Would it be the product of nature, or the result of a broken world? Sushant couldn't help but wonder if, in the end,

Mareek was just a reflection of himself—someone who had been shaped by forces beyond his control.

The time had come. The investigation was about to begin.

Sushant had spent months, perhaps even years, delving into the intricacies of Mareek's life. The man sitting before him in the interrogation room, seemingly distant and unfeeling, was a puzzle that had captivated Sushant's mind ever since he first encountered him. Mareek's descent into madness had been deliberate, systematic, and disturbingly methodical.

Sushant knew the patterns of Mareek's killings—each one cold, calculated, driven by a promise that was, at its core, not of loyalty or love, but of twisted obligation. Mareek had lived his life in a cycle of self-imposed constraints, each promise a chain around his soul. These promises weren't just words. To Mareek, they were more like sacred vows, each one made with a conviction that bordered on delusion. He believed that by fulfilling them, he would somehow be freed from his torment, even if it meant taking the lives of those closest to him. Sushant had discovered this over time, piecing together the shattered fragments of Mareek's mind.

The murders had never been spontaneous. Each one, from his sister to his father, and those strangers, had been a calculated decision. The promise Mareek had made to Sufiya to kill anyone who loved him? Sushant understood it. It wasn't that Mareek had no capacity for love. On the contrary, he craved it, needed it—but he also feared it. And in his mind, to preserve himself from the potential damage that love might bring, he had convinced himself that killing the ones who loved him was the only logical solution.

Sushant had, through his research, discovered Mareek's childhood trauma—the abuse, the neglect, the constant cycle of rejection. Mareek had never learned to properly understand love. To him, love was entrapment, a cage. His father had abused him and his sister, showing love as control, and it had scarred him permanently. And so, Mareek had created an imaginary friend in Max, someone who would teach him the twisted lessons of control and isolation, making promises that would only perpetuate his isolation.

Sushant's heart had twisted with a strange mixture of empathy and fascination as he pieced together Mareek's psyche. The man had become the sum of his fears and promises, not a monster, but a broken soul, splintered into a thousand shards by the people and events that had shaped him. Sushant had seen the path of destruction that had led Mareek here, but he couldn't help but wonder if it was too late to repair it, if it was even possible. The mind of a person like Mareek wasn't something that could be easily fixed—it was beyond therapy, beyond reason. It was tangled in knots too deep for anyone, even Sushant, to untangle.

As Sushant sat across from Mareek, he knew the truth. He knew that Mareek wasn't the simple monster the world had painted him to be. He wasn't the villain in the story, but a victim of his own mind, trapped in the confines of his promises. And in that moment, Sushant realized he had to take the next step, not just as a psychiatrist, but as a witness to a tragedy far deeper than any of them had anticipated.

"Mareek," Sushant finally spoke, his voice soft yet tinged with an underlying seriousness, "You're not a monster. But you're trapped in your own mind. You've been living a lie. The promises you've made... they've made you someone you never wanted to be. But you can still get out of this."

Mareek didn't answer. Instead, his eyes fluttered for a moment, as if the words didn't reach him, or perhaps, they scared him. But Sushant knew he had to keep pushing. He couldn't let Mareek stay trapped in the prison of his own mind.

"You have to understand, Mareek," Sushant continued, his words steady, but laden with truth. "You made those promises because you thought you had no other choice. But I'm telling you now, there's always another way. You don't have to keep hurting yourself, or others, to live up to those promises."

For a long time, Mareek simply stared at him. And then, very softly, he spoke, his voice barely a whisper.

"I don't know how to stop."

Sushant nodded, his gaze not pitying, but understanding. "You don't have to do it alone, Mareek. We can figure this out. But you need to face it. You need to face what you've done and understand that you're not the person you think you are. You've been living a nightmare, but nightmares can end."

The silence stretched between them, but in that moment, Sushant felt a faint flicker of hope. It wasn't much, but it was something. Maybe, just maybe, Mareek's mind wasn't as far gone as it seemed. And if there was any chance of saving him, Sushant was going to try—no matter how difficult the path ahead might be.

Sushant paced around the small, dimly lit office, his mind whirring as he considered the best possible course of action. Javed, his loyal assistant, sat in front of him, his expression uncertain but attentive. The pressure of the situation weighed heavily on both of them. The case against Mareek was growing more intense with each passing day, and Sushant's primary goal had shifted. It was no longer about the experiment, nor was it about his fascination with Mareek's twisted mind. Now, it was about trying to get Mareek free.

"Javed," Sushant began, his voice steady but carrying the weight of his thoughts. "I need to explore every possible legal route to get Mareek out of this mess. We have to figure out a way."

Javed, who had spent countless hours assisting Sushant in his various endeavors, nodded. "Of course, sir. We have to be careful, though. We're walking a fine line."

Sushant's eyes narrowed as he sat across from Javed, his fingers steepled in thought. "I know. But it's not just about saving him anymore. It's about understanding what happened to him—about understanding his mind and his choices. No one else sees it, Javed. They all see a cold-blooded killer. But Mareek... Mareek is broken."

Javed swallowed hard, his expression uneasy. "You're talking about going after the system itself. The legal system. You know the evidence is stacked against him. They've already connected him to at least ten murders, including his own family. How do you propose to get him out of this?"

Sushant paused for a moment, considering the harsh reality of the situation. "The evidence against him is damning, yes. But I think there's more we can do. Mareek's state of mind—his mental state—is crucial here. We can argue that he wasn't fully in control of his actions. That his psychological condition led him to commit these heinous crimes, but without full cognitive understanding. He has a history of severe trauma, and if we can prove that he was incapable of rational thought, maybe we can reduce his sentence or even have him declared unfit for trial."

Javed nodded slowly, his brow furrowed in thought. "It's a difficult argument to make. His actions were deliberate, calculated... It's hard to argue that he wasn't aware of what he was doing."

Sushant leaned forward, his eyes sharp. "But that's where we need to focus. We need to prove that while Mareek was aware, he wasn't fully aware of the consequences of his actions. His mind was fractured. The promises he made to Sufiya, the compulsion to kill anyone who loved him—these aren't the actions of a sane person. They're the actions of someone who's been mentally conditioned, who's suffered extreme psychological trauma."

Javed, though still uncertain, began to see the path Sushant was attempting to lay out. "You're suggesting that we prove he was a victim of his own mind, that he's not fully responsible for his actions because of his mental state?"

Sushant nodded. "Exactly. We'll have to bring in experts—mental health professionals who can testify to the degree of his mental instability. We can argue that Mareek was a product of his environment, of the abuse he suffered growing up, and the extreme isolation he endured throughout his life. We can't erase the crimes he's committed, but we can shift the focus. If we do it right, we can convince the court that he needs treatment, not punishment."

Javed sat back, processing the implications of what Sushant was proposing. "It's a long shot, sir. The prosecution won't make it easy. But if anyone can get Mareek a chance, it's you. We'll need strong evidence and a compelling case."

Sushant's gaze hardened. "I know. But this is the only chance we have. We can't just let him rot in prison, Javed. He's not a monster. He's a victim."

Javed hesitated, then spoke up. "And what if the court doesn't buy it? What if they decide he's a danger to society and lock him away forever?"

Sushant's expression remained grim. "Then we do what we must. But I'm going to give it everything I have. Mareek deserves a chance to heal, to understand what he's done, to seek redemption if he can. We have to try."

Javed nodded slowly, his gaze full of respect for the psychiatrist's determination. "Then we'll start with the mental evaluation, right? We'll need all the evidence we can get—medical records, psychological assessments, everything."

Sushant stood up, resolute. "Yes, we'll start there. And then we'll go to court. But the most important thing is that we make them see Mareek for what he truly is—a broken man who never had the chance to fix himself. If we can show that, then maybe, just maybe, we'll find a way to free him from this nightmare."

As Sushant walked out of the room, Javed remained seated, his mind still spinning with the gravity of the task ahead. He wasn't sure if this was the right thing to do. He wasn't sure if Mareek deserved to be freed. But one thing was certain: Sushant wasn't giving up on him, not now, not ever.

And that might be the only hope Mareek had left.

Mareek sat in the cold, dimly lit cell, his mind swirling in a disorienting haze. He had been incarcerated for days, the weight of his past actions pressing down on him like a suffocating blanket. His thoughts spiraled uncontrollably, but amidst the chaos, one question gnawed at his mind: *Was Max real?*

It was a thought that had begun to haunt him ever since Sushant's revelation. The psychiatrist had gently, but decisively, told him that Max—the one person who had always been there, offering advice, guidance, and dark humor—was nothing more than a figment of his imagination, a manifestation of his loneliness, a coping mechanism his fractured mind had created. Max, Sushant had said, was a product of Mareek's mind—a way for him to deal with his isolation and the psychological torment he had suffered all his life.

But Max can't be imaginary, Mareek had thought repeatedly. *Max is real. He's been there for me… he's been my guide. He's helped me make the hardest decisions of my life. How can he just be a figment of my mind?*

As Mareek's thoughts spiraled deeper into confusion, a sudden sound broke through the fog—a familiar, low voice that sent a chill through his spine.

"Mareek," the voice said softly, almost too calmly, "don't believe what Sushant said. He doesn't know you like I do."

Mareek's eyes snapped open. He wasn't sure if he was dreaming or hallucinating, but there, standing in front of the cell's bars, was Max—his ever-present confidant. The same man who had been with him through every dark moment, through every decision. He wore the same confident, almost mischievous grin, and his eyes glimmered with a knowingness that made Mareek feel both comforted and terrified.

"Max…" Mareek's voice trembled. "Is it really you? Or am I just… imagining this?"

Max stepped closer, leaning against the bars of the cage with a casual ease, like they were old friends catching up. "You really think I'm imaginary, huh? After all we've been through? You think I'm just some product of your messed-up mind?"

Mareek's hand gripped the bars of the cage, his knuckles white. "Sushant said you're not real. That you're just a part of me, created to… to make me feel better when everything else was falling apart."

Max laughed softly, the sound almost a whisper. "Sushant? That bastard doesn't know anything about us. He thinks he's got you all figured out, doesn't he? But he doesn't understand what it's like to be you, Mareek. To have to endure everything you've been through. I'm not just a fantasy. I'm real to you. That's all that matters."

Mareek's head spun. The words were a lifeline, and yet they felt like a web pulling him deeper into confusion. "But why didn't you warn me? Why didn't you stop me when I started killing? I did everything for you, Max. I kept my promises. I… I killed those people because I thought it was the only way to make you proud."

Max's face grew serious, his smile fading slightly. "Mareek... I never wanted you to kill anyone. But you did what you thought you had to do. I've always been here for you, helping you, guiding you. But I never told you to kill. You did that on your own, didn't you? You made those choices."

Mareek's heart pounded in his chest, his thoughts scattering in every direction. "Then why have you always been there, Max? Why have you been the only one who understood me when no one else did? Why did you help me?"

Max tilted his head slightly, his expression unreadable. "Because, Mareek, you needed me. You created me because you couldn't face the world alone. You needed someone who would listen, someone who wouldn't judge you, someone who would help you make sense of the chaos in your mind. And I did that. I *was* that for you. I helped you survive. But now..." Max's gaze softened, almost pitying. "Now you need to understand that it's time to face the truth. All of it. The killings, the promises, your father, your sister—none of it will ever change if you don't start dealing with what's inside your head."

Mareek's breath hitched. "So, you're telling me everything I've done... everything I've believed in... was just me? My own mind?"

Max stepped back, folding his arms, his expression unwavering. "I didn't tell you to kill anyone. But I never stopped you, either. Because I knew you needed to make those decisions. But now it's over, Mareek. The game is up. You can't keep living in this twisted little world you've created for yourself. You have to face the truth. You can't keep running away from it anymore."

Mareek's mind was racing, the words crashing over him like a wave. "So, you're telling me I've been alone all this time? That you... you've never been real? That all my promises, all the things I've done for you... don't mean anything?"

Max's face softened, his eyes almost sad. "No, Mareek. I'm not saying they don't mean anything. But you need to let go of this fantasy. You have to face the consequences of your actions. You can't keep pretending I'm real. It's time for you to take responsibility for everything that's happened."

Mareek stood frozen, his thoughts battling each other. *Is Max real?* *Has it all been a lie?* He wanted to scream, wanted to run, but his mind was too foggy, too tangled in the web of his own thoughts.

Max stepped back, the soft sound of his footsteps echoing in the silence of the cell. "It's up to you now, Mareek. You can keep holding on to me, keep pretending I'm here. Or you can face what you've done. The choice is yours."

And with that, Max vanished.

Mareek stood there, staring at the empty space where his supposed confidant had been. His heart raced, his breath shallow, and his mind a whirlwind of emotions. He wasn't sure if Max was real or if he had been a creation of his own fractured mind. But one thing was certain—whatever the truth was, it no longer mattered.

The damage had been done.

Mareek sat in the cold, dimly lit interrogation room, his body stiff, his mind a jumbled mess of confusion and despair. The world outside was still, but his thoughts churned relentlessly. *Max isn't real...* The words echoed in his mind, a haunting whisper that refused to leave. He had been living with that belief for so long, finding comfort in Max's presence, his guidance, his unwavering support. But now, after everything that had happened, the truth was undeniable.

Sushant had planted the seed, quietly suggesting that Max was nothing more than a product of Mareek's fractured mind, a creation of his loneliness and childhood trauma. The more Mareek thought about it, the more it made sense. Max's sudden appearances, his cryptic advice, his endless conversations—it all felt so real, so vivid. But now, staring into the void of the sterile room, he wondered if it had all been in his head.

As he leaned against the cold, metal wall, the weight of the realization began to settle in. He had built his entire life around the idea that Max was real. He had killed for him, made promises to him, and allowed himself to spiral deeper into madness for him. But now, nothing made sense. Had it all been a lie? Had he been living in a delusion?

His heart began to race as the thoughts piled up. *If Max wasn't real... then what was I doing?* He closed his eyes tightly, willing the thoughts to stop, but they only grew louder.

Outside the interrogation room, Sushant paced anxiously, the weight of the situation pressing on him. He had done everything in his power to keep Mareek from unraveling, to help him see reason, to guide him back to sanity. But it wasn't enough. The damage had been done, and now Sushant had to find a way to salvage whatever was left of Mareek's mind before it completely shattered.

Sushant had been doing his best to save Mareek, even when the odds seemed insurmountable. He had carefully crafted an image of himself as a friend, a confidant, someone who truly understood Mareek's pain and confusion. But deep down, Sushant knew that his true motives were far from altruistic. He had been conducting his own twisted experiment with Mareek, using him as a case study for his thesis on the fragility of the human mind.

But now, as he stood outside the room, listening to the sounds of Mareek's muffled breaths, he realized something. This wasn't just a study. This was no longer about research or experimentation. Mareek had become a person to him, someone whose well-being he genuinely cared about, even if he hadn't wanted to admit it.

Sushant entered the room, closing the door behind him with a soft click. Mareek didn't look up, his gaze fixed on the floor as if he were trying to make sense of everything.

"Mareek," Sushant said softly, walking toward him. "You're not alone in this. You never were."

Mareek's head jerked up, his eyes wide and unblinking. He stared at Sushant as if seeing him for the first time. "But Max... Max isn't real. I thought he was... I thought he was the one keeping me sane. All this time, it was just me..."

Sushant's heart ached at the sight of Mareek's broken expression. This was the moment he had feared—the moment when the delusion would unravel completely.

"Max was never real, Mareek," Sushant said gently. "He was a part of you. A part of your mind, trying to protect you from the pain, from the loneliness. But now, it's time to face the truth. It's time to let go of him."

Mareek's hands trembled as he reached up to touch his forehead, his fingers brushing against his temples as if trying to piece together his fractured thoughts. "But I... I don't know who I am without him. I don't know how to function without him. He was the only one who understood me..."

Sushant knelt down beside him, his voice low and comforting. "You don't need Max, Mareek. You've never needed him. You're stronger than you think. You've been through so much, and you're still here. You can face this. You can face the truth."

Mareek's tears welled up, his eyes blurry with the overwhelming weight of everything he had done, everything he had believed. He felt lost—adrift in a world that no longer made sense, where his own mind had betrayed him. But as he looked into Sushant's eyes, something shifted. There was no judgment there, no contempt. Just understanding.

Sushant reached out, placing a hand gently on Mareek's shoulder. "I'm here for you, Mareek. You don't have to face this alone. I'll help you through it. You can still make things right. But you have to face the consequences of your actions."

Mareek nodded slowly, the reality of his situation settling in. For the first time, he realized that he could no longer escape. Max was gone, and the path ahead was uncertain and dark. But Sushant was right—he wasn't alone.

Sushant stood, offering a hand to help Mareek up. As Mareek hesitated, unsure of what the future held, he took the hand, feeling the weight of his decision pressing down on him. This was the beginning of something new—a chance to reclaim himself, to rebuild his shattered life. But it wouldn't be easy.

And as Sushant led him out of the room, Mareek couldn't help but wonder: What happens now?

As the days passed in confinement, Mareek was forced to confront his reality. Every moment in that stark, white-walled room felt like a slow unraveling of everything he once believed in. His isolation was punctuated by the occasional visits from Sushant, whose questions sought to pry open Mareek's fractured psyche. The police, meanwhile, were building an airtight case against him, the evidence stacked too high to deny. But in all this chaos, one person remained determined to understand Mareek, not condemn him—Sushant.

Mareek sat across from Sushant in the sterile, dimly lit interrogation room. The hum of the fluorescent lights above seemed to echo his thoughts as he leaned forward, his hands trembling. The air was thick with tension as Mareek finally decided to speak, his voice low and laden with emotion.

"I don't know where to start," Mareek said, avoiding Sushant's piercing gaze. "My life... it hasn't been mine for a long time."

Sushant leaned back in his chair, his fingers steepled under his chin. "Take your time, Mareek. Start from wherever you think it makes sense."

Mareek exhaled shakily. "It was in college when I met Rakesh. He was... everything I wasn't. He taught me music.

Sushant nodded, remaining silent, allowing Mareek to continue.

"But then..." Mareek's voice cracked, and he swallowed hard. "He killed himself. I—I didn't even see it coming. One day he was there, and the next, he wasn't. And I—I had the keys to his room. When I went in... I found them. His songs. Almost complete but unfinished. They were brilliant, Sushant. Beautiful. They deserved to be heard. And I thought... maybe I could be the one to give them a voice."

Sushant's expression remained impassive, though his mind raced. So the music that had captivated millions wasn't truly Mareek's creation—it was the legacy of a man who had died in obscurity.

"I told myself it was what Rakesh would've wanted," Mareek continued, his voice barely above a whisper. "But deep down, I knew it was a lie. I was stealing his soul, turning it into something I could call my own. And it worked. People loved it. They loved me. But it wasn't me they loved—it was Rakesh, through me."

"And Sufiya?" Sushant asked gently, his tone free of judgment.

Mareek flinched as if the name itself was a dagger to his heart. "She...

she was the only light in my life after everything." His voice broke entirely, and he buried his face in his hands. "I couldn't let go of her. I didn't. I still haven't."

Sushant remained silent for a long moment, piecing together the fragments of Mareek's confession. The story was darker and more twisted than he had anticipated. Mareek wasn't just a man who had lost his way—he was someone who had never truly found it to begin with.

"What about Max?" Sushant asked softly.

Mareek's head shot up, his eyes red-rimmed. "Max... he's my only friend. The only one who's been there through it all."

"But he's not real, Mareek," Sushant said carefully. "He's a part of you. A creation of your mind to fill the void of loneliness you've carried since childhood."

Mareek stared at Sushant, his eyes wide and disbelieving. "No. No, that's not true. Max is real. He's real!"

Sushant sighed. "You don't have to believe me right now. But deep down, you know the truth. Max is a manifestation of your pain, your isolation, your need for someone to guide you. And now, he's pushed you to do things you never would've done on your own."

Mareek fell silent, his breathing ragged. The weight of Sushant's words bore down on him like a mountain, and for the first time, he began to question everything he thought he knew.

As Mareek left the room, Sushant sat silently, processing the storm of revelations. His admiration for Mareek's music—the very reason he had been drawn to him—now stood on shaky ground. The confession about Rakesh was a punch to the gut. Mareek, the man hailed as a musical prodigy, had built his legacy not on his genius but on stolen work. And not out of desperation, but out of greed.

Sushant leaned back in his chair, running a hand over his face. This wasn't just about music anymore. It wasn't about the murders or Mareek's fractured psyche. It was about a man trapped in the consequences of his choices, carrying the weight of lies he had spun for years. Despite everything, Sushant couldn't help but feel a pang of concern for him. Mareek wasn't just his experiment anymore—he was his responsibility.

Later, in the quiet of their shared hotel room, Javed noticed the heavy look in Sushant's eyes. "Sir, something's bothering you. What is it?"

Sushant hesitated, then sighed. "Javed, Mareek's past is darker than we imagined. He didn't just take lives; he took a legacy. The music the world loves, the songs that made him a legend—they weren't his. They belonged to his senior in college, a man named Rakesh."

Javed frowned. "Rakesh?"

Sushant nodded. "Rakesh was the real genius. He taught Mareek music, left behind his almost-completed songs, and then... he ended his own life. Mareek found the songs and gave them his voice. And the rest, as they say, is history. But he took them not because he had to—but because he wanted to."

Javed's face twisted in shock. "So, he stole the songs that made him famous?"

"Yes," Sushant replied quietly. "But this changes nothing about what I need to do for him now."

Javed blinked. "Nothing? Sir, how can you still stand by him after that?"

Sushant leaned forward, his voice firm. "Because Mareek isn't just a criminal or a thief, Javed. He's a man who's drowning in his own guilt, his own lies. He's trapped, and if I don't help him, no one else will. I started this journey thinking of him as just a case, but now... now I can't let him face this alone."

Javed shook his head, still processing the revelation. "So, what's the plan?"

Sushant's gaze hardened. "The police may have the evidence, but Mareek needs someone who believes in the person he can be—not just the person he's been. I'll do whatever it takes to get him out of this. He needs to answer for what he's done, yes, but he also needs a chance to start over."

Javed exhaled sharply. "You're risking a lot for him, sir."

Sushant gave a small, weary smile. "I know. But sometimes, Javed, people don't need to be abandoned when they're at their lowest.

Sometimes they need someone to remind them there's a way out."

Javed nodded slowly, understanding the weight of Sushant's decision. "Alright. I'm with you, sir. What's next?"

"Next," Sushant said, standing up, "we figure out how to untangle this mess without destroying what's left of Mareek."

One afternoon, Sushant arrived for yet another session. He sat across from Mareek, clipboard in hand, though the formalities had long since dissolved. Sushant wasn't here as a psychiatrist anymore. He was here as someone desperate to save the man in front of him, not from the law, but from himself.

"Mareek," Sushant began, his tone softer than usual, "I need you to talk about Max."

Mareek stiffened, his hands clasped tightly in his lap. He had been avoiding the subject ever since the revelation. Every time the name was mentioned, it felt like a dagger twisting in his chest.

"Max is gone," Mareek said finally, his voice hollow. "He was never real."

"That's not what I mean," Sushant said, leaning forward. "I want to know what Max meant to you. Why he existed in the first place."

Mareek hesitated, his gaze dropping to the floor. "He was... everything. My guide, my friend, my family. When the world felt too much, he was the only one who made it bearable."

"And now that he's gone?" Sushant pressed.

Mareek's lips trembled, but he didn't cry. "Now... it's just me. Just me and everything I've done."

Sushant nodded, scribbling something on his clipboard. He had heard what he needed. Mareek's attachment to Max was more than a coping mechanism; it was the only thing holding him together. Without Max, Mareek was crumbling.

Later that evening, back in his office, Sushant discussed the situation with Javed. The assistant was visibly torn between his loyalty to Sushant and his own growing unease about the direction of this case.

"Sir, with all due respect, you're walking a tightrope here," Javed said. "The police are closing in. They'll want your assessment soon.

Are you prepared to tell them the truth about Mareek's mental state?"

Sushant leaned back in his chair, his eyes distant. "Mareek isn't a monster, Javed. He's a man who's been broken by the world and by his own mind. I can't let them destroy him. Not when I know he can be saved."

"And if they don't agree?" Javed pressed. "If they think he's too dangerous to be let off on an insanity plea?"

Sushant's jaw tightened. "Then I'll fight them. Whatever it takes."

The next morning, Sushant returned to the police station, only to find Mareek staring out the small, barred window of his cell. His expression was unreadable, but there was a strange calmness about him. Sushant stepped closer, tapping lightly on the bars to get his attention.

"You seem... different today," Sushant observed.

Mareek turned, his eyes meeting Sushant's. "I've been thinking."

"About?"

"About what happens next," Mareek said. His voice was steady, but there was a trace of something else—resignation, perhaps, or clarity. "About whether I even deserve to move forward."

"You do," Sushant said firmly. "But you have to want it. You have to fight for it."

Mareek didn't respond immediately. Instead, he walked closer to the bars, his fingers curling around the cold metal. "Do you think it's possible to come back from something like this? To live with what I've done?"

"It won't be easy," Sushant admitted. "But yes, it's possible. You can't undo the past, but you can decide what kind of person you'll be from this moment on."

Mareek nodded slowly, as if absorbing the weight of those words. "And what if I don't know who I am without Max?"

"You find out," Sushant said simply. "And you let others help you."

For the first time in weeks, Mareek allowed himself a faint smile. It wasn't much, but it was a start.

The courtroom was filled to capacity, buzzing with whispers and stolen glances. Reporters scribbled in their notepads, the hum of their cameras filling the tense air. Mareek, once a celebrated musician, now stood as the accused, his fame overshadowed by the chilling charges against him.

He was brought into the courtroom in handcuffs, his head held low. His disheveled appearance—a stark contrast to the polished, charismatic man the world had admired—drew gasps from the crowd. Even now, his silence felt imposing, like a man resigned to a fate he knew was inevitable.

The judge entered, calling the courtroom to order. The prosecutor wasted no time, painting Mareek as a calculated, remorseless murderer. "The defendant has taken the lives of ten innocent people, including his own sister and father. These were not crimes of passion or impulse. They were premeditated, cold-blooded acts." The prosecutor turned to the jury. "The evidence is damning. His fingerprints, his connection to the victims, the body of his fiancée found rotting in his home—Mareek is not just a murderer; he is a monster."

Murmurs rippled through the room as the prosecutor presented photographs and forensic evidence. The audience recoiled at the haunting image of Sufiya's decayed body, uncovered in Mareek's home.

Sushant sat at the back of the courtroom, his hands clenched. He had anticipated this, but hearing the accusations laid bare still felt like a punch to the gut. He watched Mareek closely, his expression inscrutable but his body tense.

The defense attorney rose to counter. "Ladies and gentlemen, the prosecution paints a picture of my client as a villain, but they fail to see the man before you. Mareek grew up in an environment of abuse and neglect, which fractured his mind. He is not a monster; he is a victim of his own tragic circumstances. We must ask ourselves: is he criminally responsible, or is he a deeply disturbed man in need of help?"

The defense's argument introduced Mareek's mental health into the trial, subtly alluding to Max without naming him. The court ordered a psychological evaluation, and Sushant knew it was his moment. The prosecution didn't object; if Mareek was mentally unstable, it would only bolster their case.

The judge, an older man with a stern gaze, glanced toward Mareek. "Mr. Mareek, do you have anything to say?"

The courtroom fell silent, all eyes on him. Mareek slowly lifted his head, his gaze sweeping across the room before settling on the judge. His voice was calm but hollow. "I have nothing to say. Not now."

The trial adjourned for the day, but the storm of public opinion raged on outside. Mareek was escorted out, his face unreadable.

That night, Sushant sat in his hotel room, poring over his notes. The weight of the trial was pressing down on him. For years, he had treated Mareek as an experiment, dissecting his psyche to construct a thesis that would cement his career. But now, things were different. Mareek's confessions, his anguish, and the layers of pain Sushant had uncovered made him more than just a subject—he was a broken man trapped in a web of his own making. And yet, Sushant felt a pull—a responsibility to help him.

Javed knocked on the door. "Sir, may I come in?"

"Yes," Sushant said without looking up.

Javed entered, holding a file. "These are the police records they shared with us. They've got everything—his financial history, his connections to the victims, even witness statements from neighbors who heard strange noises at odd hours. It's airtight."

Sushant sighed, leaning back in his chair. "Airtight, perhaps, but still missing the context. None of them know why Mareek did what he did. None of them know about Max."

Javed frowned. "But Max doesn't exist, sir. He's a fabrication of Mareek's mind. How do you prove that to a court? They'll just see it as a convenient excuse."

Sushant rubbed his temples. "Exactly. That's why I have to push harder. If the court understands that Mareek's mental state—his dissociative tendencies—drove these actions, they might spare him the death penalty. Rehabilitation, not execution, should be the goal here."

"But what about the music?" Javed asked hesitantly. "You admired his work, sir. Now we know it wasn't his genius but Rakesh's."

Sushant stared out the window. "The music isn't the issue anymore. The man is. Mareek stole Rakesh's music out of greed, yes, but it was also an act of desperation—an attempt to cling to something, to create an identity for himself. His entire life has been about survival, no matter the cost."

Javed nodded slowly. "So, what's the plan for tomorrow?"

Sushant stood, his eyes resolute. "Tomorrow, I'll meet with Mareek again. I need to dig deeper into his psyche. The court will order the psychological evaluation soon, and I have to be prepared to defend my findings. If I can show them the fractured state of his mind, we might have a chance."

The next day, Mareek was brought to the interrogation room in the detention center. He looked gaunter than before, his eyes shadowed but alert. When Sushant walked in, Mareek glanced up briefly before looking away.

"Good morning, Mareek," Sushant said, taking a seat across from him.

"Morning," Mareek replied curtly.

Sushant leaned forward. "I need to ask you more questions. I know it's exhausting, but this is important."

Mareek gave a hollow laugh. "Important for whom? Me? Or your thesis?"

Sushant flinched slightly but held his ground. "For you. And for the truth."

Mareek raised an eyebrow. "Truth? The truth doesn't matter anymore, Sushant. The world already sees me as a monster. What difference does it make?"

"It makes a difference to me," Sushant said firmly. "I know what you've been through. I know about Max, about Rakesh, about Sufiya. And I know why you did what you did. But the court doesn't know any of that. They won't understand unless you let me help you."

Mareek looked at him, his expression unreadable. "Why do you care, Sushant? Why go through all this trouble for me?"

Sushant hesitated before answering. "Because you're not just a killer, Mareek. You're a man who's been carrying unimaginable pain for years. And if I can help the world see that, maybe—just maybe—you'll have a chance at redemption."

For a moment, Mareek said nothing. Then he leaned back, his gaze distant. "Do what you want, Sushant. It doesn't matter anymore."

The night before the trial, Sushant sat in his office, papers scattered across the desk. His focus was split—one part preparing Mareek's defense, the other trying to reconcile everything he had learned. Javed entered with two cups of coffee, placing one in front of Sushant.

"You've been quiet all day, sir," Javed said, taking a seat. "What's on your mind?"

Sushant exhaled, his voice heavy. "Mareek isn't just a man on trial, Javed. He's a labyrinth of trauma, guilt, and desperation. He's been running from himself for years, and now it's all caught up to him."

Javed frowned. "But do you really think we can convince the court? They're not interested in his trauma—they're interested in justice."

"Justice," Sushant repeated, a trace of bitterness in his tone. "What does justice mean in this case? Punishing a man who's already destroyed himself? Mareek didn't just kill those people; he killed every part of himself along the way."

Javed sipped his coffee, watching Sushant closely. "But what's driving you, sir? Is it guilt for seeing him as an experiment? Or do you actually believe he deserves a second chance?"

Sushant looked out the window, the city lights reflecting in his tired eyes. "Maybe it's both. I treated Mareek as a case study for too long, and I can't deny that. But the more I understand him, the more I see a man who's been shaped by forces he couldn't control. That doesn't absolve him, but it does explain him."

The next morning, Mareek was escorted into the courtroom. He looked composed, almost indifferent, as if the weight of his crimes no longer pressed on him. Sushant sat beside him, ready to argue for his life.

When the judge called for Sushant's testimony, he stood, his voice steady but impassioned. "Your Honor, the defendant, Mareek, is not a man driven by malice or greed. He is a man shaped by tragedy, abandonment, and a fractured psyche. He created a figure—Max—to cope with the isolation of his childhood, and that figure became both his solace and his torment. What we see in Mareek is not a calculated killer but a deeply broken individual who needs help, not retribution."

The courtroom murmured, and the judge raised a hand for silence. Sushant continued, "If we condemn Mareek without understanding the depth of his mental state, we fail not only him but ourselves as a society. We must ask ourselves if justice is about punishment alone or if it is about understanding, rehabilitation, and preventing such tragedies from repeating."

As Sushant sat down, he glanced at Mareek, who gave no visible reaction. The trial would continue for days, but in that moment, Sushant knew he had laid bare the truth as he saw it. Whether the court would see it the same way was another question entirely.

The prosecutor, a sharp and no-nonsense woman named Advocate Priya Mehta, stood up after Sushant's testimony. Her presence commanded the room as she adjusted her glasses and glanced briefly at the defense table where Mareek sat with Sushant.

"Your Honor," she began, her voice crisp and resolute, "while the defense presents an emotionally charged narrative of Mareek as a victim of his circumstances, let us not forget what this case is truly about—justice for the victims. Ten innocent lives were brutally taken, and the evidence, albeit circumstantial in some cases, points directly to the defendant. Regardless of his mental state, Mareek acted with intent and precision. He left no trace—indicative of a man who knew exactly what he was doing."

She paused, letting her words settle. The jury's eyes were on her, as was the judge's. "The defense wishes to portray him as a fractured soul, a victim of his own mind. But let me remind this court that fractured souls do not orchestrate murders with such methodical precision. Fractured souls do not carefully remove evidence, leaving the police with almost nothing to trace. Fractured souls do not carry out these acts over years without remorse or confession until they are caught."

Priya turned to face Mareek directly, her eyes piercing. "Mareek is not some misunderstood artist or a man consumed by tragedy. He is a cold, calculating murderer who exploited his fame and charisma to evade suspicion. The fact that his victims include his own father and sister only cements the fact that this was not about a promise or mental anguish. This was about control, about power."

She gestured toward the jury. "The defense asks us to feel pity for this man. I ask you to feel justice for those who can no longer speak for themselves. This is not a case of a man needing rehabilitation. This is a case of a man who must face the full weight of the law for his actions."

Priya returned to her seat, her face impassive but her words still echoing through the courtroom. The tension was palpable, and the stakes were higher than ever. It was clear that the prosecutor was not going to let Mareek's fame or Sushant's psychological insights sway the path of justice.

The trial, it seemed, had only just begun.

Rehan Malik, the country's most sought-after defense lawyer, rose from his chair with an air of calm authority. Dressed immaculately in a tailored suit, his reputation preceded him—a man who could dissect arguments with surgical precision and sway even the most skeptical jury.

"Your Honor," he began, his tone measured yet captivating, "what the prosecution fails to acknowledge is that this case is not as simple as it seems. Mareek is not a cold-blooded murderer, nor is he the monster Advocate Mehta portrays him to be. He is, above all, a deeply broken individual—a man haunted by an unrelenting storm of trauma, mental illness, and a world that demanded from him more than any human could bear."

He paced slowly, his voice commanding the courtroom's attention. "Let us examine the facts. Mareek grew up in unimaginable hardship, subjected to abuse and neglect from the very man who was supposed to protect him—his father. He witnessed loss after loss, from his beloved mentor Rakesh, whose music he preserved, to the love of his life, Sufiya. He made promises, yes, promises born from love, not malice. Promises that fractured his already delicate mind."

Rehan paused, his piercing gaze moving from the judge to the jury. "Mental illness is not an excuse; it is a reality. A reality that cannot be ignored. Mareek's actions were not calculated, as the prosecution would have you believe. They were the tragic manifestations of a tortured psyche—of a man driven by delusions, guided by an imaginary companion, Max, who exists solely within his mind. The very existence of this delusion dismantles the prosecution's argument of calculated intent."

He stepped closer to the jury, lowering his voice for effect. "This trial is not just about Mareek. It is about us as a society. Will we condemn a man for his brokenness, or will we try to understand it? The prosecution demands justice, but justice without compassion is nothing more than vengeance."

Rehan turned toward Mareek, whose hollow eyes stared ahead. "My client is not a criminal mastermind. He is a victim of his circumstances, his mind, and a society that failed to intervene when he needed it most. He needs help, not chains."

He stepped back, his voice rising again. "I urge you all—judge, jury, and the public watching—to look beyond the headlines, beyond the fame, and see the man who stands before you. A man who has lost everything, including himself."

Rehan returned to his seat, his expression stoic but his words carrying the weight of a man who believed in his cause. The courtroom buzzed with subdued whispers, the contrast between the prosecution's unrelenting pursuit of punishment and the defense's plea for understanding drawing clear battle lines in the trial of the decade.

As Rehan Malik took his seat, a soft but pointed chuckle echoed through the courtroom, breaking the tense silence. Priya Mehta, the prosecutor, leaned back slightly in her chair, her lips curling into a wry smile.

"Compassion," she said aloud, her tone dripping with mockery, as though she was having a private thought made public. She stood, smoothing out her black robes, and turned to face the jury, her expression shifting into one of sharp precision.

"Ladies and gentlemen of the jury," she began, addressing them with the authority of someone who had dismantled countless defenses before, "we have just witnessed an exceptional performance. Mr. Malik is, without a doubt, one of the finest orators of our time. But let us not be swayed by theatrics when we are here to deliberate on facts."

She stepped toward the jury, her voice steady and deliberate. "We are not here to decide if Mareek's life was tragic. Many lives are. We are not here to decide if his mind was troubled. Many people face unimaginable hardships and still manage to abide by the laws of this nation. No, we are here to decide if Mareek committed ten premeditated murders, including his own father and sister, and whether he should be held accountable for those heinous acts."

Turning her attention to Rehan, her smile grew sharper. "The defense paints a picture of a man driven by delusions. But delusions do not erase evidence. Delusions do not hide bodies, erase fingerprints, or eliminate CCTV footage conveniently absent. Delusions do not carefully plan every single step to ensure no trail is left behind."

She pivoted back to the jury, her voice now cutting through the courtroom like a blade. "Mr. Malik asks you to see a broken man. I ask you to see the trail of blood he left behind. Ten lives extinguished. Ten families destroyed. And in return, the defense offers us... compassion." She let the word linger, her disdain palpable.

Priya paused, her eyes narrowing. "But let me ask you this—what of the victims? What of the woman who thanked him for helping her, only to be brutally murdered? What of the high school girl who dared to profess her feelings for him, only to meet her untimely end? Did Mareek show them compassion? Did his so-called delusions spare them?"

Her voice softened momentarily, the shift deliberate. "Mareek isn't a victim of society or circumstance. He is a man who made deliberate choices. Choices that destroyed lives."

She turned back to her desk, a smirk on her face as she added, almost casually, "Ladies and gentlemen, we are not here to redeem a man's soul. We are here to deliver justice."

The courtroom buzzed again, the stark contrast between Rehan's plea for understanding and Priya's relentless pursuit of accountability leaving the air charged with tension. Mareek sat motionless, his face unreadable, as the battle between his savior and his accuser unfolded before him.

Priya Mehta adjusted her glasses and stood confidently. "Your Honor," she began, her voice crisp and unwavering, "the prosecution would like to call Dr. Sushant Malhotra to the stand."

A murmur rippled through the courtroom as the name was spoken. Mareek's expression didn't change, but a faint flicker of something unspoken passed through his eyes. Across the room, Sushant rose from his seat, his calm demeanor unshaken, though a hint of tension was visible in his stride as he approached the witness stand.

After Sushant was sworn in, Priya wasted no time. She stepped forward, her piercing gaze locking onto him. "Dr. Malhotra, you are regarded as one of the finest psychiatrists in the country. Is that correct?"

"Yes," Sushant replied, his tone professional but reserved.

"And you've been involved with the defendant, Mareek Masood, for quite some time now, haven't you?"

"Yes, I've been studying his case extensively."

Priya's lips curved into a calculated smile. "Studying, you say. Interesting choice of words, Doctor. Would you consider Mareek Masood your patient or... an experiment?"

Rehan immediately rose from his seat. "Objection, Your Honor. The prosecution is attempting to lead the witness."

The judge nodded. "Sustained. Ms. Mehta, rephrase."

Priya didn't flinch. "Dr. Malhotra, what exactly was your relationship with the defendant?"

Sushant glanced briefly at Mareek before answering. "I was his psychiatrist. My role was to understand and evaluate his mental state, particularly following the traumatic events surrounding his arrest."

"Of course," Priya said smoothly, pacing a little. "And during your evaluations, did Mareek ever mention someone named Max?"

Sushant's expression tightened slightly, though he kept his voice steady. "Yes, Max was a recurring figure in his narrative. He described Max as a close companion."

Priya paused, letting the weight of her next question settle in the air. "And what, in your professional opinion, is Max?"

Sushant hesitated for a fraction of a second, then spoke. "Max is a figment of Mareek's imagination. A construct born out of years of isolation, loneliness, and trauma. He is not a real person."

The courtroom stirred with whispers. Priya let them simmer for a moment before continuing. "So, Doctor, you're telling this court that the person Mareek claims influenced many of his decisions—someone who supposedly guided him to commit these acts—does not exist?"

"That is correct," Sushant replied firmly.

Priya stopped in her tracks, turning to face the jury. "Ladies and gentlemen, the defendant has built a narrative around a phantom. A convenient scapegoat for actions that were meticulously planned and executed by him alone. Max is not real, but the blood on Mareek Masood's hands most certainly is."

Rehan stood abruptly. "Objection! Speculation and inflammatory rhetoric!"

The judge raised a hand. "Sustained. Ms. Mehta, stick to the facts."

Priya nodded, unfazed. "No further questions, Your Honor."

As she returned to her seat, Sushant's gaze briefly met Mareek's. In that fleeting moment, it was impossible to tell who felt more exposed—the psychiatrist unraveling the mind of his subject, or the man whose demons had been laid bare before the world.

The second day of the trial was over, leaving the courtroom divided. Mareek was escorted back to his holding cell, his face as emotionless as ever. Sushant, walking with Javed out of the courthouse, muttered, "We're fighting against public perception as much as the law."

Rehan Malik, meanwhile, spent the evening preparing for the next day, determined to steer the narrative toward Mareek's struggles rather than his crimes. Priya Mehta, on the other hand, was strategizing to emphasize the victims' stories, painting Mareek as a calculated predator hiding behind his fame.

After several more trials, the courtroom was abuzz with tension. This final day would conclude everything—the fate of Mareek Masood rested on the arguments presented today. The prosecution and defense were at their sharpest, knowing this was their last chance to sway the jury.

Rehan Malik stood with a commanding presence, his voice steady as he began his closing argument. "Ladies and gentlemen of the jury, my client, Mareek Masood, is not the monster the prosecution paints him to be. He is a man plagued by his past, trapped by his own mind. Yes, he has committed grievous acts, but these acts were driven by severe psychological disturbances—disturbances that stemmed from years of trauma, neglect, and loss. We cannot ignore his mental state. This is not just a matter of law; it is a matter of humanity."

Priya Mehta rose to counter, her tone sharp and resolute. "The defense asks you to see a man who has suffered. But what about the ten lives he took? What about their suffering? Mareek Masood did not just kill; he planned, he executed, and he left no trace. This was not the work of a man lost in his mind—it was the work of a calculated killer. Fame does not exempt one from justice."

The jury was visibly torn, their expressions a mix of empathy and doubt. Sushant sat in the gallery, his hands clenched. He had done everything he could to present Mareek's psychological state, but the final decision was no longer in his hands.

As the judge prepared to give the jury their instructions, Mareek sat motionless, his face unreadable. Max, invisible to the world, sat beside him, whispering, "Whatever happens, you kept your promises."

The jury was escorted to the deliberation room, their faces tense as they carried the weight of the trial on their shoulders. The room fell into a hushed silence as they settled into their seats, the gravity of their decision looming over them.

"Well," began an older man with graying hair, the foreman of the jury, "we have a lot to discuss."

A young woman leaned forward, her voice trembling slightly. "I just... I can't stop thinking about the testimonies. Sushant Malhotra explained Mareek's mental state so well. It's clear he's disturbed—he's not like any ordinary criminal."

"But disturbed or not," interrupted a middle-aged man in a suit, "ten people are dead, including his own sister and father. Mental illness doesn't justify murder."

The group nodded in agreement, though a younger juror spoke up. "Still, the defense argued that his actions were driven by delusions and trauma. If that's true, do we have the right to condemn him the same way we would a cold-blooded killer?"

Another juror, a woman with glasses and a calm demeanor, countered, "But how do we know where the line is? He planned these murders carefully, leaving no trace. That doesn't sound like someone entirely out of control. Can we really overlook that?"

The foreman raised a hand to bring order to the discussion. "Let's focus on the facts. First, the prosecution argued that Mareek was methodical and deliberate. The evidence supports that. Second, the defense argued that he was driven by delusions—this 'Max'—and Sushant testified that he believes Mareek's actions were the result of a fractured mind. We need to decide which holds more weight."

The room fell into silence as they processed the arguments. "Can we start with a vote?" someone suggested.

The foreman nodded. "Alright. Let's see where we stand."

Hands rose hesitantly, some more confident than others. The foreman counted the votes, his brow furrowed. "It's close," he said grimly. "We'll need to talk this through more."
The deliberation stretched late into the evening, arguments circling between justice and compassion, punishment and understanding.

The atmosphere inside the courtroom was suffocating, the air dense with anticipation. Days of grueling testimonies, endless cross-examinations, and impassioned arguments had led to this moment. Mareek Masood sat at the defendant's table, hands clasped together, his face stoic but his eyes hollow. He had endured a lifetime of storms, but this was one he knew he could not escape. Beside him sat Rehan Malik, the country's best defense attorney, his sharp mind a weapon in countless battles, yet now dulled by the overwhelming tide of evidence against his client.
Across the room, Priya Mehta, the prosecutor, exuded an aura of confidence. Her crisp black robes and meticulously organized files spoke of her preparation and determination. She was the voice of the victims, the relentless pursuer of justice. Today, she knew the scales would tip in her favor. This was no ordinary trial—it was the trial of the decade, if not the century. Mareek Masood, the once-revered musician and now an alleged monster, had captivated the public's imagination. His fame had shielded him for years, but no longer.
The jury filed into the courtroom, their faces solemn and heavy with the weight of their duty. Each step echoed ominously, a drumroll to the impending verdict. The foreman, a middle-aged man with graying hair and glasses perched precariously on his nose, held a piece of paper in trembling hands. Judge Harsh Vardhan presided over the courtroom, his gavel resting silently on the bench, waiting to punctuate the final act of this tragedy.
"Has the jury reached a verdict?" the judge asked, his voice resonating with authority.
The foreman nodded, his throat bobbing as he swallowed hard. "Yes, Your Honor, we have."

Rehan Malik shifted slightly in his seat, his jaw clenched, his fingers drumming softly against the table. He was a man who thrived on control, on bending narratives to his will, but today he felt uncharacteristically powerless. Mareek sat motionless, his gaze fixed ahead, as if already resigned to the outcome. In the back of his mind, the faint whisper of Max lingered, taunting him, reminding him of promises and choices that had led him to this precipice.

The foreman unfolded the piece of paper, his voice steady but heavy with gravity. "In the case of the State versus Mareek Masood, we find the defendant guilty on all charges."

A murmur rippled through the courtroom, a collective exhalation of breath held too long. Judge Vardhan struck his gavel once, silencing the crowd. Mareek's expression didn't change; his lips remained a thin, immovable line, his eyes devoid of any spark. For him, this was merely a confirmation of what he already knew.

"The jury," the foreman continued, "unanimously recommends the sentence of death by hanging."

The words hung in the air like a guillotine poised to fall. Rehan Malik's hand instinctively went to Mareek's shoulder, a silent gesture of solidarity, though he knew it offered little comfort. Priya Mehta's lips curled into a faint, triumphant smile, though the weight of the moment tempered any sense of victory. For her, this was not just a win but a vindication for the victims and their families.

Sushant Malhotra, seated quietly in the back, lowered his head into his hands. He had watched this unfold from the sidelines, his role as an observer and unwilling participant in Mareek's unraveling. Despite his analytical mind and clinical detachment, the verdict hit him like a punch to the gut. He had thought of Mareek as an experiment, a puzzle to be solved, but now, as the final chapter of this story approached, he felt the pang of guilt and loss.

Judge Vardhan nodded solemnly, his voice carrying the weight of finality. "The court hereby sentences Mareek Masood to death by hanging. May justice be served."

The gavel struck, sealing Mareek's fate.

Mareek stood as the bailiffs approached, his movements slow but deliberate. He neither protested nor resisted, his silence more powerful than any words he could have uttered. As he was led away, Max appeared in the corner of the room, visible only to Mareek. His presence was as unsettling as ever, a shadowy figure with a sly grin and piercing eyes.

"Well," Max said, his voice dripping with sardonic amusement. "It seems our symphony has reached its final note."

Mareek didn't respond. His mind was whirlwind of memories and regrets, of promises made and lives taken. Max's voice faded into the background as he was escorted out of the courtroom, the world around him a blur.

The days that followed were a cacophony of media frenzy and public outrage. News channels replayed clips of the trial, headlines screamed of Mareek's downfall, and debates raged on social media. But within the confines of his prison cell, Mareek was untouched by the noise. The outside world felt distant, like a fading echo of a life that no longer belonged to him.

Sushant Malhotra, however, was not untouched. The verdict had ignited a fire within him, a need to understand, to reconcile the man he had once admired with the monster the world now saw. He spent hours poring over case files, dissecting every piece of evidence, every testimony. He visited Mareek in prison, their conversations guarded but laden with unspoken truths.

"Why did you do it?" Sushant asked during one of their meetings, his voice heavy with a mix of curiosity and despair. "Was it Max? Was it the promise?"

Mareek's lips twitched into a faint, bitter smile. "Max didn't make me do anything. He was... he was just a part of me. A voice I created to survive. But the choices, the actions... those were mine."

Sushant studied him, searching for signs of remorse, of humanity. But Mareek's gaze was unfathomable, a deep well of secrets and scars.

Meanwhile, Rehan Malik was working tirelessly behind the scenes. Despite the overwhelming evidence and the public's demand for justice, he refused to give up. He filed appeals, challenged procedures, and sought out any legal loophole that could save his client. For Rehan, this was more than a case; it was a battle for redemption, for a man he believed had been failed by the world long before he became a killer.

Priya Mehta, however, remained steadfast. She was determined to see the sentence carried out, to ensure that Mareek Masood paid for his crimes. Her resolve was unshaken, even as new details and revelations came to light. The battle between Rehan and Priya continued, their arguments fierce and unyielding, each fighting for their version of justice.

The night before his execution, Mareek sat alone in his cell, the silence pressing down on him like a physical weight. Max appeared once again, his presence both comforting and haunting.

"Well, my friend," Max said, his voice softer than usual. "This is it. The final curtain call."

Mareek leaned back against the wall, his eyes closing. "Do you think it was all worth it?"

Max tilted his head, a faint smile playing on his lips. "That's not for me to decide. I was just here to keep you company."

The next morning, as the sun rose over the prison, Mareek was led to the gallows. The air was heavy with the weight of finality, the crowd outside a mixture of protesters, supporters, and onlookers drawn by morbid curiosity. Inside, Rehan Malik and Priya Mehta watched from opposite sides of the room, their expressions unreadable.

Sushant Malhotra stood in the back, his hands clenched into fists. He had tried to save Mareek, to understand him, but in the end, he had failed. As the noose was placed around Mareek's neck, a hush fell over the room.

Mareek's final words were barely a whisper, but they carried the weight of a lifetime. **"All the noises are silent now."**